PHALLOS

ALSO BY SAMUEL R. DELANY

FICTION

The Jewels of Aptor (1962)

The Fall of the Towers

Out of the Dead City (1963)

The Towers of Toron (1964)

City of a Thousand Suns (1965)

The Ballad of Beta-2 (1965)

Babel-17 (1966)

Empire Star (1966)

The Einstein Intersection (1967)

Nova (1968)

Driftglass (1969)

Equinox (1973)

Dhalgren (1975)

Trouble on Triton (1976)

Return to Nevèrÿon

Tales of Nevèrÿon (1979)

Neveryóna (1983)

Flight from Nevèrÿon (1985)

Return to Nevèrÿon (1987)

Distant Stars (1981)

*Stars in My Pocket Like Grains
of Sand* (1984)

Driftglass/Starshards (collected stories, 1993)

They Fly at Çiron (1993)

The Mad Man (1994)

Hogg (1995)

Atlantis: Three Tales (1995)

Aye, and Gomorrah
(and other stories, 2003)

Phallos (2004;
enhanced and revised edition, 2013)

Dark Reflections (2007)

Through the Valley of the Nest of Spiders (2012)

GRAPHIC NOVELS

Empire (artist, Howard Chaykin; 1980)

Bread & Wine (artist, Mia Wolff; 1999)

NONFICTION

The Jewel-Hinged Jaw
(1978; revised edition, 2009)

The American Shore (1978)

Starboard Wine (1984; revised edition, 2012)

Heavenly Breakfast (1979)

The Motion of Light in Water (1988)

Wagner/Artaud (1988)

The Straits of Messina (1990)

Silent Interviews (1994)

Longer Views (1996)

*Times Square Red, Times
Square Blue* (1999)

Shorter Views (1999)

1984: Selected Letters (2000)

About Writing (2005)

PHALLOS

ENHANCED AND REVISED EDITION

SAMUEL R. DELANY

Edited with an Afterword by Robert F. Reid-Pharr

Wesleyan University Press | Middletown, Connecticut

Wesleyan University Press

Middletown CT 06459

www.wesleyan.edu/wespress

Essays © 2013 Wesleyan University Press

Phallos: Wesleyan edition © 2013 Samuel R. Delany;

original edition © 2004 Samuel R. Delany

The first unrevised edition of *Phallos* was published by

Bamberger Books, Whitmore Lake, MI, 2004.

Wesleyan University Press is a member of the Green Press Initiative.

The paper used in this book meets their minimum requirement for recycled paper.

Library of Congress Cataloging-in-Publication Data

Delany, Samuel R.

Phallos: enhanced and revised edition / Samuel R. Delany;

edited with an afterword by Robert F. Reid-Pharr.

p.   cm.

ISBN 978-0-8195-7355-1 (pbk.: alk. paper) — ISBN 978-0-8195-7356-8 (ebook)

1. Science fiction. I. Reid-Pharr, Robert, 1965– II. Title.

PS3554.E437P48 2013

821'.914 — dc23   2012033262

5   4   3   2   1

Phallos is
for Christian Bök,
author of *Eunoia*,
a novel that will drive everybody sane,
and is presented here with great thanks
to Gil Roth,
who lived with far too many versions of
this tale over many too many years, and
gratitude to Lance and Andi Olsen
and Callum James.

———

This revised edition
is for Ric Best and Louis Navarrete.

CONTENTS

Phallos

1

———

Critical Essays

125

Afterword by Robert F. Reid-Pharr

127

Discourse and Desire, Muddle and Need: Radical Reading
In and Around *Phallos* by Kenneth R. James

135

Ars Vitae: Delany's Philosophical Fable by Steven Shaviro

159

I Can See Atlantis from My House: Sex, Fantasy,
and *Phallos* by Darieck Scott

173

———

About the Author and Contributors

189

PHALLOS

IN HIS UPSTATE HOMETOWN, Bithynia, New York, a twelve-year-old African American, Adrian Rome, discovers a carton of pornographic magazines and paperbacks in the rear of his older cousin's van. The chimerical cover of one book, *Phallos,* ignites his curiosity, but, before he can read it, his cousin catches him and drives the van away.

Ten years later, in 1994, on finishing college Adrian moves to New York City's Greenwich Village. In his new Charles Street apartment, among some books left on a shelf, he recognizes a copy. Intending to read *Phallos* on his first night in the city, that evening Adrian takes a walk. When he returns, however, the books are gone. Adrian's landlady has been in, and, in an ill-conceived attempt to finish cleaning the place, she's thrown them out, and homeless folk have filched them from the alley's green trash receptacles.

Adrian becomes fixated on owning *Phallos.* He contrives to meet an elderly black man of letters, presumably the author of the anonymous text. He even goes to observe a statue that provided the artist with the idea for the cover. But though, in the course of his adventures at a pornographic movie house, the Columbia, he meets his life partner, a white ex-convict, Shoat Rumblin, the closest he ever comes to reading *Phallos* is a synopsis he discovers on the Internet.

SYNOPSIS OF A GAY PORNOGRAPHIC NOVEL

PUBLISHED BY ESSEX HOUSE PUBLICATIONS,

LOS ANGELES, 1969,

BY RANDY PEDARSON, MOSCOW, IDAHO

═══

Downloaded from a website at
www.threelegs.com/wonkers/~phallos/pornsite.html
"My Three Favorite Gay Male Porn Novels:
The Gaudy Image by William Talsman,
Mr. Benson by John Preston,
and *Phallos*."[1]

═══

Yet there is nothing more fascinating than secret wisdom: One is
sure that it exists, but one does not know what it is. In the
imagination, therefore, it shines as something unutterably profound.

Umberto Eco, *The Search for the Perfect Language*

There is always more surface to a shattered object than a whole.

Djuna Barnes, *Letter to Emily Coleman*

LIKE MANY SUCH NOVELS, *PHALLOS* was published anonymously — in 1969,
by Essex House Publications of West Hollywood, responsible for much of that
decade's most literate pornography, straight and gay. An equally anonymous
editor's "Introduction" discusses the text's history, telling of nineteenth-century manuscript copies owned by Walter Pater, by Lionel Pigot Johnson . . .
States that "Introduction," a copy was rumored to have been in the pos-

---

[1] *Phallos* (Anonymous), New York: Bard Books, Avon. $2.65. 472 pp. (2nd Ed., 1982) ISBN 380-
14373-265. (Thanks to Binky for providing most of the bibliographic data here.)

session of German classical antiquarian Johann Joachim Winckelmann in 1768 — an item that the nineteen-year-old murderer Arcangeli presumably made off with, along with the golden medals, after garroting the fifty-one-year-old scholar in a pensione just outside Trieste.

Arthur Symons was supposed to have had a copy stuffed into his boot-top ("not above the size of our current edition today") when, during his October 1908 collapse into dementia, he was arrested in his deranged wanderings on the roads 'round Ferrara and dragged from the streets to a basement cell in the Ducal Palace dungeon, with its wooden bed — and its wood *pillow!* — and its "Judas" slit in the oak door through which the jailors peered in at the mad miscreant.

Earlier that same year Frederick Rolfe (better known today as Baron Corvo) and Professor Richard MacGillivray Dawkins (polylingual Oxford don, redheaded, left-handed) carried a manuscript copy with them to Venice, we are told. It was August; and the supposed purpose of the Venetian "vacation" was to have a deluxe edition of *Phallos* printed by Italian typesetters who presumably would be unable to read the scabrous text, which would then be sold to certain wealthy subscribers in England and on the continent. The two men's September break-up came because of arguments over both the proofreading of the wretched galleys the non-English speaking typesetters returned and the photographic illustrations they had begun for the project with their adolescent gondolieri, Carlo and Ermenegildo (or "Gildo," pronounced "Zeeldo" in the Venetian dialect) — and, as was always the case with the impecunious Rolfe, money. Whether the manuscript went to Athens with Dawkins or remained in Venice with Rolfe is not known. Although, as with so many of Rolfe's projects, the Italian printing came to nothing, *Phallos* was the direct inspiration, says the "Introduction," for Rolfe's next novel (written in 1909, published posthumously in 1934), *The Desire and Pursuit of the Whole.*

Historian and aesthete John Addington Symonds discusses *Phallos* in five of his letters (claims our "Introduction") to sex researcher Havelock Ellis . . .

No existing biography of the Napoleon-sized poet Lionel Johnson is extensive enough to mention such a manuscript — given him, the "Introduction" says, by Austin Ferrand — even had he owned one. Nor is any such manuscript mentioned in Benson's authorized biography of Pater (1906). No one would expect it. But neither — more surprising — is there any mention in the more sensational and unauthorized two volumes with which Thomas Wright answered it a year later (1907). And Denis Donoghue (*Walter Pater,* 1995), with access to Benson's papers, where the juicy bits had lain entombed for near-on ninety years (Going into an Oxford barber shop, suddenly and unaccountably, Pater seized up a young barber's foot — a youth of nineteen, he wore only slippers — and, before customers and employees, removed the cloth covering to caress instep, toes, and heel for twenty minutes, while apostrophizing on their Hellenic perfection — followed by an invitation to the young man to come, later in the week, to tea. Twenty years on, the otherwise unknown tonsorialist told Benson: "If I'd 'a known 'oo he was, I mean 'im bein' a genius and all, I'd 've taken 'im up on it. But I never even *seen* the gentleman before!") cites it not.

One understands why no such item is mentioned in Pater's own account (from the *Westminster Review* for January 1867) of Winckelmann's murder — a pattern to be replayed across the centuries (older, naïve homosexuals; avaricious, predatory boys), now with the death of composer Marc Blitzstein, now with the murder of art critic Gregory Battcock.

Pater's essay sits today as the most eccentric contribution to his perennially popular *Renaissance* (1873), though readers seeking both style and substance, from Hart Crane to Harold Bloom, have, with reason, preferred his *Plato and Platonism* (1893). Nor is it in any other account of Winckelmann's life — or death.

Although the incidents marking Symons' precipitate plunge into syphilitic delirium have been recounted in many literary sketches, Symons' own memoirs, put together after his partial recovery, were not readily available — at least in this country — till George Beckson's 1977 edition. They state that, when the greatest of those English critics of the 1890s was taken into custody, he was barefoot — that, indeed, when our madman attacked his jailors, under their retaliatory brutality (and the studded boots with which they stamped on them once our man was downed), Symons' feet bled so badly that, on the jailors' departure, blood jellied half the cell's stone floor.

So much for booted copies.

From Symons (1934) to Weeks (1971) to Benkovitz (1977), Corvo biographers seem unaware of *Phallos.* Nor is it mentioned in Rolfe's *Venice Letters* from those years, first published complete in 1971.

And what of J. A. Symonds — at work on *his* sonorous five-volume histo-riography, *The Renaissance in Italy,*[2] when he become the model for Henry James's "The Author of Beltraffio"? In 1969, the year of *Phallos*'s publication, the third and final volume of Symonds' complete letters also appeared, ed-ited by Herbert M. Shueller and Robert L. Peters. The indices to the three fat Wayne State University Press volumes include no reference to the novel. The Symonds/Ellis friendship has occasioned several published studies. Yes, I've read them. No, none mentions it.

The same "Introduction" speaks of a subscription edition of *Phallos* put out by the Hermetic Order of the Golden Dawn, this in the 1920s. As far as I have been able to learn, no such edition exists. Over more than a dozen years now, I've consulted authorities on pornography, from Yale's Beinecke to Lockhaven State's Stevenson Library. None is aware of any mention of *Phallos* before 1969.

Finally, back from three weeks in London at the British Museum, research-ing something else entirely, my old friend Binky (before he had a single piercing) says there is no listing for *Phallos* in any of the three Henry Spencer Ashbee (the pixyish, if perspicacious, Pisanus Fraxi) volumes — neither in the *Index Librorum Prohibitorum* of 1877, nor in the *Centuria Librorum Ab-sconditorum* of 1879, nor in the *Catena Librorum Tacendorum* of 1885. Having buried herself nine weeks in the Bibliothèque Nationale for like reasons of research and returned from Paris last winter, Phyllis assures me it is not cited either in the 1861 edition, in the 1864 edition, or in the six-volume 1871–73 expansion of Jules Gay's *Bibliographie des ouvrages relatifs à l'Amour;* nor is it anywhere catalogued in the whole of the *Enfer* — a treble blow that reduces any possibility that *Phallos* dates from the eighteenth century or could have been well-known among the "Other Victorians" of the nineteenth. All this leads me finally and firmly to believe that, at least as it is spelled out in its "Introduction," *Phallos*'s provenance is a hoax.

While a hoax its history may be, the novel's style is rich and vivid — some-times to the point of turgidity. But though from time to time passages have a rhythm and lilt that move from the middle seventeenth to the early nineteenth

---

[2] And its two-volume supplement, *The Renaissance in Italy: Italian Literature,* 1886.

century, the diction and (especially) the syntax — lush, gorgeous, and even baroque (some of its more recondite vocabulary — "incrassate," "uliginous," "paralogical," "expilator," "diuternity . . ." says Binky, surely borrowed from Sir Thomas Browne [3]) — is much too modern for any such composition date.

PHALLOS BEGINS WITH a Greek epigraph, set on a page apart:

ἐξ ὧν δὲ ἡ γένεσίς ἐστι τοῖς οὖσι, καὶ τὴν φθορὰν εἰς ταῦτα γίνεσθαι κατὰ τὸ χρεών· διδόναι γὰρ αὐτὰ δίκην καὶ τίσιν ἀλλήλοις τῆς ἀδικίας κατὰ τὴν τοῦ χρόνου τάξιν.

Part I and the first of the novel's fifty-one chapters (none less than seven and none more than eleven printed pages) begins:

THE GLITTERING SEA; the stony shore; the friable, yellow cliffs; behind them scrub forests with green-gray leaves, where rarely a tree grew more than a foot, a foot-and-a-half higher than a man, and all threaded by thin, bright, brackish

---

[3] A notion supported in Chapter Twenty-eight, says Phyllis, when the secrets presumably contained in the *phallos* are dismissed by the under-clerk at the Temple of Artemis Nana in the Piraeus as holding "no trace of any positive science, but rather forming an astute '*pseudodoxia epidemica*.'" The *Pseudodoxia Epidemica* ([1646], "false beliefs" [*pseudodoxia*] "upon" [on, upon, widely spread (*epi*)] "the people" [commonfolk (*demos*)], Binky's translation) is Browne's major (and all-but-unread) work: an "*Encyclopædie*" of "*Vulgar Errors*" (as it is usually translated) abroad and common in the good doctor's day, i.e., the mid-seventeenth century.

[4] Binky has identified this as the "Anaximander fragment," found in Simplicius's commentary (c. 530 CE) on Aristotle's *Physics*. (After Thales [625–560 BCE], Anaximander [610–546 BCE] is the earliest of the Ionian presocratics.) Again Binky has translated for us: "*On the other hand, out of where things have their genesis, there dissolution returns them, according to necessity. For things in their decline return order for their disorders, accordingly as time charts.*" Here is his annotated gloss: "on the other hand [but; however: δέ], out of where things have their genesis [creation; source; origin: γένεσις], there dissolution [perishing; destruction: φθοράν] returns [brings: γίνεσθαι] them according to [under, down: κατά] need [necessity: χρεών]. For things give [give over, return; exchange: διδόναι] justice [order; social propriety: δίκην] for their injustices [social flummoxes; disorders: ἀδικίας] according to the order of time [a rigorous schedule; time's grid/chart/order: τὴν τοῦ χρόνου τάξιν]." As well, he offers this commentary:

"As did most nineteenth-century European philologists, Nietzsche believed this fragment the oldest example of philosophical writing extant. All else, until Xenophanes, Heraclitus, and their like, was paraphrase or synopsis by later writers who may or may not have had the original texts to hand. In his incomplete essay (or undelivered lecture) 'Philosophy in the Tragic Age of the Greeks,' written shortly after his first book *The Birth of Tragedy from the Spirit of Music* (1873), as he considers Thales (in the latter half of that century traumatized by the second law of thermodynamics), Nietzsche pauses for a

streams; the sunlight through the thatch, dappling the poles of my father's porch, on a house five of whose walls were white-washed stone, making our four rooms minutely grander than some houses closer to the road, though not so fine as others further off. Such memories return from southern Syracuse, where I was born.

Though my mother was a part-Egyptian slave, brought to those hills and freed years before by a rich family in the area, my father's folk had lived in that landscape time out of mind. However strongly the blood of Africa beat behind his thoughtful features, he gave me a Greek name, Neoptolomus, as did many under Rome in those years, in hopes I would aspire to a life more than mere toil for grain, cheese, mutton, and onions. He got me well along in the language, too, for he had a Greek text of the first seven books (you would call them chapters), the first of the three sections — on physics and natural philosophy — of Heraclitus's great treatise, περὶ φύσεως. As well, he could recite, in Greek, a dozen of the slave Æsop's tales of animals and ethics. Thus, between them, I learned my first hundred or three hundred words in that language — fire, river, resin, rust, life, copper, fish, bread, wine, site, salt, garlic, honey, song, vision, rain, bird, history, drinkable, discourse, barley, poet, laughter, belief, now, undrinkable,

---

page to muse on the fragment by Thales' slightly younger pupil at Miletus. From the linkage *genesis/ phthoran* [genesis/perishing] under *chreon* [necessity], he extracts the notion that it is too easy to read Anaximander as saying, 'all coming-to-be' appears 'as though it were an illegitimate emancipation from eternal being,' before he turns to Heraclitus (540–490 BCE), who, says Nietzsche, exclaims: 'Becoming is what I contemplate and no one else has watched so attentively this everlasting rhythm and wavebeat.'

"In his own lectures on the history of philosophy, first presented in 1805–6, Hegel (1770–1831) quotes the fragment and gives Anaximander some five pages. (Volume I, Part 1, Section 1, Chapter 1-A, II.) Most of the discussion concerns Anaximander's cosmogony (see below), though Hegel notes the early Milesian believed material endured forever, despite changes in form, which sounds suspiciously like an intimation of the conservation of matter. (Not a century later, Heraclitus's contention that all things generated from and perished as fire and that 'all things are guided by the lightning' might even reflect an intuition of the fundamental identity of matter and energy.) In his account of the presocratics that initiates *Plato and Platonism* (1893), Walter Pater (1839–94) omits Anaximander entirely, possibly because he had the least influence on Plato himself, the subject of those ten—or twelve, depending on how you read the chapter breaks—lectures constituting Pater's extraordinary consideration and critique, the more devastating for their low-key and respectful tone, coupled with their sharp intelligence and rhetorical beauty."

(Comments Phyllis: "Pater is all over *Phallos*—though I'm sure Binky feels it's the other way around. Literary fanatics can be wonderful—I'm a crypto-Oxfordian, myself.")

"In his 1946 essay 'Der Spruch des Anaximander' ('The *Anaximander* Fragment')," Binky goes on, "Martin Heidegger (1889–1976) is ready, by the end of his consideration, to agree with more recent philological scholarship, holding that the passage in Simplicius is at best an Aristotelian paraphrase, rather than a verbatim quotation: the 'genesis/perishing' opposition only becomes 'conceptual' with

then, gods, treaty, nation, change, grain, cricket, necessity, mountain, astonish, commander, beauty, thunder, all, hear, steersman, nothing, love, freeman, pain, water, good, wet, weep, slave, night, tomorrow, suffer, justice, moon, rest, sorrow, up, down, no, yes, sun, tree, branch, head, hand, clitoris, earth, body, jar, breast, bad, wisdom, city, road, root, cattle, common, dawn, tomb, none, day, when, urine, measure, gold, horse, create, deathless, shit, experience, laughter, destroy, eternal, opposite, blade, on-the-one-hand, shield, on-the-other, wasp, finger, penis, people, eye, peace, battle, journey, pleasure, exchange, strife, star, foot, sleep, sand, rectum, remain, mud, and death — the ocean of ideas and sounds from which the learning of the language itself lifted, like a wave over sand and shells and sea grass, flooding confusion with comprehension, and upon which my name was the merest foam. Often my father said he hoped I'd get to see a bit of the world, as had he, before I settled down to farming, though how I was to do this, at the time I had no notion.

As a child I fished off the rocky coast and herded our own and several other farmers' goats on the cliffs above the sea. In my fifteenth year, while I pastured our flock among isolate cypresses and beside the profusion of sumac, repeatedly

Plato and Aristotle (though the concept is found in Parmenides ['οὕτω τοι κατὰ δόξαν ἔφυ τάδε καί νυν ἔασι καὶ μετέπειτ᾽ ἀπὸ τοῦδε τελευτήσουσι τραφέντα·' *Thus according of men's opinions things come into being, and thus they are now; in time, they think, they will mature further and pass away* (DK 28B19)], the words are not), so that, Heidegger concludes, only the words 'κατὰ τὸ χρεών· διδόναι γὰρ αὐτὰ δίκην καὶ τίσιν ἀλλήλοις τῆς ἀδικίας' have the feel of Ionian Greek. Heidegger argues that until the modern reader has tried to encounter what exactly 'things/*onta*' were for the Ionians—what particular qualities did 'things' have; what was their particular relation to justice (order), injustice (disorder), and being (εἶναι), which might allow such an utterance to be thinkable—these early thinkers in general and Anaximander in particular are all-but-closed to us.

"In his studies of the presocratics, collected in *The World of Parmenides* (1993), in the 1980s Sir Karl Popper (1902–94) was much less interested in the textual fragment than he was in a theory attributed to Anaximander that the world was a vast drum, hanging in the center of the universe, equidistant—below, above, and on all sides—from everything else, in what Anaximander styled the *apairon* (the unbounded/the indeterminate). Different from the air (which his contemporary Anaximenes claimed was the source of all things), the *apairon* was an early notion of the ether. It was, indeed, the first theory to picture the universe not as a physical extension of the material world itself. In that, it is fundamentally different from Thales' infinite ocean, on which the earth—itself a form of water, as was ice—floats, occasionally breasting some great wave, which produces earthquakes.

"Thales is claimed to have mathematically predicted an eclipse. Anaximander is also credited with making the first map of the world, as well as inventing the sundial. Parmenides promoted skepticism: 'In understanding the universe, you cannot trust to appearances.' He was the first to prove Phosphoros, the morning star, and Hesperos, the evening star, one. He knew the moon was lit by the sun, even when the sky was dark and the sun was below the horizon. He knew what caused the phases of the moon; and when in his sixties he visited Athens (he was known as the Philosopher of Being), he

I'd meet a Roman gentleman, who, repeatedly — first weekly and soon daily — ca-joled me to lie among my charges, bleating raucously around us, and sucked my cock to one and another pleasurable eruptions, while I grunted and whinnied and finally fondled his bald head in thanks. Soon he became my friend. Shortly, through his recommendations, I was working on the estates of several wealthy Romans and some somewhat less wealthy (but far more interesting and friendly) Greeks, who had taken refuge in the neighborhood for political reasons.

I used to make their servants laugh, reciting the Æsop tales, which they understood better than I, even as they taught me their tongue. A bright and curious boy, soon I could speak and write informatively, if without polish, in both Greek *and* Latin.

In my seventeenth summer, a fever took many in my village and sent many more wandering. At August end it killed my father. My grief was intense and total — three days of sobbing exhaustion. On the fourth, when I awoke to hear a bird, to see the sun on the edge of my blanket, to smell the goats passing by the house, even as I realized how much of it had abated, I realized too that much of that intensity had been fear at what might now befall. Three months on, when my mother sickened and died, I realized, however unfairly, that I felt far less strongly than I had before. First, my emotions had been blunted by all the misery around us. Also, the way silver alloyed with gold makes electrum,

---

went with his younger lover Zeno, the Philosopher of Paradox: Certainly the love of Being for Para-dox contains an allegory. Democritus had a theory of atoms—he gave us the word. He believed the earth a sphere, rather than a drum, and when he calculated its circumference (at what today would be nineteen thousand miles), he was only five thousand miles short. Pythagoras with his belief in num-bers, Heraclitus with his universe of process—and Anaximander with his world separate and distinct from the rest of the universe (held in place only by an attractive force; Popper claims this is what, two thousand years later, would free Copernicus to think his theory of the solar-centric system of planets, among which is the earth, as well as prepare Newton for conceiving of the function of gravity in the universe), in which everything that is created must eventually dissolve, erode away, run out, or run down—all these preplatonic philosophers suggest a hotbed of proto-science, from Asia Minor's Ionia to Southern Italy's Elea, which took nothing from Greece proper save the language, and from which, for a hundred to fifteen hundred years, despite all their philosophical and theological acumen, Plato and Dante seem to back-slide radically. Not until Galileo, Copernicus, Columbus, and Descartes would empirical developments force thinkers to catch up to where those earlier men had gotten through ratiocination and the naked eye.

"Though he spent his productive years in the city of Miletus with Thales, a few say Anaximander was born on the Ionian island of Samos (or at least passed a number of years there), famous for its wines through classical times, and at which eight hundred years later Nivek and Neoptolomus stop, in *Phallos*, and where their relationship shifts from that of slave and master to that of mutual (if not permanent) commitment. The year after Anaximander's death at the age of seventy-four (Hegel says

this bout of sorrow was mixed with relief. For now I had only myself to fend for, which was beginning to seem possible. Yet I wonder if, finally, I was not more affected by that second passing. From time to time, even today, I recall her, turning to face the sun and uttering a little cry . . . When as a boy I had questioned it, she'd told me it had been a surge of emotion for her birth land, Egypt, which she would never see again.

While I am endlessly grateful for what my father gave me, my mother seems to have given me that memory alone — the one from my childhood than can still grip my heart and shake it. As well, when I think of the part Egypt, her home, eventually played in my life, it is almost as if her yearning were quietly passed to me at a level far deeper than my father's seemingly more valuable gifts. But these are speculations of my age, not observations of my youth.

Aware of my orphaning and feeling for my plight, a powerful merchant in the area — yes, it was my rich Roman friend of the fellatial mountain idylls, though I had not seen him for most of a year — took me onto his columned estate. Beside his own cushioned and canopied bed — frankly too soft for me to sleep in with any comfort more than an hour — I slept on a padded rug, stitched with red and gold, where a slave changed the straw beneath it each week. Through the summer he kept me for companionship and pleasure, while he entertained a succession of men and women, who, evenings after our supper, talked of great

he reached ninety), a massive Persian army invaded Asia Minor under General Harpagus, ending Ionia's intellectual and political freedom. Five to ten years later, a bit to the south, in the great city of Ephesus, Heraclitus (c. 540/'35–c. 490/'75 BCE) was born. One might assume Heraclitus would be the guiding thinker for *Phallos*. In the novel's opening pages, the Obscure Philosopher cedes Neoptolomus the very vocabulary he will use to think with and acquire what he can of classical culture. (On reading Heraclitus's περὶ φύσεως [*On Nature*], loaned him by Euripides, Socrates is reputed to have said: 'The ideas in it I understand are great. But I believe the ideas in it I do not understand are great, too. To read such a book, you must be as strong a reader as the swimmers of Delos, for this is a book you can drown in.') Parmenides's later poem περὶ φύσεως took its name from Heraclitus's three-part (so says the spectacularly untrustworthy Diogenes Laërtius) treatise on the material world, political ethics, and cosmology and the gods, and in some ways may even be a gently critical answer to that earlier work, all of it—save some hundred twenty-five fragments quoted by later writers—now lost. But in the same way that all the presocratics illuminate one another, as they also illuminate Plato after them to show up Plato's philosophical sophistication, they highlight a certain range of empirical limitations Plato was to share with—if he did not actually cede them to—Christianity, as it was practiced up to, and indeed through, much of the Enlightenment; in the same way, Anaximander's reminder of a certain dialectical relation between creation and destruction resonates with much in this novel of process (especially its opening and closing), with its intricate analysis of the ways pleasure can be integrated with life, by allowing freedom to the movement of absences through the field of discourse that is life's very map." So says Binky.

theaters and moving performances at Delphi, Athens, and Epidauros, or, sitting in the villa gardens of a morning, recited bloody speeches from Seneca or comic ones from Plautus.

Once someone recited the "Pervigilium Veneris," whose lines sound like singing even when they are not sung. On other evenings, still others recited equally musical poetry and philosophy from Homer, Sappho, Euripides, Virgil, Horace, Longinus, Plato, Isocrates, Diotima, and Archilochus, and even stretches from Suetonius or magical adventures from Apuleius's *Golden Ass,* as though all these authors were friends they'd known in their youth, and the pieces recited had been recent letters sent them personally.

One elegant woman visitor gave us the passage from Tacitus's *Annals,* about the clumsy, pusillanimous suicide of Seneca and that of the arbiter of courtly elegance, Petronius, both commanded by the emperor Nero; Petronius, learned in luxury, had been first proconsul, then consul, in distant Bithynia, and when, on a visit to Cumae, the emperor's decree that he end his own life reached him, he acceded to his lord's wish by opening his veins in his bath, then binding them up, then opening them yet again, over several days, with his retinue of friends and servants about him, listening to light poetry, and talking of witty and fanciful things, ordering one slave rewarded and another flogged, so that death came like the natural end to an elegant and civilized life.

The same woman told us she had recently acquired the sixteen volumes of the *libri Satyricon* by this same Petronius, crammed with wonderfully hilarious adventures. On her next visit she would bring one of the choicer books to read to us, as soon as she finished having the whole of it copied, for it was very valuable — as well as critical, with its acid wit, of the Roman upper classes, so that members of the aristocracy *still* wished to see it suppressed. That is why, she opined, Tacitus had not mentioned it. But, alas, she never returned while I was at the villa.

That same day, however, when he found I could speak Greek as well as Latin, one little accountant from Salistia, with a hunched shoulder and an oversized head, placed his hand on my thigh and declaimed Pericles's full funeral oration for the troops dead in the Peloponnesus, as Thucydides had taken it down in shorthand (while sunlight burned through the leaves over us, and other guests looked on, with nostalgic fondness, at my fascination), and I was left with tears in my eyes that day — and a bruised leg where, at the height of his emotions he had gripped me so tightly, while my own emotions had been too high to notice.

(For a year I was convinced great Pericles himself must have been a hunchbacked dwarf.)

Later in bed, my patron shocked me by explaining that Nero had been emperor of Rome not a decade back when I was a child too young to remember, but a whole *century* before — and that it was the cutting quality of his humor and rhetoric alone, which kept Petronius's work dangerous to this day. Pericles had addressed his troops, out on the field of pyres, in the words I had listened to only hours back, even hundreds of years before that! For all these fine remarks and expressions were from men and women dead fifty, three hundred, six hundred, even eight hundred years. And for the first of many times I began to feel myself, there in my patron's summer home, somehow part of an immortal company.

The visitor I remember most clearly, however, was an onyx-black Nubian — much of my master's export and import business were bronzes and terra cottas from Africa — who was, indeed, the tallest man I'd ever met, but who, while he knew some engaging songs and some *terrifying* dances, had little interest in literature. He was almost seven feet! As well, he took the time to explain to me that, in his own home, self-pleasure was nowhere near as private an act as it was with us. Though, for the week of his visit, he confined the practice to his room, often he left his door ajar, and, I confess, I was fascinated and regularly lurked outside to watch him labor over his own considerable flesh. When he saw me, he would laugh and invite me to assist, from which invitation (the first time) I fled, then (the second, having already told myself what a coward and fool I'd been) hesitantly accepted and happily joined him. My patron found my fascination with this randy, broad-nosed, full-mouthed fellow (he was a merchant in the market for Roman-made arms) between fascinating and funny, but seemed comfortable sharing my favors with him during the days of his stay.

The first time my patron took me to Rome, in his retinue of friends, servants, and slaves, once, on a hot day, not thinking, I left my inn room naked, to come down to the street, for, on our arrival the day before, I had seen a gaggle of filthy youngsters playing, naked, in an alley behind the square. But I received shocked and astonished looks from every guest in the inn I passed — I was so naïve at first as to think these were awed notices of my penis's warm-weather heft and stretch — till one of my patron's other servants spotted me, pulled me aside, and told me that, in the city, no one over the age of fourteen, or other than the poorest men and women, ever went about in public with loins uncovered, no matter how hot the day.

I *must* return to my room and don a summer tunic!

While, again upstairs, I pulled one over my head and belted it, I remembered our Nubian guest of a year before, back in Syracuse, and how he would chuckle at my closing of doors behind us, at my urging him to more secluded alcoves in the gardens, or my whispers to pursue our lubricities more privately. Or even how funny he'd found it that I was always exhorting him to be quieter; for while I am someone who growls toward the end of sex, he had been a man who roared.

On that same day, in Rome, I found that blowing your nose on your fingers and wiping them on a wall or a tree trunk or a stone was hopelessly offensive to the Romans, even while the finest aristocrats hiked up their toga hems at street corners to urinate in the gutter outlets. (In Syracuse we did not have pavement, underground sewers, or gutters with outlets that went down to them. We had latrines behind our houses.) So I had to unlearn the doing of one and learn to do the other. But now I had new sympathy for that Nubian stranger, come to a place where custom made such unusual demands on how the body and its ordinary workings must be pursued.

Through a recent marriage by his cousin, my patron was currently a distant relative of Sabina, Hadrian's empress, and something had occurred — in the coils of politics, so I was never sure exactly what — which had considerably improved his fortune. His Roman house, where his sister lived year round, was undergoing renovation: because of the dust, noise, and confusion, during our visit my patron had fixed those of us in his entourage at an inn half-a-dozen streets distant. Several times, along with his servants, slaves, and friends, we strolled past his mansion on one and another sunny morning, to watch *near*-naked workmen clamber over the scaffolding erected before the three-story façade, with its crisscrossing planks, towering against the Roman clouds — the only things about the city one with those of Syracuse.

I'd never seen a house before of three whole stories!

Once, when we walked by, my patron and his steward left us to go within, stopping to joke with a man pushing a barrow, now calling to a foreman loping along some high planks before an upper window. Then they disappeared inside the heavy stones, behind the beams and supports, to check the work's progress, while we continued on to the park my benefactor had suggested we explore for the noon hours, where, after we settled under the trees and opened our picnic hamper, he would join us.

Possibly because, during my own wanderings, I'd passed some street excavations (where I heard accents like my own among the workers — a handful of whom had come from my island, though when, eagerly, I began to talk with one, he turned out a not very communicative quarry worker's son, who'd never heard of my village on the southern shore, as I'd never heard of his in the central mountains) and another place where more workers hoisted up a new column before another great building (all jabbering in a language not Latin — some Teutonic tongue, I later learned), soon I felt that, in place among its seven hills more than five hundred years, since Aeneas had carried his father Anchises here, the whole grand construction was really as new as morning and had all been built in the past days for my entertainment and wonder.

Oh, I could recount hours of searing homesickness, wiped away by hours of equally searing excitement. Late one night, when I was moody and sleepless, I took myself into the moonlit street. Shortly I was at my patron's building, where, exploring the scaffolding's base, I saw three workmen asleep at the back of the site. When one woke and jokingly called from his blankets that I should join them in their rest, soon I found myself in my first Roman orgy!

It turned out those workmen had no homes of their own — though all three were friendly and generally genial. After the biggest and roughest had taken his pleasure of me, assisted hand, foot, and — yes — mouth (that service so few will admit to and yet so many of us are so hungry to get and to give) by the others, immediately he had fallen asleep again, his back to us, hands thrust down between his thighs. How matter-of-fact the remaining two were about my taking mine of them! Once, waking briefly from that pleasantest of after-climax drowses, I found the smallest astride the biggest — and roughest. "If you're still heated up, when I'm finished, banquet at his butt hole some, but leave it nice and sloppy with spit — then skewer him!" He grinned down at me in the graying dark. "He pretends to be asleep, but he doesn't mind." He fell again to bucking on the big one's back.

So that is what I did.

What truly stays with me, though, is waking later, held between their warm bodies, loosely gripped in sleep by their hard hands. While sunrise and birdsong filtered through the planks, I rose, redonned my tunic, and, delighting in the quiet glory of Roman dawn, walked out past the cart bringing bread, cheese, beer, and raisins. (It is the Roman custom to feed your workers: and beer keeps fresh longer than water.) As the city's very stones began to wake about me, I ambled back to the inn. Mulling on how much rougher and more preëmptory all three had been, taking their pleasures of me, I realized, this was different from any sex I'd known.

Yet, for all its difference and, yes, rudeness, I'd liked it as much or more than any I'd yet had!

Eagerly, the next night I was back, only to note immediately the workers slept further apart. As well, the littlest one was gone and a bigger stranger snored in his place. The one who had called me before, though he lay naked and under scaffold-checkered moonlight, now squinted up at me and grunted as roughly and as sleepily as I would have expected from the biggest — who dozed a yard away — as if he did not want someone there to hear: "Go home, young prince! We work tomorrow. We're too tired to play tonight. Come back some other time!"

I returned to the inn, confused (I, a prince? Or was that simply a laborer's irony?), rueful — and, yes, embarrassed at their rejection — but chuckling nevertheless at my presumptions. Again in my inn room, I went to sleep, but only after thoroughly enjoying — and even improving upon — the memories they'd provided from the night before.

Still, homesickness was abolished; and I'd begun to understand that, while the sadnesses and joys of travel are both quite real, the intensities behind them, the negative ones especially, were largely loaned by terror. If men like these were scattered through the empire's streets and nights, there seemed nothing in life to fear. As much as when we'd first embarked on the boat from Syracuse, the world and my time in it, now at its neap, broke and sparkled ahead.

Among his many reasons for returning to Rome, my patron wished to procure me a lieutenant's commission in the Roman army, as if I had been a son and not a servant. At least three times on that visit, over the heads of crowds along the street's edge who had gathered to wave, watch, and cheer, I saw regiments parading with horns and drums, banners and horses, metal shields, horse-maned helmets, and bright-tipped spears. Yes, the military dazzled and delighted me! Days on, while birds flew by in loose V's high over our inn's verandah, my patron told me that, yes, in his name, his steward had that morning obtained for me a three-year military sojourn. (Only much later did I learn how unusual that was.) Then it was done: and I was with a lot of very strange men, indeed — now uncomfortably crowded, first in our military barracks, then in a military boat.

Because we were jammed so close, I learned quickly who was willing to engage in sex behind this bale or in that dark corner and who was not. Soon I learned as well that, while a fair number were quite as open as I about their desires, a whole population among them was lazy enough to take whatever was offered sexually, even if it was not their first choice, while another, equally numerous, went to endless lengths — almost always futile — to make sure *no* one knew what they did, some in pursuit of women, some in pursuit of men.

In the mountains of Syria, my squadron oversaw its bit of the *pax romana,* an idyllic passage, once we arrived, where, as soon as I found him, mostly what I did was bugger or receive the oral services of an auburn-haired private named Clivus, with buttocks as neat, high, and cleanly cleft as his genitals were full, firm, and low-hanging. A Gaul by blood, in childhood Clivus had been brought by his parents to the Nile-side city of Hermopolis on the border between upper and lower Egypt, where his father had worked — and eventually died — in Rome's service. His mother still dwelt there. Late afternoons in Syria, often Clivus and I lolled together, under the pines and apart from the other soldiers. There he told me of the serenity of Hermopolis — and its temple, not to the more widely known Thoth, but rather a smaller and marginal shrine at the city's edge, sacred to the nameless god, in which, throughout Clivus's younger years, he'd worshipped. "In Saïs you will hear her wise men tell tales of long-vanished Ur, Chaldea, and Atlantis. In Memphis you will see statues of giants that will open the halls of history. Ah, but in Hermopolis . . . !" On his release from the army — his was to come the same season as mine — Clivus hoped to return and indenture himself to a novitiate with the nameless god's shaved-headed priesthood. Off in Syria, among the ferns, as he'd lain with his head on my belly, I'd listened to his reminiscences, his plans, his projects, and while I'd contemplated the Roman military machine and Roman governmental might, which brought together folk as disparate as we were, so far from our homes, in the coppery sun through the leaves I'd turned his auburn curls on my forefinger and been pensive.

How excited I was when, just weeks before my discharge my Roman sponsor messengered me money and a letter. As soon as I was my own man again, it would please my patron greatly, the letter explained — while the leather-cloaked deliverer, lighter by a sack of coins now hanging from my own waist, ambled off between the tents and trees to await my answer — if, on his behalf, I would journey to that very site of Hermopolis, to the very temple of the nameless god, and be his advocate in the acquisition of some lands across the river in the Nile-side village of Hir-wer, owned by the priests: a clutch of the poorest fishermen's hovels and shacks made from mud bricks and wattle, clustered around a half-fallen temple, once dedicated to Ramses II.

I wrote back (his letter had come from Africa) that of course I would do as he wished — that, indeed, I had already booked caravan passage down to Ephesus. On the day of my release I would be on my way. (What a shame that my friend Clivus had not been able to wait for me, I wrote my patron, for he knew Hermopolis and the temple well; but Clivus had already gone on.) I had to remark that, given the poverty of Hir-wer as he'd described it, the project seemed a bit stupid, if not silly — but in no way should he take my untutored speculation as a sign that I would bend less than my full powers toward carrying out his wishes. The unusualness of it only goaded my eagerness to see the place.

At Ephesus, once home to the Obscure Philosopher, Heraclitus himself, and the city of the rhapsode Ion, who'd argued so eloquently with Socrates, another messenger handed me another letter from my patron. I read it at a table beside an inn in the shadow of Artemis's great library (where the Obscure Philosopher once played dice with the children) — saying that he was pleased by my commitment, that my criticism of his plan only raised his estimation of my commercial acuity, but that he wished to repay an old debt to the temple priests, his true motive. Having finished some business in Tunis, he concluded, in two days he was leaving by boat for Rome.

I, too, was on my way by boat — from Asia Minor to Egypt, my mother's home — but because those were times of limited travel, I had to detour slightly from the straight course to halt for a day at the city of Heracleon in Crete, where peasants tell of the tunnels of King Minos that supposedly still worm their indecipherable ways beneath the earth. How pleased I was, when, after an hour in port, I saw my old patron strolling across the patio of the same inn at which I had chosen to stay. His boat had also stopped here for provisions. We spent a pleasant day — and night — with one another. Odd, I thought: When I'd been fifteen and he thirty-four, he'd seemed so much older than I. But now that I was twenty and an army tour older and he was thirty-nine, we seemed far closer in age than before. Toward dawn, when outside our window the cicadas had grown quiet, I remember asking if he felt he could tell me the nature of the debt his letter had mentioned. But he released me and rolled to his back, chuckling, in that country bed with soft blankets but no sheets (as we would have had in his Syracuse summer home): "Best let this one remain unnamed. We all carry far too many that have to be acknowledged. I tell you, my little Neoptolomus (who are now so miraculously three inches taller than I!), on a clear day — " his words recalled something Clivus might have said — "from the Hermopolis docks, you can look over the river and see the roofs of Hir-wer, wistfully visible across the Nile's near-mile of water . . ."

No, I did not understand, nor could I have mapped out his plans and plottings any more than I could have limned the ways of the long-dead Bull-god who, rumor held, still roamed Daedalus's littered course beneath the town, above which our inn, our wooden floor, our bed now stood — the first bed I'd slept in an entire night. (Three years in the Roman army teaches you to sleep on anything, firm *or* yielding.) But since those Hir-wer lands were what my benefactor wanted, it was not my place to nay-say him. The next day his boat nosed from Heracleon's harbor for the north, while, half an hour later, mine sailed south.

Five days forward, under rain, I stood on Hermopolis's docks, which sagged and recovered in the southern winds: But Hir-wer was wholly hidden, as if, behind the waves, that shore had sunk in mud or vanished in mist.

There is a page break, and, after this prologue, the second chapter — for me the opening of the novel proper — begins:

TUGGING UP ITS HEAVE AND SLOSH, pushing them down, spindrift wind swung and swirled above continuous discontinuity, flux, and swell, scumbled with foam and nudged by evening's slant-light through all the colors of glass. A bit of wood slid, turning, toward pilings slowly pogoing in shifting skin, then slid away but not so far. Another hump smashed to foam along its crest and, become wave, arched, spooming, repetitious motion marking an orderliness in this oscillate irresponsibility shattering shoreward.

About which, harkening again back to the "Introduction" (surely the last time for many, many pages) and prompted only by the OED, I make one comment: "pogoing" . . . ? *Not* before 1921 (the invention of the pogo stick[5]).

At any rate.

We are in a storm at the Hermopolis docks on the day of the September equinox ("a turning point as holy for rituals of the east as for any western sacramental"). Despite the wind and rain, the revels of the city's titular deity, Thoth, fill Hermopolis's main streets and squares with processions, chanting, and prayer. (" — Thoth, whose totem is the ibis, the inventor of writing and letters, draughts and dice, architecture and astrology; he is the bull among the stars, who, at the behest of Marduk the Sun, toppled Babel's grand tower and tore tongue from tongue into the mutually incomprehensible array of human languages, even as his own breath imparted life to all things living, unto quill and calamus.") In the warm and rare Egyptian rain, so far no one he's asked has been able to tell Neoptolomus where to find the temple he seeks. ("If a god has no name, what sort of a god can he be?" one man asks him, urging him to join in Thoth's celebration.) Unable to see his true object, however, Neoptolomus has found himself deviled by nameless dissatisfactions, as he walks along the waterfront to wander up this deserted alley or down that empty backstreet.

A new city never appears bigger or more confusing than on the day one encounters it.

Perhaps as he had found his patron at Heracleon, here he will run into Clivus, who could not only help him locate the shrine but might even resume their affair, "for already I'd learned, from my Roman friend, when so briefly we'd met on distant Crete, that sex with someone knowledgeable in the desireful workings of your body — and whose desiring turns you know as well as you know the stones patterning your father's hearth — though unlikely ever to reconduct you to passion's heights, can offer extraordinary relief and refuge from the stormy banks of life and lust."

Beside the roaring Nile, Neoptolomus sees a naked youth walking up

---

[5] Phyllis is responsible for this fact. Thanks again, Phyl.

Hermopolis's rainy docks. Even before Neoptolomus can ask the fellow if he knows of that elusive holy site, the well-hung, handsome youngster, perhaps a year or so younger than our narrator, tells Neoptolomus that he is from the city of Bithynia in Asia Minor and makes clear he is of a randy disposition. (All Neoptolomus can remember of Bithynia is that "I'd heard it was very near Syria — where I had spent my last three years — and, of course, that the elegant Petronius had once been proconsul there; as well, it was the home of some dancer Sappho had been smitten with nearly a thousand years before — none of which told me much about the youth standing on the rain-spattered boards before me.") Under the peppering drops, the young fellow explains that, in search of sexual adventure, he has slipped free of an older lover, leaving him behind at the city central celebration:

> "But who is he?" I asked.
>
> Droplet-speckled shoulders shrugged. "No one, really." Above his green, green eyes, be-gemmed lashes flickered, as lightning flickered over us. [. . .]
>
> "Doesn't he satisfy you?"
>
> "Oh, very well. He is elderly, kind, wise, masterful. And handsome. Yet there is always something . . . missing, I suppose, at the core of even the most ardent love — something making those of us with a certain restlessness of soul seek further, want more, yearn to explore beyond all we are given."
>
> I chuckled; and, like a grumble from a discontented god, thunder above Hermopolis obliterated it.
>
> [*All ellipses* not *in square brackets are in the original.*]

At the youth's suggestion, he and Neoptolomus take refuge in a dockside warehouse, for finally Neoptolomus decides he will have to put aside his patron's commission long enough to take some pleasure from this grim, gray town. Under the ceiling's dripping beams, on a corner pile of straw, they have sex. It goes on for several gloriously explicit pages, indeed, for the bulk of the chapter: wet, passionate, near-acrobatic — and exhausting. ("Though I thought it then and have often since, I have never written it down until today: The boy made love like a man condemned to die within the hour who wished to wrench every gram of ecstasy from the act.") Spent at last, in fragrant straw, with the boy in his arms, Neoptolomus closes his eyes.[6] Their extreme coupling has been, however, not the measured sex with Clivus Neoptolomus had been hoping for. Might he be able, Neoptolomus wonders, with later conversation, to locate a calmer strain in this impassioned ephebe, "to more-than-touch: to grasp, hold, or even determine the outline of what it was that had so far seemed absent in our encounter." Neoptolomus drifts to sleep . . .

Waking to harsh voices arguing in the alley outside (Chapter Three — but whence the need to enumerate . . . ?), Neoptolomus finds the boy gone. He goes to the warehouse door and steps from the building:

> The boards of the low storage houses were stained with lime and rain. Here and there, in a huge sky, smashed silver fell from deep blue. Down a side street before the rushing Nile, sun gilded the wet dock houses. Afternoon gold bladed into the alley. Ships' masts swayed and palm trees rocked above the shore. The street I stood on ran with orange muds and, to one side, green oil. Making my way through the sucking stuffs, I reached the corner and, a hand against drenched wood, stepped around it —

— where, at the joining of three ways, he finds a dozen ruffians, Roman soldiers, and beggars in altercation. Before he can determine the cause, they run off, leaving one hooded beggar in a rude, ragged robe. Neoptolomus begins talking with him and learns the elderly man is looking for his "prodigious

---

[6] Binky writes: "Having read through—and been somewhat lulled by—the prologue chapter's low-key sexual encounters, Randy, the first time I passed from there into Neoptolomus's love-making with the young Bithynian, the effect was as if the book went into Technicolor and simultaneously opened into the three screens of Abel Gance's *Napoleon* (1927), complete with surround sound. In these eight pages all five senses are appealed to half-a-dozen times. Here are the differing heats of palm, genital flesh, inner arm, and nape, the second finger's slip across the rucked foreskin, wet with excitement's pre-leakage, the straw's roar when you throw the side of your face onto it, how the passing tongue flexes, pressed to a thumb knuckle, the feel, the odor, the tastes of two male bodies, the hammering heart behind someone else's ribs during orgasm, hammering yours; times, hefts, shifts in weight and tautness, the slap of bellies slicked with sweat and rain, a dithyramb of rising and resonating intensities. I know you couldn't quote it, can't describe it, had to cut it. Still, it was one of my—yes—great first-time reading experiences. In one way, I'm glad you didn't try to recreate it. In another, well . . . when I read your synopsis and reached this part, the bottom fell out of my belly, as it might have had I rounded a roadway's bend, expecting to see a mountain menacing silver clouds, to find instead a graveled waste to the bald horizon."

Thanks, Binky.

young protégé. Perhaps you've even seen him — a green-eyed fellow, as handsome as yourself, somewhere along these docks."

Is *this* the young man's older lover . . . ?

Without admitting he's bedded the boy within the hour, Neoptolomus engages the man in further conversation. As they talk, though, Neoptolomus realizes, now from the fact that his hands are so clean, now from the elegance of his Latin diction, that this is no waterfront vagabond. Rather he must be a nobleman, even a rich Roman in disguise. "Are you jealous of him?" Neoptolomus asks, daringly.

"Why should I be?" the "beggar" declares — and goes on:

"I glory in his youth, his bravery, and . . . yes, his vigorous sex! Once I said to him just idly, mind you, that I would delight in seeing him tied and ravished by one of those huge wrestlers from the long island beyond Asia. Less than a week later, he whispered: 'Be at such-and-such an inn at such-and-such an hour by the back window,' and would say no more. When I wandered by the inn at the specified time, and looked between the shutters, with his black braid bound in a loop a-top his half-shaved head, one of those near-spherical easterners carried my friend over his shoulders, into the room, and tossed him, bound shins and forearms, to the thankfully cushioned bench. Removing his belt and his weapon, with an outsized member like a gnarled, yellow yam, he abused my poor boy, now one way, now another, till the blood ran from his buttocks along the backs of his thighs. Bound though he was, he was not gagged. But never, to all that black-browed colossus's tinny curses, gong-like grunts, and metallic invectives, did the boy let a syllable of complaint — till, finally, as I watched them stagger through their violent, even bloody, pleasures, I could not tell whether sympathetic lust or lustful sympathy was the greater of the twin fires within me. Another time, when I told him I would delight to watch him disport himself with a pair of yellow-haired children of the north, again he told me I should linger at the door of a certain shack that would be left a-jar. When I did so, I saw him inside with two gold-haired brothers, their eyes of old ice — and neither above a dozen years of age. Easily they could have been twins. As they poked, wrestled, and kissed, now one, now the other was more eager to impale his youthful prize upon my dark-haired champion's considerable manhood. Their Latin was heavily accented, uncouth, but inventive. As I observed the boys' boisterous jokes and jibes, I could not tell if I felt more desire or more delight at their puerile merriments, at their passages of back-arched ecstasy. Still another day, when jokingly I said it would amuse me to see him in the throes of lust with three great Nubian sailors, like the ones prowling the southern docks of the seaside port we passed through, again he instructed me to avail myself of an empty upstairs tavern room. Removing a board from the floor, through which, a night later, as I'd been instructed, I looked into the room below, I saw him already in lust's transport with three ebon-skinned fellows, the shortest of whom towered him by a head, and one of whom wore bronze rings in his ears you could easily wear on your wrists, and one of whose blocky biceps was bound, vein and muscle, by a chased band of such diameter that, were I to sport it on my head, you'd think me crowned emperor. One black sailor held him on his knees, head between dark fingers, while the other two simultaneously thrust their midnight members within him, of a thickness, the two of them, that together stretched his mouth to pain. From there they went on to every position four men might assume in maintenance of debauchery's heights. Now and again, as white as yours or mine, an essential gout cascaded teak flesh, flank or thigh, when it was not ejected within the hungering bowels or thirsting throat of my luminous lover, who, moving now between these two or those two muscular darknesses, became a dusky moon amidst their triple night. How could anyone doubt such a boy? Could there be a greater fidelity than his? His exhibitionistic adventurousness and my voyeuristic inquisitiveness are as complementary as much of the uncritical world finds to be male and female. Why, only yesterday, I told him, 'What pleasure I'd have in watching you couple with the first foreigner you meet tomorrow on this very dock!' And again, last night, he told me to visit — today — a dockside warehouse with a chink between its old boards, through which I might see what transpired on the straw heaped within."

As I realized my recent pleasures were merely an extension of his narration, this beggar coughed (from a shed across the alley, a gull flew up, down, and away), then continued:

"Only sometimes, whether by beggar or by emperor posed, the finest plan goes awry. Alas, it's happened more than once between us, where I've gone to the wrong hovel, the wrong inn, or — as I must have this afternoon — the wrong warehouse. For this time I saw nothing. All his athletically energetic faithfulness was — today — for naught. But then, in the profligacy of eggs laid by fowl or fish or spider, in the amount, the intensity, the variety of the sexual instincts themselves, we know that most of life is a riotous superfluity. Take the lusts that, along through the night journey of nations, weaves like sea-fire between woman and woman, man and man. While it contributes little to procreation, what individual or what society could aspire to civilization without it, whether at peace or at war? What woman would seriously take up arms or art without it? And what man could? At the same time, it supports all that yearns after the name of culture — sculpture, song, poetry, or philosophy. When such men and women do not create the pinnacles of culture themselves, they are sorely needed to appreciate those who do. Without us, society becomes a muddle of needy barbarians, where, whether or not his or her own desires are with the majority, any man or woman with a jot of intelligence or sensibility passes his or her bleak life sunk in the herd's stupidity. We pray to Jove and Venus and the Great God Pan, but the only gods truly great are that rambunctious pair, Muddle and Need; for their mischief straits all human endeavor, high to low, doubtless determining the actions within Olympus's very Pantheon. I have yet to decide which is the primal parent of desire."

His narrative relieved a bit of my worry, though now and again I wondered if it were only some aristocratic delicacy that prompted this old "beggar" to appease my embarrassment. Could my passionate coupling with his energetic paramour have been a mere rhetorical turn in the recomplication of their day's discourse?[7]

Neoptolomus leaves the "beggar," deciding that, should he encounter the youth again, he will warn the Bithynian ("reading things only by the most commonplace code, which says that lovers grow jealous when they see a lover entwined with a stranger") that the elderly man might have observed them — and let the youngster deal with this datum as it deserves.

---

[7] Phyllis has suggested I quote this passage because, beyond Chapter One, it is the longest section of prose in the book where the sexual carryings-on are indirectly, rather than directly, described; thus, unlike the warehouse tryst, for which it functions as a kind of rhetorical recovery, it can be reprinted without lapsing into rank explicitness.

Wandering from the waterfront, Neoptolomus rounds another corner to see a street brawl underway: beggars, priests, ruffians — and, rushing in from an alley a moment on, again Roman soldiers! Someone shouts. The brawlers break up. On the cobblestones, a knife in his neck, lies . . . the naked Bithynian, his green eyes wide.

He is dead.

While Neoptolomus stands, astonished, the "beggar" runs from a side street to the center of the square, recognizes the slain boy and cries out, throwing off his frayed robe — yes, from the toga beneath it, clearly he is a Roman lord: "No! No . . . ! Not here — take him across the river, to Hir-wer!" He begins to shout orders, which the soldiers fall to obeying. With a jagged scar down his face, a great bemuscled fellow snatches up the beggar's abandoned cloak from the muddy walkway, then, with it over his shoulder, goes to yank the knife from the corpse's neck. Could *he* be the murderer? wonders Neoptolomus. The former "beggar" cries out: "Why? *Why* — ? Oh, my Antinous! I chose you myself. But why must it have been you?" Neoptolomus is dumbfounded — when a young priest with a shaved head takes his arm.

"Quick! Come, my old friend . . . !" It is his army lover, Clivus, now serving in the priesthood of the nameless god! As the soldiers carry the body of Antinous away toward the water, Clivus leads Neoptolomus off. "But didn't you know? That was the Emperor Hadrian, Pontifex of the Empire of Rome! For six months, now, his imperial flotilla of fifty ships has anchored a few leagues down the Nile from here — but then, you have only just arrived in Hermopolis."

For a year and a half, from Bithynia to Egypt, the love of Hadrian for Antinous has been a focus of gossip, rumor, and scandal. Both have been consorting with scandalous types at low inns and waterfront dives. Now and again the emperor borrows some ragged vestment to disguise his profligacy. But it no longer fools anyone. Talking of the revenge the murder of the emperor's favorite might now bring to Hermopolis, Clivus takes Neoptolomus to the city's edge and the temple of the nameless god. As they enter —

Piled a-top one another to make a corridor whose ceiling I could not see in the upper dark, the wall stones were the height of short men perched on one another's shoulders. With undressed faces gray-black as true beggars' feet gone barefoot in a foul city, the rocks were lapped by mossy tongues, up from the floor. Here and there water trickled beside our shoulders. Ahead, at a turning, on a scrolled iron tripod, fires reeled on the coals within it.

Clivus is afraid the emperor will raze Hermopolis, burn it to the foundations — even the temple — scattering salt on its ashes, as his ancestors had done once at Carthage.

Well, Neoptolomus counters, as they pass among the temple rocks, he can perhaps conclude his patron's business before then. He needs to see the High Priest about some lands across the river in Hir-wer, the town the emperor spoke of. In the main hall, a ritual is in progress, however; and, some sitting, some standing, the worshippers sing their hymn.

There were fewer than I would have thought. Also they seemed far poorer. Some were ragged. Most were naked, as was I (for Hermopolis was not Rome), displaying both their poverty and their humility before the god. Suddenly I saw, among the unclothed, in the shadow of one square temple column, the great bemuscled ruffian from the melee in the street, with his head shaved like one of the priests and the scar dropping across his right eye, staring at me with his left. Catching his gaze, I felt a deeply sexual surge, so that I turned away, wanting to hide my response to him, having already seen him start to rise in the temple's half dark.

Before the altar, the High Priest completed the prayer. As he started down the steps beside the statue on the chapel alter, I pulled away from Clivus to accost him. "My name is Neoptolomus, noble Priest, and I have come on a commercial mission to see about some investments in your properties at Hir-wer — "

But the High Priest interrupts:

"My friend, the temple has suffered a catastrophe today. This very morning, infidels broke into our hold here and raped the sacred *phallos* from the statue of our nameless god. [. . .] Bandits invaded our hall and, from its sacred socket, removed the deity's golden *phallos*, encrusted with jade, jewels, and copper. They have carried it away. We know not if it be in the city, if it has gone across water, or even if it is unto the desert. Those who changed moneys from foreign lands and those who sold doves have turned up their tables, put them against the walls, and gone home. Here at the temple, howsoever, we can conduct no commerce until its return." [...]

Over the heads of the supplicants, some seated on pews, some kneeling before them, across the hall, on the raised altar, ringed with braziers, I could make it out. [...]

"See him there," another voiced intruded. Thinking it was Clivus, I looked aside, to see it was the one-eyed ruffian who spoke! "Oh, he is a terrible god, with spined wings, one foot human, one clawed like a carrion bird, one hard hand of a huge workman and one with a dragon's talons. His head has horns; his maw holds the tusks of a demon. A god of fertility, death, construction, and abundance, he is also a god of lust."

Again, so as not to see or be seen by the man, I turned to gaze at the god.

Even violated, the statue is imposing; although, Neoptolomus comments, in its raped state, with its vacant genital socket, it seems oddly effeminated — rather, a winged and monster-headed goddess. Acolytes pull a silver gauze before it. "The god will remain thus curtained," the High Priest announces, "until the *phallos* is again in its place." A shadow behind its bright scrim, the statue regains its former virility, Neoptolomus notes, once its violation is veiled.

The High Priest offers our narrator a meal of wine, brined olives, cheese, bread, and figs — and a room in the monastery cellars. (The one-eyed ruffian has moved away.) As the priest gives Neoptolomus over to the acolytes who are to take him to his room, his parting suggestion is that, after some indeterminate time, perhaps, when they are able to retrieve the sacred member, Neoptolomus can proceed with his real negotiations.

In his stone cell, having eaten, Neoptolomus lies on his hard bed, trying to put aside thoughts of the scarred ruffian and wondering if Clivus will visit later that night to resume their army affair. As time passes, however, Clivus does not come. Still alone, Neoptolomus drifts to sleep.

As dawn breaks through the brazen leaves on the vines about the high granite window, Neoptolomus wakes. Shaking his shoulder, Clivus kneels beside his bed, clearly upset. He has come not to make love — but to warn! The High Priest has found someone with power, wealth, and wisdom enough to retrieve the stolen *phallos* for the temple. He has sold Neoptolomus to the man as a catamite in exchange for his commitment to return the *phallos* to its right and proper place.

"Flee, flee from here before you are taken — "

Neoptolomus tries to rouse himself. Immediately, however, soldiers and priests invade his cell, push Clivus away, and, chaining Neoptolomus, drag him into the temple courtyard, where, his monies all taken, he is handed over to a caravan, clearly made up of brigands — or, perhaps, imperial soldiers in disguise. For, in the cool dawn, with the band, as a distraught Neoptolomus begins his trek across the sands, he realizes the caravan is headed by a man in a rude robe — a beggar's cento, its cut, color, and patches familiar to Neoptolomus.

Though the man is never too near, Neoptolomus recognizes that soiled and ragged raiment.

Could it be the disguised emperor, who is leading these rude fellows on this quest?

Now and again, Neoptolomus overhears comments that certainly sound as if the caravan seeks some treasure — surely the purloined *phallos*.

Could Neoptolomus have been purchased as a replacement for Hadrian's slain lover? How, he wonders, would *he* be at creating the imperial diversions the emperor had described on the Hermopolis docks? As Neoptolomus trudges along the sand in chains, he decides that worse fates could have befallen him — and that his situation might have some advantages. Thus he is eager to undertake whatever sexual tasks his imperial lover — however incognito — might have for him. That evening, after they camp, Neoptolomus's chains are removed and he is brought into the pavilion of the caravan leader.

The man pushes back his hood to disrobe, however — and it is *not* Hadrian.

Rather it is the scarred and bemuscled fellow who had stared at him in the temple, the robe's rightful owner, his knife again in its sheath.

Without his dress, I saw, now that I had a chance actually to observe him, he had ornamented himself like the wild man he was: up the back of one ear he wore six silver rings. From the other hung a grooved gold nugget in a much distended lobe. He wore rings through both his teats, so that they had grown, from the all-but-constant stimulation of them, to the size of the first joint of my thumb — indeed larger than the nipples of most women.

Peremptorily the man grasps Neoptolomus, who, disoriented, blurts: "But the *phallos* has been stolen — and you know where it is!"

This halts the ruffian. After a moment, he answers: "Yes. That's true." Then, over a welter of wondrously lapidary pages, he seizes Neoptolomus, who resists at first. But his bandit paramour tells him gruffly: "You cost me thirty silver dinars — and a night's sleep. Come here!" — and ravishes our narrator.

Like the passage describing his love-making with Antinous, I cannot quote it.

But though it is different in mood, detail, and affect, it is possibly even more vivid and intense; and is quite a sexual set piece.

This is what precedes it:

As he was neither Jew nor Muslim, his prepuce was of an inordinate length and width. It flopped about the rim of his grip when he'd brought himself to climax, while he rooted deep in my face with his tongue or held me to his chest to gnaw the distended teats on his brazen breasts. His hand a-pump between us, there, he'd push me down to lick up his uliginous discharge as it overran the boulder of his fist, suck away any liquid pearls a-linger in his groin, or tongue what dribbled his belly . . .

When their coupling (ten pages over two chapters, with half-a-dozen orgasms between them, which starts in the tent, moves out under the stars, then returns within . . .) is done, Neoptolomus's owner, lover, and master turns out to be a committed son of the desert.

This is what follows it.

He — and, indeed, all the other sub-chiefs in his brigand band — had no sense of privacy in intimate matters. One might walk into his pavilion, on any scene between us, asking for advice or orders, and, from the man, however curtly, receive them.

Indeed, during or just after the communal meals we took outside around the evening fire, he and his chiefs gained an exhibitionistic delight in casually demonstrating what one or another youngster — this camel groom, that provisions loader, or, indeed, I — would do for his lord. And I must tell you, there at the fire with the others talking lazily of this and that, I have done as much, in my way, as did Antinous for his emperor.

Still, the basic servicing this rough fellow demands is nothing like the erotic theatrics Neoptolomus had been expecting to engineer.

Besides his scar (which, he told me, even as it disrupted his already coarse and sun-darkened features, had lost him much of the vision in his right eye, though his left, as sharp as a peregrine's, made up for it), his other "deformity" was his huge and slab-like hands. On fingers now thick as hatchet hafts, he'd gnawed the nails, thumb to little, since childhood, so that, while they banded his broad nubs right to left, from leathery cuticle, all teeth-thickened, to crowns ballooning a whole half inch before them, scarred and hardened in sand, he could never allow the nail proper to grow greater than they'd been when, as a child of four or five, he'd commenced the habit.

At first I found them hideous. Then, as he took great delight in sinking one, two, or three fingers, now down into my mouth, now deep up my fundament, I found myself thankful they were not, indeed, the foul talons of some of his fellows, however more prepossessing they were in other aspects than he. After a month, I began to find them, to my fascination, brutally erotic, so that he only had to touch me, or, indeed, bring one sand-hardened finger anywhere near my body, and I was aroused.

Nor did he miss that arousal.

In the evenings, as we ate out at the fire, he on his chair, I naked and cross-legged by him, his bare foot on my thigh, he would hold forth to the men on this or that raid they'd planned, till, at one point or another, absently he might brush his hand across my face, then interrupt his commentary to point out to the others: "Look there, how he loves me! See him, risen as proud as a desert adder!" The others would laugh. I would smile. He would go on. Then some other bandit would try to outdo him with an even coarser joke at the expense of one of our other young men.

Once, during an evening's after-dinner session of braggadocio among the older fellows, the narrator is traded to one of his lord's lieutenants for another youth and spends three rather sexually full days with his new master in a smaller, less opulent, smellier tent. But, in the end he is traded back: "You're much better," his old master tells him, when they are alone. "As pretty as the little fox was, all he did was lie there and whimper when I grabbed him. Now — ! Fall on your knees before me, friend, and lick the salt from my flesh until I am raised to the plateau the gods have given all men and women to ascend to called pleasure . . . !" After only a few more days, impelled by a combination of their sex's oddity and directness, Neoptolomus finds himself, to his surprise and even distress,

filling the space of any disappointment in my new lover, who, on my return, had become my old (he smelled like a camel and delighted in thrusting his tongue, at the oddest moments, deep into my mouth like a boar after truffles, while he stimulated himself to climax, and in general made love like a rutting ox), with a bounding tenderness for this scar-faced, steel-armed, granite-thighed, and finally fascinatingly ugly fellow, who, as long as he was sexually satisfied himself, was actually, if roughly, quite obliging. Basically he was pleased for me to do anything and everything with him — as long as I initiated the things I liked to do only in private . . . and did them often — though much of our congress, in its heat and intensity (interruptible as it was), was all-but-without words. Above all, I realized, one morning when, for the third time before dawn, he poked me awake to ask if I *wanted* to make love to him as, sprawled on my back across the cushions, I had once more gotten an erection in my sleep, my desert colossus wished to be thought sexually irresistible!

But the desert men are dreadful exhibitionists:

Often I was called in from under the blue, bronze, and mackerel sky, from among the camels and into the tent, where the seven chief brigands met to map out their routes and strategies — and, in one or another twenty-minute break from their negotiations, I would service my master — or, on a few occasions [. . . service orally][8] his chief lieutenant, who had grown too excited and exercised during the discussion; and so, decided my lord, needed some relaxing, some calming down. All this occurred while the others wandered about or stood and watched, munching dried figs. (I believe more than once his lieutenant feigned such a tantrum because he knew I'd be called in to calm it.) Now and again, others of them would summon their boys in as well.

For all their play with us, there were moments of high jealousy. I have seen a boy out in our encampment with a black eye, or walking with a limp that came from a beating over some presumed sexual infraction.

I never suffered any such, however, because — I can only infer — I had the good sense to make clear to whom my first allegiances lay. Whenever, always at my master's orders, I finished with one man or another, I would return, drop to my knees before him, and kiss his broad and sand-hardened foot, or, if he sat in his chair talking with the other men, crouch at his feet and nuzzle his granite thighs, lick his salty testicles (often he told me how much that pleased him, when I did it in front of his fellows), while he gave my head an acknowledging pat, called me his "little gentile hedgehog," and went on with his conversation.

You call it self-abasement? It was simply common sense. And it achieved the desired end. I survived my desert stay sans injury — at least from him.

While it has its pleasures, the bandit's day-to-day life is without anything approaching intellectual stimulation. (When, one night, Neoptolomus attempts to recite a poem to his master, first he gets sniggers, then chuckles, and finally outright guffaws.) Their several violent encounters with other bandit bands, vividly described, terrify Neoptolomus. (Each may or may not have something to do with the return of the *phallos*.) After his first question to the bandit leader, however, Neoptolomus is unable to get another clear answer from the man. On one such raid, Neoptolomus sees his master coldly cut the throat of an enemy Neoptolomus's own age — reminding him that, after all, the man was, most likely, Antinous's actual murderer. (That night, Neoptolomus has the first of several dreams that will regularly revisit him throughout the novel: he is

---

[8] Actually this bracketed ellipsis covers three pages and contains a description of oral sex to rival (and perhaps surpass, because it is so different from, save in its rhetorical richness), one of Guy Davenport's scenes of adolescent masturbation. [Phyllis's evaluation.]

set upon by a huge creature that seems some form of the nameless god: "part manticore, part minotaur, part chimera . . ." — often a terrifying presence but as often an astonishingly tender lover.) On another, the one friend besides his master Neoptolomus has made in the band — another lieutenant's catamite — is wounded mortally and, though not yet dead, must be left on the sand without water to die under the sun — because he will be dead in a day or two, anyway. When they pillage a peaceful settlement, Neoptolomus is appalled at the sexual atrocities some of the men in the caravan, both younger and older (including, indeed, his lord), commit on the women. Hours before he had been musing on how civilized his master and the men of the desert, in reality, were. Now he is shocked by what a narrow notion of civilization has called forth his judgment. Perhaps, he goes on to consider, it is the notion of civilization itself, with all the crimes it excuses and disguises, which is shockingly narrow. The bandits' actions seem insufferably barbaric to Neoptolomus and completely unlike the lazy peace-keeping duties he'd performed with his squadron above the idyllic mountain town, when, in Syria, Clivus had been his lover.

The brigand's men respect their brutal leader, however, and he

ran his caravan of expilators and cutthroats with a metallic discipline that often verged on iron cruelty — though, let me say it, to me he was never outrightly cruel. Rather, I found myself the recipient of all the privileges and comforts you might expect with my position: extra food, my own tasks in the camp now and again reassigned by him to others, and more of his companionship than most.

Though only when we were alone, he would ask my advice on this or that about our band, an honor over which I was popinjay proud — natural enough, I suppose, when there were no others.

Occasionally, as, in my daytime djellaba and sandals, we trudged the dunes, I'd muse that, were we in a more domestic surround and not raping, pillaging, and looting across the wastes, this might have been a pleasant relationship, since my master found my attentions both physically and socially a delight and thought me amusing and clever (as long as I did not broach actual poetry) while I — even if we had nothing else in common — found him generous, friendly, passionately masculine, and, by now, scar, smell, and hand, jaw-clenchingly attractive as only the wholly alien can be or become.

At a stop beside a market in Alexandria ("I arrived in Alexandria as a barbarian, without any knowledge of its social laws and formal legislation, up and as alert as a king to an early change of government scheduled for that day, in my sandy finery and bronze bangles, given me by my desert lord, listening for an elegance and an oratory that, in each street as I looked for it, remained silent to me; but as I searched for some problem I was there to solve, I saw only untroubled versions of myself in the gates and the avenues around me"[9]), Neoptolomus learns that his master has sold him off to a man of the city!

"You were not happy in the desert," his gruff paramour declares, when, back at the encampment, Neoptolomus demands to know why. "You get no pleasure from our violences in the desert — because you are a child of the town. Besides, I have found a young man here who is not happy with town life — and who might be more pleased than you with our desert regimen. No, he is not so clever as you. But, then, he does not talk as much. Go and try to be happier, little hedgehog." The rejection hurts, but on reflection Neoptolomus realizes he has actually been very lucky.

Neoptolomus assumes his new master is some city cut-throat, from whom, perhaps, he can escape. His new owner is a scholar, however, at work in his neat stone house, editing texts from Pergamum to replace Alexandria's library, long-ago destroyed by Caesar. Having seen Neoptolomus with the outlaws, he's taken pity on him, and paid for his release. After their first night of sex, gentle, passionate, yet moderately restrained, under the canopy on the roof (the kind of sex Neoptolomus had once hoped for with Clivus—but our narrator has been spoiled by the more violent and gritty commerce he'd found out in the sands), next morning his scholar-lover explains, Neoptolomus is all-but-free to go:

> "How, in all consciousness, could I keep you? I might employ you as a secretary, if you found the work amenable." Though, as I heard him say it, I noted—more silently than I would have days ago—my late lord of the desert had had little difficulty keeping me as such and had only sold me away because his heart was

---

[9] Binky notes that this passage makes an interesting comparison with one of Constantine Cavafy's best-known poems, "Waiting for the Barbarians."

as kind and noble as his exterior was rude and primitive—nor had I much difficulty being kept.

It seems, however, the scholar knows something of the *phallos*, whose-whereabouts Neoptolomus is still hoping to trace. It is not so important for its jade, gold, and jewels, the man tells Neoptolomus.

Rather it takes its worth from the papyruses rolled up and kept in it.

Those ancient texts tell of philosophical, mathematical, and astrological wonders, whose import dwarfs the material value of the object itself — simply a more or less elegant casing for the marvels of knowledge and power within. The temple back at Hermopolis would easily forgo the gold, jade, copper, and jewels, opines the scholar, for the secrets inside.

Various points of both the plot to steal the sacred object and the reason behind the murder of the emperor's favorite now come to light. Fearing young and unsophisticated Antinous had far too much influence, the scholar tells Neoptolomus, the emperor's advisors engineered a plot where again and again Hadrian would discover his favorite in flagrant unfaithfulness — till the emperor himself, unable to stand his own jealousy, had ordered the boy murdered on the day of the revels of Thoth. It's a possible explanation, thinks Neoptolomus. Though he objects —

"The emperor himself told me, however, there on the Nile docks, that these acts of 'unfaithfulness,' as you call them, had been put together at his own request and for his own pleasure."

"Did you believe him?"

"No — at least not while I thought he might still be a beggar."

"Why, then, would you believe that, as an emperor, he spoke for any other reasons except to preserve appearances?"

"But — ?"

"Doubtless that's why you were sold off — to the boy's paid murderer himself, you now tell me. Probably you were not supposed to survive either. Surely you endured only through some intricate combination you could not follow of necessity and chance, through conversations and orders delivered, misunderstood, or disobeyed, conveyed by messengers you never saw in alleys or taverns or rich palace chambers you were never fortunate enough to enter."

Recognizing the scholar's "chance" and "necessity" as the emperor's Muddle and Need, the possibility sobers Neoptolomus.

From friend to lover, from lover to friend, Neoptolomus moves around the Mediterranean. During these pages, the book's erotic content rises to peak upon peak. With a true beggar Neoptolomus has brought into a prince's silk-hung bedroom back at Ephesus — then with the prince himself, rolling in the gutters outside the palace wall — Neoptolomus has passionate sex, both scenes rising to their several sorts of prose poetry, in their descriptions of what one male body might do with another.

In the detritus of a massacre by the Romans, Neoptolomus makes love to a thirteen-year-old Jewish soldier, Moises, one of the survivors of his regiment, in the charnel field itself, while another, shyer boy looks on, bewildered. ("I can kill. I can make love. But now that there is no reason to kill further, why will you not take me with you . . . ?") His lovers go on to include a one-legged man, a blind boy, a temple dwarf, and a hulking gladiator three times his weight and size, who guards the treasury of a rich Greek at Corinth, into which, the gladiator tells Neoptolomus, the *phallos* has found its way. But after several nights of love-making, the randy giant tells Neoptolomus he's only concocted the tale of the *phallos*'s presence to lure Neoptolomus into sex — and now Neoptolomus must get out. Only half believing the man (as easily and instrumentally the big fellow could have concocted *this* tale of the *phallos*'s absence), Neoptolomus leaves.

Each time, however, Neoptolomus expects one sort of lover, only to find himself with another, even when, several times, he carefully chooses: "Does it perhaps not matter whom we take? I fared no better by choice than I did by chance."

Thus the opening part (and the novel's first seventeen chapters) concludes.

CERTAINLY THIS IS AN ODD MOMENT at which to intrude a note on the principles by which I have tried to control paraphrase, excision, and synopsis. But better here than nowhere. Let me reaffirm for my readers what will, to most, however, have already become obvious: Anything presented either in quotation marks (brief sections of dialogue, mostly) or as excerpts (passages of narrative or description unencumbered by desire's detailed distractions) are unaltered quotes, bracketed ellipses excepted.

Observational obsession by the author of *Phallos* is at once the source both of the text's poetry and of its prurience (" . . . blinking about in the hirsute, rich, and slightly sour odor, I found myself observing a lone freckle among the tangle of enlarged veins at the thick, left-curving base of his rigid . . ." " . . . despite a pliability in the dwarf's gluteal musculature, which, under my kneading, prompted a thought that, pursed as it was — pulled tight as if with a drawstring — under my tongue's urging soon he'd as easily allow our donkey's log to enter him as some bit of human kindling . . ." " . . . across my cradling palm a prepuce, dark as ripe olives, in its overhang longer, thicker, and looser on the left than . . ."), which, besides the fact that, in full context, they would result in this website's being struck by our university monitors, I have excised because, I suspect, along with most modern editors, such cascades of detail finally slow the reader — who is eager, at least on first acquaintance with such a text, for its overall shape.

As well, many such minor incidents simply flesh out an atmosphere of sensuality without advancing the story in any way I can discern; and atmosphere is not where, on first encounter, interest is likely to fall. Brazenly I have omitted them, many without mention — though it is only fair to say that some of the excisions have been contested by both Binky and Phyllis. You will find their reasons, at least — if not the restorations — in ensuing notes.

Anything printed not as an excerpt or not specifically in quotation marks has supported enough of my editorial paraphrasing and condensation so that I cannot, with conscience, attribute any such sentences to the anonymous author of *Phallos*.

The prose of *Phallos* — even in the three extraordinary scatological chapters toward its end — is written in the past tense of most normative fiction. In order to achieve what registers with me as a more contemporary mode, I have put my own synopsis into a neutral present — to mark it current, if for no other distinction.[10]

We continue.

---

[10] "Come on, Randy. The present tense hasn't been 'current' since 1974." (Binky)

IN LIKE MANNER, THE BOOK'S Part II (*sive* central third) covers several more years.

Neoptolomus still desires the *phallos*, so that he can return it to Hermopolis in Egypt, complete his old mission, and repay his own debt to his former patron back at Rome. But strong forces war for the sacred object. Various people involved seem only fronts for various others, more powerful than they. Now and again, all sides seem to mistake Neoptolomus for one of their own — or, from time to time, for an enemy to be eliminated. Finally, however, the identity of these forces — or their motivations — remains a mystery.

Over these pages the sex moves from the relatively uncomplicated encounters described above, where the variety, styles, and emotional tone are the most notable aspects, to take in sadomasochism, urine, group sex, and more.

His adventures bring him to Rome, where (this is Phyllis's favorite part), in the storage district, Neoptolomus reconnects with his Roman patron, who is only happy to learn the young man is still alive.[11] (Apparently once Neoptolomus was carried off by the desert rogues, the priests returned his money to his Roman patron, with whom they had long had dealings.)

Neoptolomus begins work as a broker at three of his former patron's warehouses. At a tavern called Vulcan's Forge, he takes a second-floor room.

---

[11] Phyllis writes: "You're glossing over Neoptolomus's entire reunion with his patron—an emotional high point of the book, Randy. After searching for his patron three days, finally in the warehouse district Neoptolomus sees him down the street. They recognize each other, run up to one another, and embrace, in the midst of which Neoptolomus decides he is going to have sex with the man right there, and wrestles him into an alley, and into a doorway, where he forces the older man to have both oral and anal sex. His patron protests, 'No . . . ! No . . . ! Stop . . . ! No . . . ! We mustn't . . . ! Please, not here . . . ! Not now!" A young man comes by, and Neoptolomus tells him roughly to stop looking and get away. When they are finished, his patron thanks Neoptolomus and, straightening his tunic, tells him, 'I am so glad you are a barbarian outlander from the islands and not a civilized young Roman who respects his elder. It's wonderful to see you again, my son. Would you like a job?' Neoptolomus is overjoyed. His patron advances Neoptolomus some money, shows him which warehouse to come to the next day, then leaves, and Neoptolomus wonders how and where he learned that his patron would respond so well to forceful sex. He thinks briefly over some of the incidents from his past few years, but at once remembers a time from his island childhood where he and his patron were among the goats and Neoptolomus had been upset by something that had happened with his father. His patron had forced him to have sex anyway—and afterwards, Neoptolomus had surprisingly felt much better. Walking through the streets, looking for a cheap inn, Neoptolomus laughs, feeling he has repaid a debt. Now, come on, Randy. Why would you elide that?"

Well, since you asked: however well it works out, it is a rare moment in the book of non-consensual sex, and I didn't think it would be good to stress it in, what for most, will be a first-time encounter. Many would simply not appreciate that aspect, today. But perhaps we can leave it here, *en passant.*

But someone warns him: While the rooms at the Forge are fine and the fire warm, the food in the tavern below is poor, and only thieves, pimps, and worse come to drink and connive at its counter. Though it might serve as a place to live, Neoptolomus would do better to eat — and certainly to socialize — in one of the inns a few streets away. Thus Neoptolomus begins to spend his evenings at a tavern only a little distant, Hebe's Chalice. There at the bar he falls in with a group of small-time businessmen and artisans, who eat, drink, and socialize at the Chalice after work. All these men, Neoptolomus soon learns, trace their troubles to absent women — a wife who has run off with someone else, a domineering mother recently dead, a traitorous girlfriend who has done one or another of them out of most of his business profits.

Meanwhile, at his warehouse work, Neoptolomus begins what seems a satisfying affair with the young son, Lucius, of a rich Roman merchant. At Lucius's elegant townhouse, not far from the warehouse district, at first their Roman siesta-time idylls, filled with Lucius's imaginative sex-games, greatly please, and even flatter, Neoptolomus.

In the evenings, however, because Lucius's social life does not allow room for him, Neoptolomus returns to the Chalice and his new straight friends.

As they drink, joke, and laugh in the tavern, their extreme misogyny, recalling that of the men he'd known in the army, makes Neoptolomus wonder if, as a group, they don't all share secretly his sexual tastes. ("Their hostility to everything feminine, whether in art or in life, was far greater than any I had ever entertained — I who had so little to do with women.") As they yearn after the women who, now beside one man, now on the arm of another, sometimes alone or even in pairs, come through the Chalice, all these men protest their heterosexuality, now to each other, now — it would seem — to every stranger, so that Neoptolomus hesitates to reveal his own predilections, even as he finds himself becoming more and more friendly with them. Among themselves, they are quick to make fun of any male obviously homosexual who enters the place. Now and again some even demonstrate open hostility toward the prac-tice — though always in a manner ambiguous enough to leave Neoptolomus unsure if, indeed, some statement of his own proclivities isn't called for. Still,

they assumed that I was, as was each of them, a lover of women — though what conflicted love was theirs! I said nothing to make them think otherwise. I said a few things, even — a phrase here about an attractive matron, a grunt of approval there at a passing prostitute, no more — to deceive them into continuing to think so. I confess: today I know that was cowardice. Then, however, I called it curiosity — from my desire to further learn what I might of their practices.

Over these same weeks Lucius was not particularly interested in letting knowledge of me into his social circle; nor was I particularly eager for knowledge of him to become common in mine. Therefore, on those nights when, after some party, my wealthy lover would drop into the Forge and mount the steps to my room to pass the remainder of the dark hours with me above the late-drinking cut-purses, reprobates, strumpets, hustlers, and poor women below, I decided that I had, by passing my evenings at the Chalice and my nights at the Forge, alighted on the most convenient of living arrangements.

During his Chalice evenings, Neoptolomus takes to two men in particular. The first is an even-tempered and intelligent man in his late thirties, Jason, the illegitimate son of a senator's valet. Jason's deceased mother had been a weaver of fine cloth. Jason works as a carpenter, with two other men in the group. Neoptolomus is impressed by Jason's genial temperament, friendliness, and observational powers. One evening, when they are walking alone through the quiet Roman streets, Jason tells Neoptolomus that he enjoys having things pushed up his rectum during sex. Surprised, Neoptolomus assumes Jason must like getting fucked by men. (Here, aping the author of *Fanny Hill*, the author of *Phallos* does all this without a four-letter word. I mention it because in other sections he scatters scatology abundantly and brilliantly, often for effects I have simply never seen before in pornography. I am, however, neither so lucky nor so skilled in my *précis*.) Jason explains, however, that, no, he means by women. Indeed, he has tried sex with men: it does little for him. ("Sometimes I've even wished I *was* that way," Jason tells him, with a grin. "Certainly it would have made my life simpler. But, no, my solitary dreams are all of women.") The second is a sharp, lively, and rambunctious youngster, Lukey. At twenty-three (he is two years younger than our narrator), his eyes all-but-shoot from his head at every woman he sees, but he is too shy to approach them and seems too unsure of himself to realize that women find him attractive — as does Neoptolomus, though after two or three drunken evenings (when Neoptolomus leaves his hand on Lukey's shoulder or thigh seconds too long, and Lukey, seemingly without any thought, shrugs or brushes it away), Neoptolomus resolves not to push his attentions further on the young man. ("Certainly I would not wish some woman — or, indeed, a man to whom I did not respond — to paw and pet me beyond the point where I'd made my lack of interest clear, as had happened four or five times back at the Syracuse villa, forcing me to learn how to tell men — and one woman — 'No,' a valuable art and accomplishment, which, as soon as one really learns it, one rarely has to use again, since there are so many ways to suggest it, at least among the civilized.") The mascot of the circle, Lukey takes odd jobs among them, at times with Jason's carpenters, at other times with Saul's launderers, sometimes with Gaius's cart drivers, and at still others delivering messages for Costas, the Greek clerk. The men all worry that Lukey will fall in with bad company, for now and again one or the other has seen him consorting with outright thieves — the sort who hang out at the Forge. More and more he has been showing up with money or finery they cannot believe he has come by honestly.

The next time Neoptolomus goes for an afternoon siesta at Lucius's townhouse, Lucius complains that, though he would like to introduce Neoptolomus into his social circle, it is not the same-sex nature of their relationship that forestalls it. Rather, Neoptolomus is too provincial in his manners and habits.

But that's silly and stupid, Neoptolomus points out: His somewhat rough and country manner is precisely what attracted Lucius to him in the first place, when they met at the warehouse. Neoptolomus reminds his wealthy lover that Lucius has frequently told him this.

Yes, Lucius admits; but if Neoptolomus could learn to turn that country manner on and off, as it were, depending on the social situation, it would further Neoptolomus's business ventures, and it would mean they could see much more of one another. Injured by the complaint, Neoptolomus finds himself wondering if perhaps he isn't already seeing too much of Lucius. As he leaves the townhouse, a friendly groundsman smiles at him and gestures good-bye. What does it mean, Neoptolomus ponders, when my lover's servants treat me better than my lover?

Indeed, that evening, back at the warehouse, Neoptolomus asks to meet with his patron. "Do my provincial island habits, gestures, and turns of speech stand in the way of my carrying out my business tasks for your profit?"

His patron responds: "Come to my house tonight, Neoptolomus. My sister is away at Milano. When she's not there, I keep only a skeleton staff, for me and my current favorite — I don't think you've met Yin. But you might enjoy him. He sleeps on the same sleeping rug I had made for you, back at the summer place on Syracuse. We'll dine together — and you and I will talk. Come a bit before sunset. You remember where I live."

I thought I did.

But that evening, though I found the neighborhood easily, I lost my bearings among the great houses and once had to ask directions of two women and a boy lugging flower baskets for some party and, fifteen minutes on, again of a fat man driving a donkey cart heaped high with garbage and lashed across with hides, which he was taking to an outlying refuse pit.

It did smell foul.

When Neoptolomus finds the house, no longer covered with scaffolding, it looks smaller — and older, as does, in fact, the entire city. Though this urban mansion is far larger than Lucius's, Neoptolomus notes how much smaller the grounds around it are than the lawns and walled gardens at Lucius's townhouse. Here no more than six yards of shrubbery and a few statues separate it from the buildings either side.

When Neoptolomus climbs the wide stone stairs and rings the bell pull, the servant who answers the plank door is not one Neoptolomus remembers from seven or eight years ago. Still, she says he is expected. His first time actually within his patron's Roman home, Neoptolomus follows the elderly woman through high-ceilinged halls and across inner courtyards under the darkening sky, with the curiosity and trepidation of a man entering a labyrinth.

Finally, Neoptolomus hears harp notes. At a high bronze door, the servant stands aside and Neoptolomus enters a room with tall windows, a fountain in a pool to one side and, along the other, a table and several banquet couches, on one of which his patron reclines. On the floor beside the couch, crossed-legged on a bearskin thrown over the tile, a boy sits playing a lyre. He's a wonderfully muscular and lively youngster. "With eyes close to the front of his face, behind little folds down over their inner corners," he hails from somewhere in Asia. In the first minutes of greetings and introductions,

Neoptolomus finds the youngster a bit too talkative (it makes him smile. . .), but winning in his enthusiasm and curiosity, which he expresses in oddly accented Latin, and his patron perhaps too indulgent of him, but clearly happy.

> Within minutes I learned that the Syracuse villa was as much a mystery to Yin as this same Roman mansion had, in my boyhood, been to me.

Declares Yin: "But our friend promises to take me to Syracuse, this summer!"

"It's a very beautiful place," Neoptolomus tells him, "as is this."

Neoptolomus's patron chuckles:

> "I find Yin quite as delightful as I found you when you were his age, Neoptolomus. His music and his affection are both a joy." (And I had the sudden feeling I had been called here as much for Yin's benefit as for mine.) "Because the older families of the city consider me no more than a too-successful shopkeeper, when I'm in the city my social life is never at its peak — we rather used to enjoy our summer guests on the island, though, didn't we? I hope you still have a young man's appetite; and that you'll still enjoy my table."

The kitchen staff rolls in carts with a tureen of fish soup in which float circles of green onion and sliced mushrooms, a platter of roasted partridges, a bowl of mango slices and cherries, flavored with lemon juice and honey, a bowl of spinach with roasted pork cracklings and bits of salt like crushed gravel, and several kinds of breads with pieces of onion and green and black olives throughout, as well as wines — both dry and sweet, pink and red.

While they eat, once more Neoptolomus puts his question to his patron and employer.

As Yin takes up his harp, his patron says, "No — you must let us talk awhile. I'll want you to entertain later." He gestures for a servant to refill their metal goblets, while Neoptolomus reflects on how grand, even overwhelming, all this had once seemed to him, when he first worked in the Syracuse villa — and how working for the Greeks had prepared him to be a guest of the Romans; and how, in turn, his months among the Romans at Syracuse had prepared him for Lucius's city dwelling; and how life at Lucius's had prepared him . . . well, for this — so that even though it is not Neoptolomus's day-to-day fare, it does not feel particularly unusual. His patron repeats Neoptolomus's question: "You want to know if your island origins as a farmers' goatherd on Syracuse present any defects in your person that decrease your value to me as a broker of warehouse space here in the city." His patron smiles in the flicker of the braziers.

While reclining on his own couch, Neoptolomus sips his wine. ("On the bearskin, listening intensely, and, though he was from half a world away, reminding me, in that intensity, of no one more than my younger self, Yin hugged his knees.") His patron answers Neoptolomus: "On the contrary. You are alert, personable, and astute. Generally we Romans romanticize the country and island working classes — we think of them as good, honest stock, unlike the city-bred swindlers around us. If anything, I believe your island manners make our Roman clients trust you a little *more* than they otherwise might and probably work to your advantage — and to mine. At least — " and he smiles again — "that is how they have always made *me* feel about you." After a pause, still smiling, he concludes: "When you were a child, however, I remember, Neoptolomus: Any time you did not understand something, you used to laugh at it and were quick to call it stupid and silly — and, in a child of whom one is fond, that can be an engaging trait. But, you are a man, now. And, in a man, that is the one mark of a provincial you might consider an impediment to your advancement. But I tell you this only because patience is a virtue in us all — and because you have asked. But, Yin, perhaps — now — you would play some music . . . ?"

Taken by the criticism, as Yin plucks his harp strings, Neoptolomus decides to bide his time with both Lucius and his job.

Later that night, when Neoptolomus returns to the Chalice, the men continue to blame their misfortunes on women who've loved and abandoned them. (It's Lukey's too severe mother who, they declare, has made her son rebel and seek out bad friends. Exclaims Gaius, "The only way you can trust a woman is if you've tied and gagged her, up in a mountain cave away from all humanity, where you can have your will with her as you wish — and wall her in and abandon her when you're finished!" at which Jason and the others laugh, finding it a fine joke.) That evening Neoptolomus discovers that their ill will focuses particularly on the priestesses of the Shrine of Bellona — a war goddess whose women worshippers have actually changed some of the laws in Rome, so that now women can own their own property, instead of having it fettered to fathers, husbands, and brothers. Jason allows that, were the laws of the old-fashioned sort, his carpentry business would be far more successful than it is now, thanks to his greedy, evil, and scheming ex-girlfriend, who recently took him for so much. Just then, lustful but embarrassed Lukey refuses to go after a pretty woman at the bar (because he knows "she would reject me: I am poor"), though, as she leaves with another woman friend, Neoptolomus inadvertently swears "by the *phallos* of the nameless god, boy," he himself has seen her watching the handsome young man all evening.

But here the men fall to talking of the *phallos*. All the men of Rome know (or, it would seem, all save Neoptolomus): that famous and fabled object has been recently stolen by the very priestesses of whom they've been speaking. Surely, speculate the men in the tavern, the captured *phallos* is the source of the women's newfound power. The city's gossip is that the secrets once hidden within the *phallos* (certainly they are political and legal) have been removed and secreted in the vaginal cavity of the statue of Bellona herself. Raped of its secrets, the vacant case — the nameless god's great member — is now regularly demeaned and desecrated by the priestesses, emptied of its wisdom, as the all-but-valueless trinket it has become.

Lukey suggests that if they could steal those secrets, rightfully the property of men, back from the goddess, to hold that knowledge for themselves, then they would ensure that they had wealth, power, and the love of beautiful women who would respect and cherish them and keep to their proper station. Neoptolomus laughs at the idea, wondering if Lukey intends the observation as a joke.

The next afternoon, at his townhouse, again Lucius begins to harp on Neoptolomus for his provincial mannerisms. But now Neoptolomus halts his lover. "Perhaps our friendship no longer pleases you. Certainly having you disparage me for things I can't control and have no wish to change is not fun." And, to a spluttering Lucius, he leaves.

On his way back to work, Neoptolomus takes some of his mid-day hours off to engage in conversation a group of naked, dirty adolescents, rough-housing in the street. About fifteen, with bright, dark eyes and matted hair, one hangs back to talk with him. Neoptolomus is feeling bold and openly tells the boy — whose name is Maximin — of his sexual tastes, going into, and even exaggerating, some of the more outrageous acts he had recently performed with Lucius.

(Those absolutely *filthy* three pages are the ones *I* keep coming back to — so there! From here on in, though, I'm only going to tell the story . . .)

Surprising Neoptolomus, Maximin tells him that he has heard of men with such tastes and would like to try doing some of those same things. Neoptolomus tells Maximin to come to the Forge late that night, after Neoptolomus has returned from the Chalice, and pass the dark hours with him — thinking, of course, that the boy will be too frightened, or think better of it, and so do no such thing.

That day, when work is finished, instead of going to the Chalice, however, Neoptolomus decides to go directly to the Forge. While he is walking home, about a block away, he glimpses young Maximin begging a coin from a well-off merchant, who, a moment on, Neoptolomus recognizes as Lucius's father. Merchant and beggar leave in different directions. Seconds later Neoptolomus nods first to the one, then, a block later, to the other — Maximin returns a grin, and Lucius's father a nod — while Neoptolomus strolls on, as if he had no special relation with either, even though he is greatly pleased that, in truth, he does.

That he's exchanged words with both the wealthiest and the most impoverished of the city makes Neoptolomus feel he has begun to be a true citizen of Rome.

Back at the Forge, as he enters the kitchen, Neoptolomus spots a thief and stops her in the midst of stealing the little bronze goddess that looks down from a shelf over the pots, pans, and cookery — the landlord's tutelary deity, which Neoptolomus knows the man values greatly. The thief tells Neoptolomus that she — Ihelva — is a favorite of the High Priestess of Bellona, in turn a favorite of the Empress Sabina, Hadrian's wife. When Neoptolomus mentions what the men at the Chalice have said about the *phallos* and the goddess Bellona herself, Ihelva tells him, yes, what they say is fundamentally correct.

"Or, any rate, having men think such things of us rarely hurts us — and often helps."

Neoptolomus is surprised by her "us." But Ihelva goes on: If, during the up-coming dark of the moon, he and his friends will go out beyond the twin temples of Juno and Lucina, the little thief tells Neoptolomus, and take the path away from the Temple of Minerva toward the Field of Mars and on to the Shrine of Bellona, they will find themselves welcomed by the High Priestess. In times of peace, the statue of Bellona may not be looked upon by men. And, however uneasily, the *pax romana* still reigns. If his friends, singly or together, can sexually satisfy the priestess, when she sleeps, deeply and comfortably after her sexual exhaustion, they can go behind the veil, into the shrine's keep, and steal back the secrets of the goddess from Bellona's very statue.

"But why are you telling me this?" Neoptolomus asks.

"Because I am a thief; because I like mischief; and because I like to see things change . . ."

Neoptolomus makes her put back the statue, then lets Ihelva go. When, that evening at the Chalice, he meets his friends and tells them what Ihelva has said, all are enthusiastic. Only Jason pooh-poohs the idea; while Lukey (who has heard that the priestesses are all lesbians and is excited by the notion) urges them to it. The dark of the moon, just passed, will return, the Chalice bartender tells them, three Fridays hence. The men agree to meet.

Late that night, when he returns to the Forge to sleep, Neoptolomus comes into his room on the second floor to find Maximin already within, sitting cross-legged on his bed. Maximin explains that he found out which room Neoptolomus rents, then climbed up the back wall to come through the window there . . . When they commence to make love, Neoptolomus discovers the boy is even more willing, inventive, and sexually curious than he had imagined. The little guttersnipe is wonderfully pleased with himself and proud of his own willingness to try everything that Neoptolomus suggests. (I wish I could let you read it. It's another of the novel's choice sexual set pieces — again so different in feel from the others . . .) The only flaw for Neoptolomus in his passionate night with the unlettered youth is his own fear that Lucius may knock at any moment.

But it does not happen.

Toward dawn, as Neoptolomus and Maximin drift into sleep, Neoptolomus decides perhaps Lucius has felt himself freed from an unpleasant affair just as has Neoptolomus.

For the next ten days, Neoptolomus passes his afternoon siestas from work as well as his nights back at his room at the Forge with wily and willing Maximin. Three times Maximin shows up at one of the warehouses in the morning and, even as he's flustered by the boy's arrival, Neoptolomus takes a few minutes for hurried sex behind some pile of goods on store or in a closed-off storage space. (Since Neoptolomus does not want to be discovered, rarely can they complete their acts — these encounters are comic.) By now Neoptolomus knows that Maximin — the bastard get of a soldier from the Tuscan area, and a North African whore who now works in Rome — has recently been turned out from his house by a cruel uncle and has been sleeping in the street, because his family is too poor to care for him any longer. He would seem to be in awe of Neoptolomus and appears devoted to him both sexually and personally. At the warehouse, Maximin is all curiosity; and Neoptolomus shows him the letters and orders he receives, as well as the stores of precious cloth and carved furniture the warehouse holds. One such letter, indeed, is an offer to store a large amount of grain in one of his patron's other warehouses, for which the merchant is offering an exorbitant amount of rent. Two or three phrases in the letter suggest to Neoptolomus that something illegal might be hidden within the grain. The wording hints that it may be the *phallos* that will reside there, which has Neoptolomus intrigued — an intrigue he explains to Maximin.

Impressed, Maximin looks at the letter, turning it over and over as if he might even read it.

Eagar to run errands for Neoptolomus, indeed to do anything he asks, Maximin exhibits a devotion and commitment to Neoptolomus that clearly goes beyond the sexual. Once when Maximin has left to take a message from Neoptolomus to a nearby warehouse, as he sits back, relaxing in his office, Neoptolomus reflects: Certainly it is more fun having a lover who thinks you are the most worldly and sophisticated of men, rather than having to put up with one who thinks you are a provincial yokel and country clown. To pursue the latter would simply be stupid and silly —

Which is when Lucius stops by. He is haughty, arrogant, and says several things to Neoptolomus that verge on the insulting: "To reject my friendship, and for a . . . Well, it's what one might expect from an ignorant island fellow." But Neoptolomus holds his tongue. ("Yes — and I found myself smiling over it — I had every urge to tell him he was acting silly. And stupid. But, no, I did not say that I missed his groundsman's smile more than I missed Lucius's carping; and was proud of myself for my forbearance.") There is no invitation, however, to return to the townhouse.

After Lucius leaves, Neoptolomus notes that the letter about the great grain shipment that was on his table is gone. He remembers showing it to Maximin — indeed he remembers the illiterate youth turning it and looking at it . . . Where in the world, he wonders, could it be?

After work, back in his rooms at the Forge, Neoptolomus notices some coins that he'd left that morning on his bed have also vanished. He frowns at the window, through which Maximin had climbed, over these last days, so eagerly and agilely — and through which, yes, minutes later, Maximin crawls again for sex. They fall to love-making, and, though for moments he considers it, Neoptolomus fails to confront Maximin with his suspicions, distracted as he is by the intensity of their passion.

After the boy leaves, again Neoptolomus recalls the missing coins. Going into one of his cabinets now, he realizes several *more* trinkets are gone! Where, he wonders, frowning, does the naked youth secret his pilferings? Neoptolomus vows to himself that, as fond as he is of the guttersnipe, he can not let this situation go on.

To continue allowing the boy to steal from him *is,* yes, silly and stupid.

Indeed, the next day, when the boy again comes by the warehouse, ready for both sex and to offer his services to run errands, Neoptolomus takes Maximin into his office, shuts the door, and accuses him of the thefts. "Don't you realize," he explains, "how silly and . . . well, stupid you are acting, filching coins from my table, trinkets from my drawers, and letters than you cannot even read from my desk — and for what? To sell or trade or boast of in the street to your friends? Don't you realize that I *like* you? I do — really! You are very close to being a fine young man — and I would be happy to give you moneys and gifts worth four, five, ten times as much as what you've taken from me. But how can I bring you to meet my friends, for example, knowing that you might snatch up a coin or so, should one leave it as a tip on a table for a waiter?" Neoptolomus has hoped for Maximin's contrite confession.

Instead, though, Maximin grows indignant. "You think I *steal* from you? I, who feel only gratitude toward you, who am honored by every word you speak to me, and who have kissed your body, head to toe — you think I am a thief? I, who want only that you love me and let me stay near you . . . ? No, *you* are the stupid and silly one!" Angrily, the boy turns and runs from the warehouse.

Though his feelings are conflicted, Neoptolomus decides: "If he had only admitted the thefts — or at least returned the order letter — I would have been willing to go on with it. But how can I involve myself in an affair that damages my business?" Perhaps it's better that this pleasure, Neoptolomus thinks, no matter how animally satisfying it is, with a bad sort such as Maximin, should end now rather than drag on while he robs me of all and whatever.

Taking off from work early, back in his room at the Forge, Neoptolomus ties his window shutters together with a rope. Going downstairs a few days later, however, he notices the thief Ihelva. She is sitting at the bar, drinking and laughing with the pimps there. When she sees him, she approaches Neoptolomus, chuckling. "So, you have managed to wound your rich lover."

What, Neoptolomus wants to know, does she mean?

Well, the first night your little guttersnipe stole into your room, Ihelva explains, down here we all watched your young merchant — isn't his name Lucius? — come to visit with you, only to stop and listen outside your door, while those fires called jealousy, which alone are worse than those of the Christians' hell, fanned his features and made his fist shake near his hip, as he lingered and listened beside your chamber. Since then, he has been back at least three times and, when you were not there, has even gone in and out of your room . . . "Oh, two or three times now, I myself have seen him, and once when you and the boy were inside: Again he stayed to listen and flay himself with those cruel feelings from the sounds of your lubricities within — "

"In and out of my room . . . ?" Neoptolomus frowns.

"And, always, he left with some bauble of yours," Ihelva goes on, smiling. "Oh, doubtless he wished some little remembrance of you, to hold him over the tidal dissolutions of your love: some coins, perhaps; some trinkets from your wall cabinet — and, perhaps, he wanted you to think a little worse of your low lover from the streets."

"How do you know this?" Neoptolomus demands.

"Because, once, I broke into your room *for* him," Ihelva says. "I tried to climb in through your window — as has the boy, at least three times now. But you have permanently tied that up against him — and me. Yes, I took the coins Lucius offered me to remain silent." She laughs. "But I tell you anyway, because I like to see things change . . ."

Neoptolomus realizes that he has misjudged Maximin.

Distraught, he confesses to Ihelva what has happened.

But she only laughs. "Come with the others during the dark of the moon to Bellona's shrine," she says. "There, a whole new arena of love awaits you that as of yet you have no intuition of. That is the time to judge the worth of one lover or another."

That Friday, beyond the temples of Lucina and Juno ("where cypresses darkly feathered the plum and copper sky"), wearing his spring cloak, Neoptolomus joins the other men from the Chalice, including Jason, Lukey, Costas, Saul, Gaius and the rest, as they go along the sun-reddened road.

As Minerva's temple falls behind, the group hurries toward the Campus Martius's far edge to arrive at the Shrine of Bellona.

At the top of the steps, the door is open.

Entering, they find themselves in a well-appointed chapel, with a beautiful middle-aged woman — decked as a priestess — attended by Ihelva, now arrayed not as a thief but as a priestess herself, clearly the older woman's lover.

The two women offer the men fruit, wine, and wonderful food, treating them the way, notes Jason, "true men might wish to be treated by women." Soon, indeed, it becomes an orgy.

Singly and in groups, Neoptolomus's friends have sex with the pair. On second and third encounter, one man after another passes out. Lukey seems to be holding up best. Neoptolomus hangs back, watching now one or another of them at their pleasures, his feelings oscillating between jealousy and lust. When he comes across Jason performing cunnilingus on Ihelva, he reflects that several of the men have had the women in pairs; thus Neoptolomus begins to bugger his friend — who clearly enjoys it, as does Neoptolomus himself. Before he can climax, however, he feels someone pulling him away. It is Lukey, who seems almost jealous. Neoptolomus leaves his older friend (though not before Jason gives Neoptolomus's forearm a fond squeeze), to go with his younger. In the midst of these sweaty engagements, Lukey urges Neoptolomus to come make love to the elder priestess. Having found the whole confusion of sexually excited straight men highly arousing, somewhat half-heartedly Neoptolomus consents — and when, in his excitement, Lukey seizes Neoptolomus's cock in his fist to guide it into the High Priestess's vagina ("as though he were a groom helping a stallion mount a mare"), and while the little thief Ihelva kisses the High Priestess and strokes her breasts, Neoptolomus's own excitement overcomes him.

Lukey leans above him the whole time, a hand on his shoulder, now and again stretching up to kiss the little thief. Now and again reaching down with the younger woman, to feel one or another of the older woman's breasts, Neoptolomus ("with passion borrowed from the boy") climaxes, then rolls off, feeling rather proud of himself, as Lukey takes his place for a final bout.

With the "secrets" of the *phallos* apparently forgotten, the men are asleep about the hall, stretched on various mats and cushions — even Lukey snores near Neoptolomus, who absently strokes the young man's hair. ("And, yes, I confess, I held in my hand and even kissed of him, what he had so excitedly grasped and guided of me. Lukey snored on — and I maintain I did him no more harm by it, even as he briefly stiffened within me, than he had done to me.") But Neoptolomus desists, realizing that, with the women, he has already come as close to having sex with Lukey and Jason as he will ever be able to in any reciprocally pleasurable way. Drowsily, however, Neoptolomus is aware that the two women are up and moving about.

Blinking himself awake, Neoptolomus sees the little thief/priestess Ihelva pull back a black curtain. Could this be the veil, he finds himself musing, before the goddess's terrible statue — the statue forbidden to men's gaze — that they have so ineffectually come to rob . . . ?

The High Priestess goes into the darkness.

Moments later she comes out — and Ihelva again drops the drapery.

Now the High Priestess is wearing what is surely an erect *phallos,* jaded and gemmed, copper and golden, strapped between her legs and about her hips. ("Perhaps she saw me, beside sleeping Lukey, lift my head from the silk cushion, still moist from our exertions. Her Sapphic acolyte and she came toward me.") The priestess stands above him, laughing. Suddenly Neoptolomus is convinced that the object she wears must be the *phallos* — the thing that all the sleeping men about the hall are seeking: indeed, that will allow him to return it to the temple at Hermopolis and complete his patron's mission.

The High Priestess demands that he turn over and present his bottom to her — and, there, she buggers him in the hall. ("For my friend Jason this would have been high pleasure — while, for me, it was a barely tolerable nuisance. But she seemed to enjoy it.") When, finally ("like Jove letting Leda drop from him"), the priestess is finished, she lingers with him.

Neoptolomus collects himself enough to ask if that is, indeed, the precious *phallos* so many desire.

For answer the priestess removes the strapped-on dildo. "Do you think I would bring something so valuable as you talk of into such a night's play? No. This is the merest trifle, only an ornament — indeed, I have heard that the actual *phallos* is currently in the possession of a rich cloth merchant, who seeks for a place to store it in Rome." (Lucius's father deals in fine fabrics; for a moment Neoptolomus remembers the missing letter.) But the priestess goes on: "No, look here — its 'jewels' are paste, its 'jade' green marble, and its 'gold' mere plating. The copper work suggesting intricate inscriptions on it means nothing in particular. Here, see — it is completely hollow: empty." She turns it around to show Neoptolomus its void interior. "It's only a vacant casing. I'm surprised it didn't simply collapse in on itself and bend every which way instead of standing up to the pleasure that joined us, moments back."

"Then — " Neoptolomus hazards — "it is *not* the stolen member of the nameless god of Hermopolis, which so many men and women speak of and conspire to possess."

"This . . . ?" The priestess laughs, presumably at the suggestion's absurdity. "Here. Take it, if you like. It might make a memento of an evening's pleasure. But — no — it holds no special secrets, no secret powers. It cannot guide you to uncountable wealth. It is only a toy that, in the dusk or in the candlelight, glints now and again, recalling that true and sacred object to the minds of some, who have, perhaps, come closer to it than you or I can ever hope to — even as it confirms the impossibility of anyone but the greatest and most powerful of men — or, indeed, women — seizing and wielding the power of the original." But, she urges him, Neoptolomus had best leave now. His young friend — Lukey — has already gone. (Neoptolomus turns around: it is true. The lusty young man has awakened and slipped off. From another cushion, head propped on his hand, Jason watches . . .) Soon she must turn out the other men, here — as more will be coming.

Neoptolomus mentions their scheme to exhaust her sexually.

Again the priestess laughs: "No — I do not think there is much chance of *that*. For woman is always the master of the *phallos;* the *phallos* that men believe they have or almost have or might have someday . . . It goes out from women. It comes back to us. We do not even have to bother with it — or ever really think about it. For us it is the smallest thing. You and your friends will never win it like that. Oh — " and here she adds — "and here I add: please, from now on, my friend, forget the lusts of these men and follow your *own* desires — as much as desire can be said to be 'owned' by anyone, or that anyone can own what chains us all, one to another. Do not try to take upon yourself the wishes of these men, who slumber around you when you yourself are awake. For you to try to mimic their lusts is as pointless as it would be for them to try to mimic yours. Love and cherish whom you would, man or woman, when you would. For lust is never fixed. Its variety is as glorious as its superfluity. But do not treat it as a scarcity, fixing it within the straits of convention and law. Believe me, you'll be happier. Let this petty and pretty token you take with you tonight forever remind you at least of *that!*"

Neoptolomus looks at the glittering thing he holds. (Across the hall Jason puts down his head, rolls over on his cushions, and, it would seem, sleeps . . . Ihelva too is gone, Neoptolomus notes.) He thanks the priestess, pulls his cloak around one shoulder and the other, then leaves.

As he walks down the shrine steps and starts away from the grounds, Neoptolomus decides the evening's orgy is a good end to his fascination with these fellows — good-hearted as some of them are. He will be friends with them. But the unfulfilled sexual obsession that, he realizes, has held him so close to them, he can turn loose.

He feels the object beneath his cloak to be certain it's there.[12]

As he makes his way back toward the Forge through the Roman night, however, someone runs around a corner. For a moment, Neoptolomus thinks it is the street boy, Maximin. But others follow: it's a gang of a dozen-odd thugs, who approach him from a nearby alley. As the men surround him, three hold up torches. ("If this one doesn't make us rich tonight, we'll cut off his cock and balls," one gang member jokes — *could* that be Maximin among them . . . ?) Another demands, "All right. What have you got — ?"

Neoptolomus splutters that he has no money, but, at a thought, he pulls out the priestess's gift from beneath his cloak.

Holding it high, the straps hanging down his forearm, so that its fake jewels, its gold and copper plating, its bits of green stone glint in the torch light, Neoptolomus calls: "But here is the true and singular *phallos* of the nameless god of Hermopolis, crafted of gold and copper, set with gems and jade, and containing the secrets of the ancients." (Behind the shoulder of one of the torch holders stands a young man, who . . . no, he only *looks* like Lukey! He wears a rag around his head that Lukey wasn't wearing back at the shrine.) "Any nobleman would give you a thousand dinars for its workmanship alone. A wiser man would pay ten times that for the secrets within it. It is all I have. Take it — !" He flings it over their heads and out of the circle; and the thieves break apart to run after it, as Neoptolomus turns in the other direction and flees.

Delighted that he has tricked the ruffians with the priestess's "worthless trinket," soon Neoptolomus reaches his boardinghouse, Vulcan's Forge.

Upstairs, though he is still somewhat unnerved, as Neoptolomus sits on his bed he consoles himself with laughter: Will any of the bandits notice that the precious object, still unwiped after its recent use, besides its cheap make, also stinks of shit?

---

[12] "Phyllis, here, Randy. Given the page-and-a-half of thoughts that accompany—or, more accurately, absorb—this relatively simple gesture (that is to say, Neoptolomus's Proustian musings on what is present and what is absent, what is certain and what is uncertain, what we carry with us from—and what we leave behind us in—any such potentially embarrassing social/sexual encounter, such as Neoptolomus has been through), you've given this moment short shrift—though I confess, *I* wouldn't want to have to condense it into four or five sentences, much less one. I'm going to sit out for a while, I think, till I actually have something constructive to add. Really, despite my quibbles, so far you're doing a fine job."

After an hour, however, outside his door a familiar laugh draws Neoptolomus from his room. He starts for the head of the stairs, where, down through the rough beams, at the bar, he sees a drunken man, his arm around a woman — it *is* Lukey! And, yes, he *is* wearing the head-rag Neoptolomus saw him in with the street gang. The woman with him is Ihelva. Drunken Lukey continues to harangue the thieves and pimps along the counter, calling out, as he hugs Ihelva, "And how often, now, has some luckless fool tried to make off with it from the priestesses of Bellona? Each time the priestesses hire our gang to get it back. Each time we find and return their priceless object to the hidden goddess in the veiled keep of their shrine. And we have succeeded once more! Thus, again, we are rich. Drink up, friends!" and he releases his little consort to turn and slap a gold coin on the wood, which causes an indrawn breath from all around — including Neoptolomus — in that "rough and impoverished establishment that so rarely saw silver."

Neoptolomus returns to his room, to sit on his bedside and ponder. At first he thinks Lukey — still drunk and back from the priestesses — was only boasting, exaggerating to aggrandize himself, in much the way Neoptolomus had boasted of his treasure to the street gang. But what about the gold coin; and the young priestess, still with him? Is this the Lukey terrified of all women? But then, Neoptolomus has already seen that pose in the boy vanish under strong drink at the shrine . . . Once again, all around the *phallos* seems to suggest endless conniving, dissembling, and machinations more complex and insidious than anyone up till now might have thought. (Suppose Maximin — or, indeed, Lucius — had taken the letter, not for himself, but for Lucius's father . . . ?) Slowly, as sleep refuses to come, the thought creeps into Neoptolomus's mind that the High Priestess has only toyed with them all — that Lukey as much as Ihelva (and possibly even Maximin) has been in league with the priestesses of Bellona all along, "and that, if only for minutes, I'd actually held — and even had it thrust into my body's hidden centers — the true and material *phallos,* only to fling it from me, like a coward and a fool, at the first presentiment of danger!"

Once more Neoptolomus reconfirms his decision to distance himself from these men. Was it only Lukey who was part of the plot? Or Lukey *and* Jason . . . ? Indeed, were they all ranged against him in some way that he did not understand? Or was this all the work of Muddle mistaken — in some muddled and manic way — for the plottings and plannings of Need?

The next day, at his work, Neoptolomus is given the opportunity to go on a business journey. Indeed, Neoptolomus has just decided to go searching for Maximin to apologize, when he learns from Lucius's father, who has stopped by that day, that the "scientific" secrets contained in the *phallos* are only a ruse. ("For in fifty years, or in a hundred, or in a thousand — does it matter? — all such knowledge will be superseded and rendered trivial.") Rather, encoded among them, in symbols, cryptograms, and ciphers, are mystic and eternal laws that pertain to the achievement of spiritual peace and to even-handed dealings with one's fellows — a level of wisdom that, as it concerns human contentment directly, makes scientific pursuit (at least in this age) trivial.

That evening at the Chalice, as he says a friendly good-bye to Jason, Neoptolomus notes that the men go on as if nothing unusual has happened the night before: They still worry about Lukey — alone among them the one not there that night. They still blame their misfortunes on evil and absent women. Perhaps they are embarrassed, Neoptolomus thinks, to speak of last night's orgy, though he wonders what *they* are embarrassed over. He alone had behaved like such a coward with the *phallos* . . . if that, indeed, was what he'd thrown to Lukey's gang. Could their silence be part of the plot a-swirl about the sacred member? At any rate, it merely confirms for him his decision's rightness.

The day after, having failed to find Maximin, Neoptolomus leaves on his trip to the Abruzzi — and is soon involved in another affair . . .

Time and again throughout his adventures Neoptolomus thinks he himself might actually steal the *phallos* from its course, as it moves among the rivals who contest for it. At night come dreams of the nameless god, mixed with memories of sex with the Roman street boy. Once, back in Heracleon, he hears that the *phallos* has been seen in a jeweled casket in the treasure store of another great merchant. In the city of Lutetia, he's told that the *phallos* has been hidden in a wooden crate in a warehouse on the Seine.

During a comic sequence, when he finds the crate empty, Neoptolomus is forced to hide *within* the box as ruffians enter the warehouse to steal it away!

Through the dark they carry it off on a donkey cart. Inside, Neoptolomus hears them talking about the "magic statue" the crate is supposed to contain. Later, by the campfire, a young lout — a tow-headed farmer's boy with blue, wild eyes — lifts the cover; and Neoptolomus convinces him that he *is* the magic statue, come to life, and — after he has been blown by the younger and buggered by the elder, a gruff older man with missing fingers, bad breath, and a patch on his blind eye — gets loose; but he overhears them, even while the delighted hoodlums talk with each other of how they have "possessed" the mystic god so that its power will be theirs forever. Clearly the elder realizes it's a ruse, but has gone along with it for the sex, though he thinks it best to get rid of the evidence by any means possible. The younger is absolutely taken in, however, sure that holy magic is a-foot among them. Laughing, the elder explains what a wonderful tale their congress with the god will make. The younger claims he is too in awe ever to speak of it with anyone again. Together, they vow — clearly for their separate reasons — to wall up the "living statue" within a secret cave where no one will ever find it . . . as Neoptolomus slips beyond the fire-lit camp's dark edge into the Gallic night to pursue his own ends.

Back on his business trip, at Cumae, with a bunch of young fellows, Neoptolomus stops to visit the famous sibyl's fuming cave. While she writhes in a great pot chained above a smoking cleft deep in the Cumaean cavern, the drugged and decrepit Hirophilia — who, according to legend, three hundred years before had begged from the gods eternal life and been granted it, but had failed to ask for the eternal youth that might have made it bearable — declares in the cave's fumes that the secrets of the *phallos* are not hidden within it but are rather written on its surface for all to read, having been incised there by "the master craftsmen of Atlantis who survived the continental decline. They roamed the globe and harvested its mysteries, built marvels as they went: Solomon's Temple, Diana's Temple at Ephesus" — and, presumably, inscribed their wisdom on the *phallos* of the nameless god. During their interview, to the young men's taunts — "Σίβυλλα, τί θέλεις;" — Hirophilia croaks the answer Petronius Arbiter made known and T. S. Eliot made famous: "ἀποθανεῖν θέλω."

When, back in Ionia, he visits the cellars of the Temple of Diana at Ephesus to oversee the unpacking of a shipment of tools, in a passing conversation with a young novice about the temple mysteries Neoptolomus learns that the secrets within the *phallos* are magical. Three months later, when his work takes him north to Byzantium, he is told by a talkative and careless old watchman in a waterfront warehouse that they are medical. In each new location he samples the sexual provender: some of it is brutal and filthy, some of it pristine; or (for all its filth) near divine. But even with the sibyl's words to guide him, the *phallos* continues to elude Neoptolomus, who, as he has several times before, determines finally to forget about it, only to have it appear the more fascinating for his efforts to put it out of mind.

Now, says Phyllis, once Neoptolomus leaves the ancient sibyl's cave at Cumae, in eliding the whole of his Byzantine adventure (in the last half of Chapter Twenty-four) I've elided as well the entire novelistic reason for Neoptolomus's doings in Rome with the men of the Chalice and the Bellona priestesses.

She has a point.

All right. I'll include it here.

In Byzantium, during Neoptolomus's first meeting with the proprietors of a great warehouse on the Marmara wharf, the buzz is that, besides the goods Neoptolomus brings up from Ephesus, something else strange, mysterious, and greatly important is housed. Neoptolomus smiles to himself. If he hadn't had all the experiences he has had with it till now, he would think — as, probably, would any dozen others — that the greater treasure is the *phallos*. But why should it have come east, as if following him? He is just not that important.

That evening Neoptolomus stops into a waterfront tavern for a meal, where he overhears two men talking at the next table. One is a frail student, Egon, who strikes Neoptolomus as very smart. The other is a fellow with a beer gut and big arms, named Blutus, who ogles the women about the place, is already half drunk, and is probably stringing black-haired, blue-eyed Egon along for the drinks the boy is buying: It is clear to Neoptolomus that Egon is quite taken with the muscular, if none too bright, but friendly and expansive fellow, whose brazen buttocks, now and again showing from under his loin rag, strike Neoptolomus as quite handsome, though buttocks are not Neoptolomus's usual object. Garrulous Blutus draws Neoptolomus into their conversation. Soon Blutus tells Neoptolomus that the two are planning a burglary the next night — and it is, of course, the great warehouse they intend to rob. Egon is clearly worried by Blutus's talkativeness. But Blutus declares that, since Neoptolomus is a foreigner anyway, no harm can come from his knowing their plans. Blutus was once a loader at the warehouse, he explains, and he knows that most of the time the old watchman, with whom he is great friends ("We're like *that!*" and Blutus holds up a hand, two callused and meaty fingers crossed), forgets to lock the corridor to the room where only the most important and valuable things are stored. Neoptolomus does not mention that his own business is on another floor in the same building.

The next day, *at* the warehouse, Neoptolomus is concluding his affairs, as an aging watchman comes by on his rounds, shutting up the various passages. (The old man is as "frail" as Egon, and Neoptolomus begins to see a pattern among Blutus's friends.) The watchman mentions to the warehouse clerk with Neoptolomus that recently he has been chided by the owners for leaving some of the passages unfastened, and he's planning to be particularly careful and lock them all that evening. As the clerk leaves, on a whim, standing before the very door the watchman is about to close, Neoptolomus engages the elderly man in conversation. "What could be behind it?" Neoptolomus wonders aloud — and they begin to talk. Neoptolomus suggests that it might be the *phallos* of the nameless god. The old man tells him, no. He's heard of that object, which is reputed to hold medical formulas that will cure all the ills of age, unto dimming sight, dulled hearing, painful joints, failing memory, and fading virility, stopping only short of death. Surely nothing so valuable would be hidden here. ("If it were, would that I had it for my own!") His chuckling suggests to Neoptolomus, however, that he might be prevaricating. The watchman leaves with Neoptolomus, having forgotten, in the course of their conversation, sure enough, to lock the very door on which Egon and Blutus's robbery depends — which Neoptolomus now admits to the reader was his mischievous intent in distracting the old fellow in the first place. As the watchman and Neoptolomus walk away, their talk turns to sex, and the watchman tells Neoptolomus of a waterfront bathhouse, free to all the men in the city, where the dockworkers and warehouse loaders go for quick blowjobs before returning home and where, further within its halls, throughout the night, the city's wilder young men have extraordinary orgies. "It's a place even an old man like me can snatch a bit of sexual relief—though sometimes it costs me a coin or two." Neoptolomus thanks him for the information and returns to the tavern.

There, later that night, Blutus and Egon come into the place. They are dejected. They tell Neoptolomus that, yes, at the warehouse the door had been left unlocked, but when they'd gone within, someone had beaten them to it.

Nothing was left in the inner treasure room—

And when Blutus thought he'd heard a sound outside, Egon had urged him to flee. They'd run away empty-handed. (The fact that the treasure has been usurped convinces Neoptolomus for a moment it *could* have been the *phallos* they were trying to steal—although, as he points out, no one has mentioned it directly.) Neoptolomus says nothing, although he is aware that Egon is more upset because of frustrated and exasperated Blutus (who is all-but-ready to return), than he is for the failure of the theft. Neoptolomus is touched by Egon's affection for his coarse and loud-mouthed friend, and somewhat saddened because he is sure those feelings are not reciprocated. He urges the gruff fellow not to go back. "Earlier this afternoon, I heard rumors—" Neoptolomus goes on, inventing a tale—"that a gang of Nubians, all of them black as the night itself, with a young Greek among them, were planning a major theft there. Were you to run into them, I don't think they'd hesitate a moment to kill you!" Neoptolomus goes on to tell Blutus that Egon is doing him a favor keeping them away. After all, nothing was left. "You don't want those black thieves to think you've got what they wish to steal—that is, if they haven't already got it."

That halts Blutus; Egon seems relieved.

Later that night, Neoptolomus goes in search of the baths. During his wanderings through the building's outer colonnades, he sees a man lingering suggestively by the wall. He falls to his knees to fellate the fellow. When the man finishes and moves off, another, waiting behind, steps forward to take his place. Because the man has a small cock, Neoptolomus turns him around and rims him a bit. Turning him back and finishing him off, Neoptolomus stands up—and sees it is Blutus, who recognizes him: "Oh it's you—the foreigner from the tavern! Well, that's good. You'll be gone tomorrow. No one need know I sometimes come here." Neoptolomus asks him why he does not make use of Egon. "Oh, no," Blutus explains, retying his loin rag. "Egon's just someone who'll keep me drunk and loan me some coins when I need them. Probably he wants me — that kind always does. But I'd never go with him. If I did, everyone would know. As long as women are so expensive in this city and this is free, I'll come here for what I need." And Blutus hurries away.

Wandering into the inner bath halls, with their yellow oil lamps hanging from blackened chains, an hour later Neoptolomus is in an orgy making love to an extraordinarily well-hung youngster, when, in the three-quarters dark, he realizes it's Egon. When, into Egon's ear, Neoptolomus whispers, "Blutus . . ." Egon recognizes Neoptolomus: "*You* were the foreigner in the tavern with us!" In shifting from buggering the boy's bony butt to mouthing Egon's truly monstrous member, Neoptolomus says: "You wish I were he, don't you?"

Returns Egon: "Everyone who enters me, I dream is Blutus. But he has only friendship for someone like me — and I must learn to accept that, with Blutus, friendship is enough, though if his great cock, which he has never even let me see, were to spill into my mouth or my fundament, it would transport me to paradise."

Neoptolomus forbears to tell Egon that the boy is far better hung than his friend (and that, moments later, he spills a great deal more), but holds his silence — both about having himself blown Blutus and the part he has played in their pointless robbery. He finishes, first with Egon and finally with the orgy.

(Parenthetically, at the incident's end Neoptolomus remarks that when he has told this tale to friends, often he has given Blutus Egon's cock — and Egon Blutus's butt. But in this rendition he has no reason to bend truth.)

As Neoptolomus leaves the baths, he meets the old watchman entering the place — and tells him he believes the old man might have forgotten to lock the passage. Flustered, the elderly fellow turns away and hurries back to the warehouse to check.

Shaking his head and laughing, as he walks back to his inn, ready to quit Byzantium at dawn, Neoptolomus thinks: "In holding my silence as much as I had, perhaps I was actually guarding the *phallos*." Is silence or indirection, he wonders, the more effective protector of the *phallos*'s secrets? "Or have I, too, become someone else who merely likes to see things change . . . ?"

His contentment is only disturbed, the next day on the boat home, when

Neoptolomus finds the passengers all gossiping about a great robbery per-
petrated the previous night back in the Queen of Cities at a wharf-side warehouse: a handsome young Nubian presumably distracted an old watchman
from locking the door to the inner chamber, so that a gang of Greek thieves
could break in and loot it of some nameless and mysterious treasure — their
footprints were found all over the dirt floor after they had made off with
the booty. Hearing all this, Neoptolomus wonders if this needs be the theft
of the *phallos* . . . or if it is merely the muddled account, with the inevitable
distortions of gossip, of what he already knows — even as he finds the idea
of the handsome Nubian fascinating: which is what Byzantine gossip seems
to have refined from Neoptolomus's fantasy gang.

Well, Phyllis is right: In the novel Egon and Blutus clearly replay an extreme
version of Neoptolomus's former relation with Jason, Lukey, and the straight
men at the Chalice, a relationship which, I can see, Neoptolomus, by treating
it casually, as he does in Byzantium, might actually come to have mastered.

Phyllis says the fact that Blutus was not so well hung as I might personally
have liked is probably why I first omitted him and Egon from my synopsis.

Remembering something I told her happened to me half a dozen years ago
(a six-foot-eight Polish-Scots lumberjack; two and a half months of pursuit
over an Alaskan summer; our final, drunken, two-in-the-morning encounter
in the back of an suv, seventy miles north of Ketchikan, with a midnight sun
at the window: three and three-quarters inches — cut at that — which wouldn't
have been so bad if I hadn't been *expecting* so much more . . . regretfully and
today, I still think of him as "sparrow-pecker"), she believes the incident hit
too close to home. Well, the fact is Phyllis knows some things about my sex
life even Binky and I have not discussed. I won't argue.

I try only to make up for it above.

In my defense, I point out that the full version in *Phallos* is only three
times as long as this abridgement. Something had to go. Mostly what I've
omitted are accounts of Neoptolomus's masturbating (repeated like a chorus
throughout the book, a supplement easily omitted), prowlings along the
bathhouse colonnades, as he looks over the star-lit Bosphorus, now in his
amble within the lamp-lit corridors with their green marble walls and the
susurrus of heated waters falling into cool pools beneath, where with some

dozen men that night Neoptolomus pursues his debauches (blow job and buggery details, the scent, the sound, the *feel* of . . . Oh, never mind!), and now his musings as he leans on the rail to watch the seamen laboring at the sails, before he heads on to Iberia, among whose hills Hadrian himself had spent his boyhood.

By the novel's midpoint (Chapter Twenty-six), the plot has maneuvered Neoptolomus, by now a successful merchant, to the craggy Pyrenees. There, with black braids and studded leather bands about his shins and arms, an iron-thewed highwayman (on whom Neoptolomus is spying because he believes the man has stolen the *phallos* without knowing its worth) captures our narrator and manacles him in a mountain cave with dripping walls, here and again visiting to inflict on him brutal sex over its leaf-strewn floor. Remembering his desert lover, Neoptolomus keeps hoping that a more noble side will eventually emerge from this rock-striding murderer. He determines to be wholly sexually obliging and please his new master in every way — and possibly even trick the *phallos* from him. When a rival redheaded bandit sneaks into the cave one night and offers to free him in return for an amorous encounter, Neoptolomus refuses — afraid it will only muddle his plan. After his third highly masochistic encounter with his captor, however (I confess, because these acts are *not* my particular thing, this is the first place where, because the writing is *so* detailed and vivid, I got a bit upset on my first time through; Binky and Phyllis *both* giggled and said I was a wuss), he overhears the villain explaining to the same bandit rival, outside the cave, that he plans to kill his half-Egyptian catamite in a day or two, as soon as he can replace him with a woman. Since women are the cause of all the world's problems, the mountain bandit opines, "The only way you can trust one is if you've tied and gagged her, up in a cave away from all humanity, where you can have your way with her as you wish — and wall her in and abandon her when you're finished" — an idea Neoptolomus recalls Gaius had put forth as a joke during tavern talk back at the Chalice.

Chained in such a cave and threatened with actual death, now, to Neoptolomus, it sounds very different.

Neoptolomus realizes (one) he has misjudged his mountain man — who is nothing like the desert bandit — and (two) he needs to escape if he is to live! The next time he hears the rival redhead pass, Neoptolomus calls him in. The man enters. With Neoptolomus still in chains, they have sex — and, after laughingly explaining that the other bandit does *not* have the *phallos* after all, the redheaded rival turns Neoptolomus loose, making it appear a real escape. (Briefly Neoptolomus wonders if this one would have been a better sexual master, and might even be worth staying with — but quickly puts the thought from his mind.) As Neoptolomus runs free and hurries down the mountain trail, he ponders his own obtuseness: "With each of my adventures, I had thought I'd learned a lesson about love, only to discover, with the next, I'd merely learned a lesson about a lover — now no longer mine."

During his flight, Neoptolomus manages to halt a caravan traveling through the mountains and warns them of the bandits waiting for them in the pass ahead. The caravan doubles its guard, and they break out their weapons.

As they go in opposite directions, Neoptolomus reflects that, while he has probably saved the lives of the women within (who, indeed, thank him with a much needed bag of coins), likely he has doomed *both* his mountain lovers to death — the one who'd planned to kill him and the one who'd moved to save him — and that, he realizes, was not his intention. But there is nothing to do about it. He makes his way through the brambles down the rocky cliffs.

On reaching the shore, Neoptolomus soon finds himself back in southern Syracuse, in competition for a grain franchise with his old Roman patron, employer (again visiting his summer villa), and one-time lover.

An Asian Neoptolomus has met in the town turns out to be Yin, his employer's secretary — and still his old employer's lover, as well. When Neoptolomus explains to him the story of the *phallos,* Yin, who is now in his twenties and who provides entertainments for his master like those that Antinous once provided for Hadrian, explains to Neoptolomus that he has long suspected that what the *phallos* really contains — which is why his patron is so eager for it to be returned to Hermopolis — are the deeds to the land around Hir-wer, across the Nile on its east bank. By now everyone in the empire knows that is where poor fishermen finally found Antinous's corpse, floating in muddy water. When, a little later, Yin comes by the cottage where Neoptolomus is staying and delivers him an invitation to the villa for the evening to meet with his old patron, Neoptolomus and Yin agree that these deeds are what the elderly Roman is truly after. Yin stays long enough for sex — throughout which is woven one of Neoptolomus's more extraordinary disquisitions, on the delights of making love with new lovers in old settings.

Then Yin gets back into his cart outside to ride on to the market.

That night, as the full moon appears to crack among the branches of southern Syracuse's stubby trees, Neoptolomus walks under them and along the cliffs on a path he has not trod since he left the island at seventeen. As he walks, he recognizes trees, boulders, turns in the road he has not thought of since then and has forgotten he'd even known. The trip is a double journey through past and present: Now he recalls the look of a mountain off on the left, now a stand of cypresses to his right — is there one less of them than before? Or is that short one, there, new growth? But the night road's smell is identical to his memory of it. He comes upon the villa gardens and sees the old carriage barn. Beyond the hedges rise the familiar columns of the remembered central building. On its porch, in the upturned mouth of a bronze dragon, burns a fire — often lit, Neoptolomus recalls, when guests were expected after dark.

As he approaches over the lawn on which, as a youngster, so often he'd run and wrestled with the younger slaves and played ball, Neoptolomus sees two figures come out on the porch, beside the high brazier. By the flames, one is a young man, with taut muscles and a neat figure, surely the Asian whom, only this morning, he'd made love with down in town. The other is an older, balding figure, shoulders more rounded than Neoptolomus remembers, belly heavier, but certainly his patron, whom so often Neoptolomus has held and laughed and hugged and rolled with, spilling so much of himself into that body years before, in a bond that had always seemed to Neoptolomus the stuff of the eternal. Yet, for a moment — perhaps because the fire does not show, just then, the face of either, but only their silhouettes — though he knows who they are, both seem the essence of the unknown to Neoptolomus. These two, younger and older, Neoptolomus thinks, should be the *most* familiar things in the whole of his journey to this most familiar of grand houses. But even as first his patron, then Yin, moves into the light to greet him warmly, Neoptolomus feels — possibly because of his sexual relation with each — they are the wholly mysterious nodes in this journey into the past's overwhelming familiarity.

The evening's immediate news, his patron tells Neoptolomus, from a message delivered to the villa only hours before, is that the grain shipment has been stolen from the warehouse down at the port! Neoptolomus is astonished — and distraught. At first, when they go within to dine, Neoptolomus's patron confesses he was suspicious that Neoptolomus himself had something to do with the theft — perhaps in pursuit of the *phallos,* in order to get the deeds. But, when Yin retires early, leaving Neoptolomus and his patron, his patron assures him that because Neoptolomus has accepted the invitation, he is now convinced of Neoptolomus's innocence — though neither of them has the grain. (Is it Hadrian who is after the *phallos?* Only the emperor could be powerful enough to bring off the plot by which it must have been stolen.) Both Neoptolomus and the old Roman, as they sit talking in the villa garden that night, deride the young secretary's imaginative tendency to over-read all situations — though Neoptolomus realizes the *phallos* has once more disappeared, having reëntered the mysterious circuits that keep it from them both.

Despite the setback, over the next months Neoptolomus finds himself amassing both wealth and wisdom. In a reversal of fortune, when a boat fails to dock at the island of Lemnos in a storm ("that cave-riddled scarp where once lame Philoctetes leaned on his bow to rail at my namesake against his treatment by both gods and Greeks; and, feeling myself as wounded as that great warrior, I, too, railed at fickle Fortune's failing"), it appears that Neoptolomus has lost most of his funds. To escape his creditors, he catches another boat that abandons him on a new stretch of the Iberian coast, where, at the Pillars of Hercules, some artists, philosophers, and rich nobles have established a colony, around a store of secret wisdom they keep in their central ruling house. The elder sages believe that, with the right weather, across the ocean they can glimpse the ruins of risen Atlantis. Working there as a servant, Neoptolomus is allowed to leave only because he recites to his most recent lover (a sculptor in the colony, who, while he enjoys Neoptolomus for sex, does not think our narrator handsome enough or young enough to use as a model — which brings home to Neoptolomus that he is growing older) the words of the drugged sibyl. He realizes, even as he leaves, that the *phallos* is most likely within the colony: in the central house itself — but his plans are set, nevertheless.

Neoptolomos must leave.

The sculptor tells him before he departs: "You seem a troubled man — as if there were some absence at the center of your being that sends you wandering about the world. It is as if you search for some blue flower, or even a monstrous black one, to fill the vacancy. Why not rest, friend, here with us? Haven't you learned yet that such quests as yours can never be fulfilled?"[13]

Neoptolomus laughs — and leaves, happy to be again on the ocean, standing on deck beneath the summer evening's orange and violet clouds.

How odd, Neoptolomus thinks, that a lover can read one so wrongly. He is certain the *phallos* — or its all-but-exact equivalent — is in the colony. Yet he is leaving it, not running after it. The boat heads back along the beautiful coast.

Again at the Sicilian port, Neoptolomus learns that his ship came in only a week after he departed. He is a rich man.

On a return visit to Rome — it has been six years since Neoptolomus was last in the eternal city — as he comes from a meeting with his old patron at the warehouse (in which they speak both of the *phallos* and of the rising value of the lands at Hir-wer), in an alley a naked beggar limps up to Neoptolomus

---

[13] For anyone who still cares, Phyllis and Binky report jointly this passage is another confirmation that *Phallos* is of relatively recent composition: In his series of poems commemorating his young protégé Maximilian Kronberger, who died the day after his sixteenth birthday from an acute attack of meningitis, April 16, 1904, the German poet Stefan George (1868–1933) called him Maximin. Certainly the blue flower comes from Novalis's novel *Heinrich von Ofterdingen* (published in 1802, a year after the twenty-eight-year-old author's death), while the black one comes just as certainly from George's dark inversion of that image in his decadent novel *Algabol*. Published in 1892, *Algabol* is based on the life of the last of the Antonines, the Syrian emperor of Rome, Elagabolus, who, along with his mother Julia Soæmias Bassiana, was assassinated when he reached age eighteen, after a four-year reign (218–222 CE) of baroque depravity, during which he brought to Rome a towering baetylus, i.e., a meteoric black stone sacred to the Syrian sun god Emesa, reputedly fallen from heaven, and set it up in a temple where he married and abandoned numerous wives, including a Vestal Virgin, and a number of well-hung male slaves and athletes. He liked to be pulled, naked, through the corridors and halls of the palace in a wheelbarrow harnessed to beautiful naked women. He smothered to death a banquet hall full of pesky aristocrats under a ton of rose petals that he caused to flutter from the ceiling after the meal (a scene painted famously by Sir Lawrence Alma-Tadema) and had his own private orgy room built behind a wall of the soldier's section of the Baths of Caracalla with a number of glory holes in it. (Some claim Varius—the young emperor's first name—was the bastard of Caracalla Antoninus with whom his mother had had an infamous affair.) He assigned high government positions to slaves and commoners with the largest penises he could find, the first general practice in the east from which he hailed (far more successful than the Roman practice of handing out such posts to the rich and indifferent sons of hereditary nobles), which was carried on into the Ottoman Empire. The large penises were his personal spin on the custom: Such men, he felt, were more likely to put pleasure before power

on a crutch, stinking of wine and asking drunkenly for alms. The man is filthy, probably mad — and one of his eyes is sealed, leaking, and blind. His front teeth are gone, and his leg has been broken and has healed crookedly. The hand he holds out for coins is missing two fingers. At first Neoptolomus is too repelled to give him anything. With a curt *noli me tangere*, he is about to step around him, when he realizes the beggar is Maximin! Astonished, he takes out his purse and, removing a silver denarius, is about to say the boy's name, when Maximin, with his remaining eye, seeing Neoptolomus is near-paralyzed, snatches the money pouch, leaving in Neoptolomus's hand the coin.

Maximin staggers off down the alley with his lame gait and Neoptolomus's purse.

Startled and confused, Neoptolomus continues on through the Roman streets. Clearly the boy, now twenty-one or so, did not recognize him — surely he was too drunk. But the discrepancy between his dreams of the boy, the god, and the man Maximin has become — crippled, half blind, all-but-deranged by drink, still naked, filthy, and hobbling among the foul Roman alleys — has shocked Neoptolomus. How much am I responsible for this change? he won-

---

and be whispered about by the populace in awe. He served ostrich and flamingo brains, camel dung, pearls, rice, sows' udders, pieces of amber, camels' heels, bits of onyx, and pickled fish for dinner. He was the first person to have made for himself oyster sausages—and resinated wine, which is drunk in Greece to this day. After having the royal doctors surgically create a vagina between his legs so he could accommodate a particularly well-endowed slave, on their marriage he had himself publicly declared Empress of Rome. He established a women's senate, gave profligately to the poor, and fought no battles—with the result that the army, growing irate at his cross-gendering pranks, rose up, slew him in a latrine (and his mother just outside it), dragged his corpse through the streets and around the Circus, and made several attempts to stuff the body into several sewers. Because it wouldn't fit, finally the soldiers weighted it with stones and flung it into the Tiber, then elevated their own favorite to the throne, after which they erased Elagabalus's name from all public records and monuments.

Elagabalus's horrid twelve-year-old cousin, adopted son, and successor, Alexander Severus, whom the emperor had been trying unsuccessfully to murder for a couple of years, was straight, a mother's boy, and banished his single wife, Sallustia Orbiana, to Libya after only two years of marriage, in order to indulge in some heterosexual philandering his mother felt was more in keeping with his imperial status than simple monogamy. (Gibbon calls Alexander "modest and dutiful." *Feh!*) Sallustia's father tried to kill him and was executed for it. Alexander liked to fight and was bad at it, losing battles to both Persia and Germany. Alexander and his mother, Julia Mamaea, were also assassinated by an unhappy and rebellious army, after an ill-starred battle with the Germans in 235.

Maximin was also the name of the young illiterate "barbarian of gigantic stature" (writes Gibbon), who worked his way up the ranks to become the Tribune of the Fourth Legion who maneuvered Alexander and his mother's overthrow at the unhappy end of their German campaign. He was himself briefly emperor—the first of the empire's emperors who did not read or write. He was quite touchy

ders: Was I the first one to call him "thief" — so that now he has actually *become* one? How unfairly I withdrew from him my love, the opportunity to engage in honest work for me, the pleasure of our joined bodies, and finally my protection — to go running off (so futilely!) after the *phallos* — only to find that, without those, he has now been wounded to all-but-criminal madness. Even while he lingered in my dreams, preserved there by the nameless god, these evil streets have turned him into something that I cannot want. Recalling when he had suspected that Maximin had been a member of Lukey's gang, Neoptolomus reflects:

> To the extent I had thought of it at all, I had assumed that in my absence the forces of the *phallos* would have protected and preserved him in health and in strength, only to find on my return that those very forces had, rather, beaten and battered him to a travesty, not even of the street boy he had been, but of what any dozen men and women of Rome would have assumed him to be already — a thieving, drunken, and hideous wastrel — without knowing that he had ever been a strong, clever, loyal youngster, passionate, cheerful, and affectionate.

about his social failings—literacy, art, and music, not to mention table manners, only head the list—and has been described as a "paranoid murderer." Since the rulers either side of Alexander were such monsters, the years tended to soften the reputation of Alexander himself, till he was purported to have been something of a pagan saint.

He wasn't.

But he didn't leap across the banquet table and slash his guest's throats, either.

Alexander's ashes were held to have been buried in the Portland (née Barberini) Vase: a nine-inch container of cobalt blue glass etched with figures in white glass overlay. It was said to have been found inside a sarcophagus in the tomb under the Monte Grano on the southern outskirts of Rome by Fabrizio Lazaro in 1582, an erstwhile antiquarian, lowered into the tomb on a rope though a hole in the roof. After it spent a century or so as the property of various popes and, finally, as part of the Barberini family collection, eventually Charles Hamilton (consort of Emma, Lady Hamilton; yes, *that* Charles Hamilton) sold it to the English Duchess of Portland, who loaned it to the British Museum, where it became one of their prime exhibits. First crafted probably during the reign of Julius Caesar, the Portland Vase is *not* the "urn"—Keats's "still unravished bride of quietness"—that inspired the twenty-four-year-old poet, a year before his tubercular demise in the second-floor rooms looking out over the Spanish Steps of Rome, to his astonishing five-stanza meditation on art and time and death and their productive relation to truth. For openers the Portland is neither an urn nor Greek; it's Roman—and rather small. But many commentators have assumed it was, especially in the early years of the nineteenth century. They should have known better.

On the afternoon of February 7, 1845, in Gallery 9 on the British Museum's second floor, a disaffected student, recently of Dublin College, William Mulcahey (a.k.a. William Lloyd), walked forward among some eight visitors to the museum, grabbed up a Persian basalt sculpture from a nearby display

No, Neoptolomus decides. Rome is not my city.

As for the *phallos*, however, the reader, if not Neoptolomus, will have begun to suspect that, like fair and responsible love itself, the long-sought-for object is as much an illusion as the young and healthy Maximin of Neoptolomus's dreams — a failure made sharper by memories of faithful and conscientious Yin. That is to say, it is always something someone else possesses — never oneself: wealth, power, brilliance, knowledge, a bigger cock than yours, fame, a faithful or a beautiful lover, personal beauty, talent, wisdom, social assurance, a way with women or with men . . . something that only functions *as* the *phallos* once the seeker realizes it *is* an illusion — that, indeed, the other does not have what once you thought he or she possessed. The author of *Phallos* even identifies the revelation of its illusory status with "castration." Reflecting Freud and anticipating Lacan, he shows that the "*phallos*" (unlike an actual erect penis or clitoris, which only lends the *phallos* its most common images) works *only* through castration, frustration, and desire — the growing suspicion of its non-existence alone allowing it to serve as an ideal. Neoptolomus begins to intuit all this from the fantastic schemes he is always learning of, the competing webs of power and deception among nobles, priests, scholars, merchants, philosophers, criminals, and peasants that, now in one place, now in another, the theft of the *phallos* entails.

New business would take Neoptolomus to Athens. He rents a cabin on board

stand, and, with a single heave, smashed the vase—and its glass case—into some two-hundred-plus pieces. It's possible that Mulcahey himself was under the misapprehension that it was Keats's inspiration and had been seized by a sudden and hostile urge to "ravish" the "still unravished bride . . ." (A comma crept in and out of the first line, after "still," through various early editions of the poem, as did wandering quotation marks in the poem's final identification of the source of science and useful knowledge in general with the aesthetic register—and later found it too trivial to confess; if he even remembered.) Cloaked in the shock of the horrified patrons, Mulcahey managed to leave the museum but was arrested a few blocks away. He claimed no political motive, only that he was in his third day of recovery from an epic hangover. A few months later he was released when an anonymous benefactor paid the very stiff fine. No one knows what happened to him.

The vase was restored—it took almost a year (and has been reconstructed several times since)—but it has never been the same.

With the military slaughter of Elagabalus, however (or Heliogabalus as he was sometimes known), the most peaceful period in Roman history ended, and the decline of the Roman Empire could get seriously underway. Of course (suggests the ever inventive Binky, who now has *three* barrel collars in his right ear and whose left brow practically clanks), *Phallos* might have been the source for both George *and* Novalis's novels.

But *pogoing . . .* ?

a ship scheduled to reach the Piraeus during the dark of the moon — and, in a dockside tavern the night before they sail, he overhears the captain tell the first mate a mysterious passenger will be aboard, who is not planning to come out during the voyage, but will eat inside, away from the rest.

At dawn next day they haul up their sails, take the breeze, and move out.

Once, when she passes on the other side of the deck, Neoptolomus sees a woman who reminds him of Ihelva — but then, he thinks, that is only because she is short, shapely and, from what he can of her see under her hood, blond.

On his first night, Neoptolomus descends into the sailors' quarters and catches a sailor masturbating. He fellates the man, whose name is Grekor. The next night, with two of his sailor friends, a rangy older fellow, Fronin, and a gigantic young man, in all proportions, of twenty-two or -three, called Otho, Grekor comes into Neoptolomus's cabin (with a key, for the door is locked). First Neoptolomus fears robbery or rape.

But the sailors are looking for an orgy!

This occasions another of the book's better comic passages. Of the three sailors, the huge and happy Visigoth is seven and a half feet tall, well over three hundred pounds, and all-but-retarded. With his blond beard and barrel-thick thighs, the German giant loves to fuck (the messier the better), and at first seems little interested in anything else. Our narrator, however, gets him to kiss — which, to everyone's surprise, Otho takes to with a passion and a vengeance. All through the next day, whenever Otho sees Neoptolomus on deck, happily the giant grabs him up and thrusts his tongue deep in Neop-tolomus's mouth, scandalizing the ship's officers and reducing the other sailors to knee-slapping hilarity.

Indeed, enthusiastic Otho is finally locked up — and it is only through Neoptolomus's intercession with the captain that the poor Visigoth is freed from spending the rest of the trip in the brig. The third night, the three sailors again come to Neoptolomus's cabin, grateful for his help and eager for another bout of sex. In the midst of it, Neoptolomus learns that the secret passenger who never comes on deck is the High Priestess of Bellona — which confirms that the woman he has seen, several times now, is, yes, Ihelva.

Late the next evening, the ship docks at the Piraeus.

A cook's assistant from Bohemia, the third sailor in the trio, Fronin, has been taking meals to the priestess's cabin. Though I cannot go into details here, Fronin is one of the book's three truly remarkable portraits of a shit pig — which is what binds his mates, Grekor and the great Otho, to him. Apparently he is teaching the young German to be the same. Regularly, after Fronin has demonstrated something excremental for their pleasure, he dares the hulking German to do likewise — eat his or their own waste, or flood them with his stream as heavy as a breeding bull's. With fingers as thick as axe handles and his belly like horizontal barrel slats, Otho meets these challenges gleefully, delighting equally — as does Fronin — in both the excitement and the disgust he elicits. On deck that evening, Neoptolomus intercepts Fronin with the dinner cart and, in Fronin's place, goes with it to the cabin door. He knocks. Ihelva lets him in.

Yes, the High Priestess sits on a sumptuous bed. Stretched naked behind her is Lukey — who, when, in sudden recognition, he smiles, Neoptolomus notices now lacks a front tooth. At the same time, in the richly appointed cabin, the sexual trio composed of a man Neoptolomus has himself lusted after and the only two women he has ever touched sexually seems a more elegant version of the makeshift, violent, and primitive sexual quartet, with Grekor, Otho, and Fronin, from which Neoptolomus has just emerged.

Yet the High Priestess is older, heavier — and that is some gray in Ihelva's hair. They seem friendly, though. But they want to know what he is doing there. Immediately Neoptolomus's mind is flooded by the web of plottings and counter-plottings. Finally, stepping to a table at the side of the cabin, where a piece of patched canvas covers some object, the High Priestess asks finally, "Certainly you are not *still* looking for . . . ?" and she pulls the rude cloth away.

Upright on the table it stands, gilded, inscribed, bejeweled . . .

But is it the real and actual *phallos* of the nameless god — or merely a hollow dildo of plate and paste? "I would have thought," the High Priestess continues, "that you would have learned by now how valueless and unimportant such a trifle is — most recently I have heard that the actual *phallos* is with a rich and powerful entrepreneur who seeks a warehouse in which to hide it, somewhere in Athens. But this? I gave it to you once. If you wish, I shall give it to you again — " and, again, with its harness dangling, she lifts it and holds it out.

Declining it, Neoptolomus returns the question, "But why have *you* come *here* — and why have you brought that with you? If it is not the *phallos,* what is it?"

"It is a distraction, a simulacrum, an image — " and here she turns it to show him, once more, that it is empty — "a scabbard without a sword. It holds no secrets, no wisdom — either of magic or of history. We have carried it here, and though everyone knows it is a fake, a bogus, an imitation, meant to draw attention away from the real and actual *phallos,* a city, a nation, a world away, still the wheedling rumor that it might be the real, the true, the authentic — full, rich, and replete with its treasure — always precedes it, always accompanies it, always follows it, always makes its way about and around it, fulfilling precisely the task we require of it. Thus, you see, it might as well be in your hands as in mine. Hollow and empty as it is, it's a wonder that it hasn't broken and collapsed before now, given all the adventures it has gone through, tossed around and thrown about. Yes, I gave it to you before. And I give it to you now. Take it . . . if only as a memento, a memory, a symbol, if you like, of what it could have been, might have been, of the power that inheres in the original."

This time, however, Neoptolomus laughs. "If it is just as useful in my hands as in yours, let it *stay* in your hands!"

Smiling, the priestess shrugs. Replacing it on the table, she asks him: "But why *did* you come, then?" Once more she covers it with the canvas, as rude and threadbare as a beggar's cloak. "Certainly, you must have come after . . . something?"

"No," says Neoptolomus. "It was only because of . . . a dream." (He means the several dreams he's now had of congress with the nameless god, of sex with the phallic monster — a dream that Maximin has only recently quit.) Glancing at naked Lukey, who has one hand on little Ihelva's thigh, while Ihelva herself watches the High Priestess, Neoptolomus nods to them all.

Leaving the priestess and her two acolyte lovers, Neoptolomus steps out on deck — to find Otho passing, on his way to the sailors' quarters. With a preoccupied greeting to the grinning Goliath, Neoptolomus decides to leave the docked ship and secure a room on shore that night, so he can return to the boat the next day with hired porters for his bags and commercial goods.

Now, it would seem, Neoptolomus knows the secret of the *phallos:* it is a ruse, a lure, a distraction. But wait, he thinks, standing on the damp deck boards, realizing as he looks up, that it is, yes, the dark of the moon. If the *phallos* is simply a set of multiple imitations and distractions, of markers in a plot of plottings that web together the material world, an extraordinary fiction disseminated over the land to net a host of other fictions of power, then, at once and suddenly, Neoptolomus is convinced of it:

There *is* no original.

Any of its imitations is, in fact, as real, as actual, and as authentic as any other. Perhaps I should have taken it, he thinks, and kept it — even become its guardian, or at least the guardian of the knowledge I now have of it: a knowledge not contained within its empty hollow, or even written on its surface, but rather a knowledge that it *is* — by virtue of its position within the web of fictions, from the various horizons it creates about itself. Because I have this knowledge, I have the power to seize it from its endless circulations, and that way I could . . .

But, no, he decides. Such an act would be madness.

Back in his cabin, Neoptolomus takes up his store of spending money and starts out — though, at the ship's gangplank, he pauses. Is it wise to walk through the night streets of a strange Greek port carrying that much wealth? But then, the sailors (he now knows) can get in and out of his cabin — not to mention Lukey and Ihelva, who, however much he remains fond of them, he realizes, are only more or less charming thieves. Finally, his money would not be much safer there. No, he is worrying over nothing, he decides and, with his money purse at his belt, walks down the plank and over the Piraeus's darkened dockside cobbles.

After some ten or fifteen minutes in the waterfront streets, Neoptolomus looks into one place but decides it is too dirty and untidy. He starts along a foggy alley, seeking another that someone in the former has mentioned. After a few minutes, though, he hears running feet and, a moment later, sees ten or twelve men come around a corner — three with torches — who, in seconds, surround him.

With fear and a failing heart — and anger at his own stupidity — Neoptolomus realizes that, once more, he has been accosted by thieves.

"All right. What have you got?" one demands.

Indeed, another shouts a threat of castration . . .

Neoptolomus starts to offer up his purse, in a sort of anger-filled and hope-less replay of the last time this happened. But — again he glimpses a familiar face. Could it be — again — that Lukey is part of the gang? For, certainly, just behind one of them, stands a man who, among these Greek ruffians, looks as if, under the flickering torches, he might be a Roman. No, Neoptolomus thinks. Not this time. But he takes it nevertheless as an omen.

Neoptolomus remains silent.

After a few seconds, again the leader calls: "Have you got the *phallos* of the nameless god, perhaps?" A moment later, it *is* Lukey who steps out and declares: "No. *He* hasn't got it — can't you see? If he did, he would have told us by now — and probably thrown it over our heads to set us running after it. Believe me — " and he gives Neoptolomus a sly, dark-eyed look ("Did he wink at me? Under leaping torchlight, I could not be sure — as, I confess, I could not ascertain for *certain* the man's missing tooth.") — "I know this one's sort."

The gang breaks up around Neoptolomus to hurry off into the fog. Both relieved and apprehensive of further moon-dark mischief, but with purse intact, Neoptolomus moves on through the waterfront, finally to enter the next inn he sees.

Having taken a room at what turns out to a Piraeus brothel, Neoptolomus hears that, only a little while before, the actual *phallos* has been secreted in a niche behind a tapestry in the cellar of the local temple of Artemis Nana. It would, indeed, be simple for him to steal it. All he would need to do . . .

Again within the coils of his business dealings, Neoptolomus finds him-self entangled in a plot to purloin the sacred object. This time he assents not because he believes any longer that the *phallos* will bring him power or wealth, but because he has a wheedling suspicion that the possession of one of its surely all but infinite simulacra, however worthless and debased, will nevertheless close off a certain circuit of desire that the original theft of the *phallos* has, for whatever set of reasons, opened up in him personally.

But, again, the plot fails.

Each time, when the crate is pried open, the tapestry ripped away, or the jeweled lid thrown wide, nothing remains. Someone else has beaten Neoptolomus to it — if it was ever there to begin with.

The *phallos* has always — already — been stolen by someone else.

The moon is a chalk disk up on the October dark. On another boat, Neoptolomus leans a forearm on the damp deck rail, to gaze by the ropes across the obsidian sea, while the island of Delos ("on which it is forbidden any woman give birth") pulls from before the smaller isle of Rhenia ("sacred to the fertility cult of Pan"). As they sail past Delos's rocky plain, Neoptolomus can see, before its diminutive temple and ranked beside the island's necropolis, on their several dozen pedestals, above their pairs of meter-thick testicular stones, the island's fabled ten-foot phalluses slant starward.

> I have no memory of leaving the deck or returning to my cabin. I recall only clambering over moonlit clay, skirting chest-high plinths, dashing through sea-black shadows flung down by the moon behind them before the tall fertility symbols, my breath held as though I were diving into night. Now, I followed a dark youth, who, himself, tried to elude the even darker bull-headed creature who lunged up between us with wings a-clap like wind-filled canvas. As he scrabbled up the shale, now on a human foot, now on a condor's claw, he reached for me with a hand like that of my desert lover's, while from the fingertips of the other erupted talons, bright, brass, with verdigris about their base, which tore the leathern cuticles, till, of a moment, I blinked—
>
> A blanket tingled under one cheek, while, through a porthole, a circle of sunlight beside a weathered beam reflected off the waves outside and made me squint.

It is morning. Along with the plenitude of phallic statuary, the island's bay, once home to the whole of the Athenian navy, has slipped behind the world.

For all its affected archaism, the narrative of *Phallos* moves quickly and colorfully. The passages of sexual rhapsody make the book, however, an extraordinary prose object and verbal performance — those pages that, in an on-line document such as this, and at a university site, I hesitate most to quote.

Toward the end of the novel's middle third, in Chapter Twenty-nine, contingency and necessity again return Neoptolomus to Syracuse, where he comes to recoup a fortune and purchase for his own the house and lands where he and his parents had once lived and labored.

At a town several days' ride from his own, Neoptolomus stops for an afternoon at a village wedding of a local farmer and his country bride. Among the celebrating peasants, he spots a strong young man from the back, of perhaps seventeen or eighteen, whom he wonders if he might seduce. When, at one of the feast tables, Neoptolomus sits next to the youth and contrives to start a conversation, the young man turns to face him — he is a wall-eyed hare-lip!

To avoid appearing arrogant, Neoptolomus pursues the conversation anyway. The hare-lip is an orphan of the town, a grubby outcast who, though strong as an ox, has dirty hands and bitten nails, and is of a sullen and resentful disposition. All lust for the young man has disappeared, however, as Neoptolomus realizes also that this unprepossessing boy, seemingly eager for any attention, probably *is* sexually available . . . which, if anything, renders him even less appealing.

As his own thoughts wander, Neoptolomus remarks to the youth: "I wonder if, finally, for the smiling and giggling newlyweds over there, happiness will turn out to be as elusive as the *phallos?*" — though he is sure all possibility, if not desire, for a sexual adventure of his own has vanished.

In his uncouth country rhetoric ("his sibilants and fricatives a windy — even splattering — confusion, which left both his weak chin and his wide nose running, and which I recast here as best I can in a mode my readers might follow"), the hare-lipped boy responds surprisingly: "So, you are another searcher after the secrets of the nameless god's stolen cock."

Astonished that, barely tolerated at a Syracuse village wedding, an ugly outcast knows anything at all about the *phallos,* Neoptolomus questions him further.

"The secrets of the *phallos,*" [the youth tells Neoptolomus . . .] as I grew more and more acclimated to the distorted vagaries of his speech — his winds, his rains, his several passionate heats, his semantic aridities, when (the fewer and fewer of them I found the more—and more carefully—I listened)—I could make out a little, as in a roar of sand and cactus grass, blown through the deserts of his articulation, "are spiritual; are abstract; are philosophical. Only a few mad romantics—and a few naïve women—believe in an actual, graspable, material *phallos*. That is, they think that one person, one thing, a single situation—and the women, the possession and surveillance of a single penis—" with a nod he indicated the laughing bride, clinging to her husband—"will content them. The rest of us—those, like you, whose wealth gives them the world's range of pleasures, or those like me, with no prospects and who must make do, therefore, with whatever we can get—learn that desire always turns on a constellation, with endlessly repeatable elements, which can come from anywhere, which can be found any number of places, elements that create a situation that can occur with any number of people, things, or other situations a part of it. The philosopher might say: 'We desire to command the discourse of desire itself.' The poet might say: 'What we desire is not the wonderful, beautiful, specific thing, but the higher thing its wonder, beauty, and specificity suggest.' For it's only the constellations specificity makes visible, and not the specificity itself, that enkindle the passions—and that is why desire is as endlessly unquenchable as it is repeatable."

Considering the run of his adventures till now, Neoptolomus finds this profound. "Where did you learn this?" he inquires, as their conversation separates them more and more from the drunken guests around them.

"From a wise and aging gymnosophist whom I serve," the hare-lipped boy explains. "He dwells a hermit, there on Etna's smoking slope. If you wish to learn about the *phallos,* he can tell you more of it than I." Yes, the boy answers Neoptolomus, the hermit was once in the shorn Egyptian priesthood of the nameless god—but he quit their company at Hermopolis and came here to this village. Long since his hair has grown back in and (the boy quips) fallen out again.

That evening, leaving the wedding celebration, the hare-lipped boy takes Neoptolomus up the mountain to see the humped and naked hermit, who lives in a cave on Etna's heights.

When, high among the volcanic peaks, they meet the hermit in the moonlight and the boy leaves, Neoptolomus is somewhat surprised when the crooked-back old man asks for a night of sex in his cave on the volcano's shaley flank in exchange for his knowledge. For moments Neoptolomus hesitates.

But the hermit explains: "I first came here determined to stand on my heel and spin upon Etna to take in all the world below. But today I only gaze down pensively, now in this direction, now in that. [. . .] You have come to learn of the *phallos,*" he goes on. "You would not have come seeking such knowledge if you did not need it. What I can tell you of it may well save your life. Easily it can turn a life of hopeless misery into one of potential happiness. The price I ask is not great. When in the past have you been truly satisfied with a lover? Now, you would balk because there seems so little possibility of satisfaction with the likes of my ugly boy — or me, who adds age to ugliness and deformity." The hermit shrugs his twisted shoulder, then turns away. "It is of little matter. The decision is yours."

Neoptolomus calls him back: "No . . . ! Yes, I will lie with you!"

As they enter the cave, fumes drift from glowing cracks in the floor. In the cricket-loud evening, as they stretch out together on the rock to couple in the cavern's fog-heavy vapors, the hunchback explains to Neoptolomus: every ritual, every representation, every law, every sign, every symbol, every word — even to the Word itself worshiped by the Christian Gnostics — functions as a *phallos,* since each is a stand-in, a rehearsal, a model, a symbol for something not there. The little fires along the rock wall as well as the scent and fumes they secrete recall the cave at Cumae where Hirophilia gave her prophecies. As he embraces the wrinkled ancient, Neoptolomus asks, "But what do you mean, something not there . . . ?" only to realize that the fumes have transformed the deformed grey-beard, who turns in Neoptolomus's arms into Antinous, who, as their coupling continues, metamorphoses into the nameless god from Neoptolomus's dreams, his giant member restored. Erect between the god's thighs, however, the *phallos* is no longer an object of pleasure, but has become a terrible torture instrument set with blades, little ones fixed to the blackened length at the front, with greater ones further along it, which is rammed painfully into Neoptolomus. As he forces his body upon it, further and further, driven by some appalling parody of lust, it cuts him into chunks and bloody gobbets. Even as the nameless god (in other dreams so monstrously tender) viciously ravages Neoptolomus's corpse, a horde of demons and dragons, male and female, continue the rape as a bevy of thunderous hallucinations — humans, gods, and demons — converge in a climactic *Walpurgisnacht.* The orgiastic celebration with hundreds of revelers is a monstrous parody of the marriage down the mountain, between a pig and goat, both beasts sacred hermaphrodites. Together the celebrants take the nameless god itself, who presides over the revels and who, by now, has transformed entirely into its own *phallos,* carry it up the volcanic slope, and fling the god or its representation into Etna's cone, while the god's laughter bleats out like the cries of a clumsily slaughtered beast. Finally Neoptolomus, who seems to have transformed into one or the other of those sacrificial animals, passes out from a pain, within which certain throbs and pulses intimate a nameless merging and pleasure . . .

The next morning, crawling from under his still drugged, weak, and stringy arms, I untangled myself, in the mountain breeze, from the drowsing old man, who opened his eyes, smiled with toothless gums, between which, now I could remember, earlier in the dark, I had so pleasurably — yes — spilled. We said our thank-yous and farewells. He turned over and, I assume, slept. My wounds magically healed — if they themselves had not been dreams — I pushed unsteadily to my feet and stepped from the cave mouth to start back down the mountain trail. On both sides, fumes crept from crevices between bush and rock. With Etna's grumbling brim, smoking and spitting sparks above me, I descended.

All hints of the night-before's celebration, with its numberless celebrants, had vanished.

On the path, walking down, I passed the boy, walking up, who served the hermit and who last night had brought me here. Glancing at me, as we neared, he lowered his skew eyes. For a moment I saw, in his split-lipped face, under the dirt, something first of my lost Maximin, and even, then, of Antinous, till it became one with the demonic — an effect of the ability of something so hideous to come so close to the handsome . . . a lesson that I'd learned in the desert long ago, brought back to me in a moment on the mountain's smoky hip.

With a sense that some incredible energy glitters between them, Neoptolomus stops the boy to thank him for bringing him to the old man — moments later they are embracing, kissing, and having sex on the ashy leaves heaped beside the road, a coupling frightening in its intensity. The boy is so excited, uncontrollably he begins to urinate all over the two of them. For while, the day before, as best he can remember, Neoptolomus had found nothing appealing about the youth; now he finds his sullenness, his strength, even his dirtiness all but irresistible.

Once past their orgasms, however, the boy is as embarrassed as Neoptolomus — though both manage a deferential thank-you. The boy continues up the slope. Neoptolomus continues down. ("I'm only glad he did not ask me to stay, for at that moment I would have thrown over all the comforts of the world to remain with him — and his master — as easily in whatever hovel, or garbage heap, or pile of pig shit he called home as I might have taken him on with me to mine — in much the way I had once fantasized — I confess it now — seeking out Maximin to live with him in the streets, even in his half-blind, crippled state, sleeping together in the gutters of Rome, the two of us, in the embrace only of the god, beneath its spined, protective wing.") Wondering at his own feelings ("was it the effects of the fumes . . . ? a result of the night's vision . . . ? or something other . . . ?"), Neoptolomus makes his way beneath the ashy trees and down the mountain path.

As he descends the gravelly ruts, Neoptolomus pauses at a clearing to gaze over the great and little houses at Etna's base in the shadow of the sometimes-lethal cone. On the rocky slope, he recalls the priestesses of Bellona. Standing on the stones, Neoptolomus realizes: power itself is fundamentally phallic, in that it is a consensus-illusion that stands in for a material strength, many times not there. (And could someone like that boy, Neoptolomus wonders, the old man, or, indeed, any of us, ever know the true power he or she possesses?) Unlike strength, "power" is something you must always be thought by others to have in order to wield it. To be appealed to and deferred to as *if* you have it *is* to have it. Neoptolomus recalls Ihelva's words from years ago about the Roman women's possession of the *phallos* — " . . . having men think such things of us rarely hurts us — and often helps." That is as good as having it, if you would be a force to change the law. That is why the weak can sometimes rise in the world, and why — when the veil is removed and the discrepancy between power and strength revealed — the great and terrible are so often brought down.

Beneath twisted branches, as again he starts to walk, Neoptolomus considers the oscillations of appetite and satisfaction; the play of knowledge and unknowing; the way love can consume the edges of ugliness, even hostility; the passion that can erupt in any stalled state and the gift — beauty — that inheres in their transformations, one into another.

CHAPTER THIRTY-FIVE BEGINS the novel's final third, which, in defiance of Nabokov's observation about the serious literature of sex, turns out to be the book's *most* sex-drenched section — which means, alas, it's the one about which I can say the least.

Fourteen years have passed since the murder of Antinous. Now a man of wealth, Neoptolomus has returned to Hermopolis, summoned by Clivus. Again it is the autumnal equinox — and the revels of Thoth fill the city (" — Thoth, who, with his gray swamp crane, the ibis, was the creator of poisons that heal and cures that kill, the god of death and secrets and the moon, the psychogogue, the consort of both the goddess Maat, the Truth, and Sashet, Mistress of Libraries; the guardian of speech and reason and wisdom, the single being whom the great creatures of sky, earth, and sea — kraken, dragon, and roq — will let come, wailing, soaring, singing, through their gates"), only now the sun is bright, the clouds are crisp and sparse, and, as Neoptolomus, to get away from the noise, walks down to the dilapidated docks, the sky and the water reflect each other's blue. Across the wide, wide Nile, recalling an Atlantis risen from the sea, Hir-wer has long since been transformed from a clutch of backward hovels into the gold and marble columned city of Antinopolis, built by order of Hadrian and sacred to the memory of Antinous the Good.

Only, like Trajan — the emperor before him — Hadrian was now dead. The empire was six years into the reign of Antoninus Pius, a rule so peaceful that fleetingly one might believe the horror called history had itself ended. During the final eight years of his pontificate, however, Hadrian had raised a hundred shrines, five hundred temples, and a thousand monuments to the memory of his dead favorite, Athens to Rome, Heracleon to Byzantium, Barcelona to Lutetia.

Brazen and silver, the clouds break up, under the sunlight, over the Nile. Though, by messenger, Clivus has sent a call to Neoptolomus to meet at the temple of the nameless god, Neoptolomus finds himself looking about the waterfront and recalling the handsome "boy from Bithynia." In an eerie moment, he thinks he *sees* Antinous, but . . . it is only an Egyptian youth — a naked Nile fisherman — who, as they begin to talk, has a wily look in his dark eyes, and explains he has often gone with men from among the visitors who arrive to honor the sacred memory of the young Bithynian, now, across the Nile, become a god. For a few dinars, for a handful of lepta, the fellow will gladly go with Neoptolomus into one of the rickety warehouses and, on the straw there, make love. But Neoptolomus thinks: For himself such a coupling could only be a ritual, a stand-in, a sign, a gesture at best, in memory of the long-dead boy — as much so as the marble and gold city across the water, glittering in the sun. Neoptolomus tries to talk with the youth.

For, as I'd once found a fragment of volcanic beauty in a hare-lipped laborer on Etna's ashy slope, and had learned the cruelty of compassion withheld from a grubby Roman guttersnipe, secretly I hoped that this boy, smelling of fish and the river, might lead me to knowledge, if not to pleasure, as profound as had those others — but I knew, if I knew anything at all, that the pursuit of such hopes for sexual repetition would doom me to even greater disappointments than the normal lay of commercial lusts invariably leads to.

The randy young man is, however, importunate:

"If I am not to your taste, perhaps there is some entertainment you would like me to arrange for you? Do you want to come with me across the water, and observe me in congress with black-haired Asians, golden Norsemen, ebon-muscled Nubians? I can find any of them just as easily, for all flock to the shrine of the boy-god of love! And the truth is, it would lend fire to my passion to know that a man as mature, handsome, and masterful as yourself found pleasure in observing me. Or perhaps your desires are even more earthy [. . .]"

His offer both touched and tempted me. Could the complex and intricate feelings awakened within me now, composed equally of recollection and expectation, repeat the feelings that, six years taken by eternity and the gods, an emperor might once have felt on these same, sagging boards?

Still, Neoptolomus declines the youngster — who immediately goes off to proposition another man further down the docks. As he makes his way to the temple, Neoptolomus answers his own rhetorical question: "No. I would have been disappointed . . . for I'd have expected him to *be* an Antinous — when he was only a dockside prostitute."

Dwelling on his unsatisfactory chain of lovers, Neoptolomus decides that the emperor's feelings, whatever they were, must have been stronger than his, since Hadrian had raised shrines and citadels all over the land to the perfection of his love.

> But then, hadn't the object of that love, Antinous himself, a shy hour before his death, told me there was a lack at the center of the most ardent passion? If the glittering city across the river was a memorial to anything, it was a memorial to that lack.

During this visit, however, Neoptolomus has no problem finding the marginal temple. There, worshippers tell Neoptolomus, this very day, Clivus is to be instated as High Priest of the nameless god. Pleased at the honor befallen his friend, Neoptolomus enters the shrine, where the ritual is in progress. As soon as he is within, the first thing he sees is that there are far more worshippers today than there were fourteen years ago. The success of the new and named god in his own bright polis across the Nile has clearly redounded on the attractions of the older, unnamed, marginal sect. Supplicants have come from all lands, north and south, east and west, surely en route to Antinopolis. Many are dressed richly, displaying their wealth, though many are respectfully naked, as is Neoptolomus (save for his money pouch at his waist and a few neck chains), to show their humility, if not their poverty, before the deity. The erection of Antinopolis has clearly brought better times to the god.

Among the naked, an extraordinary young Nubian brushes against Neoptolomus. Both men stare at one another, and Neoptolomus sees the youth's considerable endowment lift slightly, as does his own. But the black man turns his attention to the ritual at the altar, and Neoptolomus observes him further:

His face and flesh were as dark as a blue-black plum — and exquisite. His arms and shoulders — and what I could see of his chest — were tightly muscled. What you'd usually call the whites of someone's eyes were, in him, the gray of winter cloud, a-swirl about irises so dark they seemed to have no pupil. His nose was wonderfully, spatulately broad. Below his heavy, heavy lips, his chin was fox-like — as was his gaze.

This young fellow from the equatorial realm stood a bit apart from the others, and I found myself paying no attention to the ceremony but rather putting all my energy into staying near him without appearing obvious. Once, people pushed between us. But again beside him, I contrived to nod a greeting. Glancing back, with the faintest smile, he barely acknowledged me, his face — familiar as a dream — both immobile and complex.

As the hymn went on around us, quietly I asked: "Do you worship regularly at this temple?"

He did not answer, but something like a smile emerged, then retreated among his features' dazzling darknesses.

As the newly instated High Priest Clivus comes down from the altar, with its demonic statue, Neoptolomus is about to approach him, but the black youth moves eagerly ahead, accosts Clivus, and Neoptolomus overhears this conversation:

"My name is Nivek, noble Priest — and I have been sent on a commercial mission by the Chiefs of the Seven Great Tribes of Ethiopia. I have been hoping to speak with you — "

"But, my young friend," High Priest Clivus interrupted, turning to this dark diamond of a man, his hand upon that ebon shoulder, "perhaps you have not heard. This very morning the temple here has suffered a catastrophe. Infidels broke in and, from its sacred socket, stole our tutelary statue's golden *phallos,* enriched with jade, copper, and jewels. They have carried it away — "

Eager to speak, I stepped up to break into the conversation: "Do you see him there? Oh, he is a terrible god, with spined wings, with one foot human and one clawed like a carrion bird, one hard hand of a huge workman and one, monstrous and terrible, with a dragon's talons. His head has horns. And his

maw is tusked like a demon's; he is a god of fertility, death, construction, abundance — and lust!" Clivus glanced at me, though if his glance held recognition
or not, I could not tell.

"We do not know if it be in the city, if it has gone away across water, or even
unto the desert. Those who changed monies from foreign lands and those who
sold doves have turned up their tables, put them against the walls, and gone
home. Here at the temple, howsoever, we can conduct no commerce until its
return. [. . .]"

Clivus turns back to the altar, where, indeed, the young acolytes, to complete
the ceremony, now pull a gold gauze before the statue. "The god will remain
thus curtained," High Priest Clivus continues, "until the *phallos* is again in its
place." A shadow behind the scrim, once more its violation veiled, the god
seems to Neoptolomus wholly to repossess its right and proper virility.

Clivus goes on to promise Nivek a meal of wine, brined olives, bread,
cheese, and figs — and a room in the monastery cellars. The acolytes and
other young priests will see to his needs. His parting suggestion is that maybe,
after an indeterminate time, once the sacred member is returned, Nivek can
proceed with his negotiations.

Nivek leaves with the acolytes, while Neoptolomus does not know for sure
if the black youth seriously desires him or not.

But Clivus turns to Neoptolomus: "Ah, and you have returned, too — my
old friend! Let us go and converse about times long past. In my own cell an
equally sparse meal awaits us, but we will enrich it with talk of our times
apart as well as our shared memories."

In Clivus's room, not very different from the one Neoptolomus stayed in
fourteen years before, priests bring them wine, bread, olives, cheese. As they
sit to eat, Neoptolomus exclaims:

"But that was a ritual, wasn't it? The things you said to the Nubian, about the
theft of the *phallos* — and the ban on commerce."

Clivus smiled. "Yes. That's true." He nodded over his joined hands, so much
older and leaner than the hands of the young soldier I had not held since back
in the army. "The original phallic theft was doubtless carried out somewhere
before the dawn of time and history, for, while all take part in the stories based

on it, that theft is older than Osiris, Seth, Hather, Horus, Inanna, Typhon, and Thoth, or even the great Sky-mother Nut herself. You are right. This is a ritual that we perform each autumn, with the first stranger to the temple who approaches us in a commercial quest on the day of the equinox." Clivus's smile became a long sigh. "It is a sad, a violent, and, yes, a cruel ritual with which we celebrate our newfound success, as we once used it to commemorate our old, old poverty. But we are still an ancient religion, and the nameless god is an old, old god, with an old, old thirst that must be slaked."

I frowned. "But why do you —?"

"The real and material *phallos* has not, of course, been kept in the sacred socket of the god for more than a thousand years. It is housed in the chapel below — in the temple's cellar crypt. Years past, perhaps, it was a public act — carried out in front of all. But even with our increased congregation we are still not so powerful as to perform such bloody sacrifices openly: we must do these violent and ugly things under cover — with a sacrificial victim who passes the night of the equinox with us."

"A victim, you say? But what is it that will happen?"

"The wine sent to Nivek's cell, unlike yours and mine here, has been drugged. Moreover," Clivus explained, "at midnight, a group of our priests, helped by hired ruffians, will drag Nivek out, take him to that basement hypogeum, where, in chains, doubtless thinking he is in the midst of a horrifying dream, he will face that terrible object, black with the blood of a thousand murders. In that chapel of black stone, with chains turned on wooden wheels, he will be hoisted into the air by his wrists and ankles, then lowered onto the actual, material, and sacred *phallos,* its metallic tip introduced into his fundament. The chains will haul him slowly down its length. As it stretches and widens him, the small blades set about its circumference will cut into his innards, then, as he is pulled further and further down its thickening diameter, his intestines will rupture and split, and the scimitars set below will sever him into pieces, until his screams and his pained gulpings for air cease, and — as he is drawn still further along that barrel-fat, blood-drooled, foul and holy rod — only chunks and bloody gobbets lie in the gore sloshing the trough encircling its base."

"But that's horrible!" I declared. "That's barbaric! No you can't do that!"

"We have no choice. The ritual is older than the temple itself for it is the true meaning of the real and material *phallos*. Easily it could have happened to you," Clivus told me. "If chance had put you here first, though you are today my oldest friend and were once my fondest lover, there is nothing I could have done to prevent it."

"But why didn't it happened to me — ?"

"Because, by chance, today you were the *second* visitor to the temple to approach me."

"But — but fourteen years ago . . . !" I countered. [. . .]

Clivus blinked at me, gravely. "There is one way that you — and you alone — can prevent this. You may purchase the victim for thirty dinars." Clivus shrugged. "If you wish to do this, then [. . .] we shall substitute a pig or a goat for handsome Nivek in the crypt. We always have a few ready. Believe me, its bleats and painful raspings will be almost as poignant as the screams of a slowly murdered youth — you will hear them, if you agree and pass the night with us. Thanks to the drugged wine, however, Nivek will be too deeply asleep. [. . .] At dawn a priest will enter his cell and wake him, all groggy from his night of drugged slumber — not very differently from the way once I was sent in to wake you, these many years past — to warn him that we have found someone with power, wealth, and wisdom enough to retrieve the stolen *phallos* for the temple. He will have been sold you as a catamite to do with as you wish, in exchange for your commitment to return the *phallos* to its rightful place — for it's not really a lie, if you accept the truth of religion. The ruffians who would have taken him into the cellar chamber at midnight will come instead to seize him at dawn, lead him into the courtyard, and, in chains, hand him over to you or to your agents. If you so choose, he may reenter the humble circuits of life, for at that point you are free to do with him as you wish." [. . .]

"Thirty dinars?" I declared. "Of course I will buy him from you! You are insane, here! What you do is unthinkable."

"Can you really say you have never thought before about such horrors?"

The memory of when I had silenced me a moment, as I stared at this priest, this man, this friend. A moment on, however, and I sputtered: "But a farm beast — ? And thirty dinars — ? You say no commerce will be enacted while the *phallos* is away from its place! How can you take such rituals so seriously if you will violate them so cheaply?"

"The price I ask is not great. Who knows? Perhaps he will please you. When before have you been truly satisfied with a lover? Besides — haven't you learned anything since you left this temple? Whether fully in view upon the body of the god or hidden within a putrid and reeking crypt among its maze of bloody troughs, the *phallos* is always in its place."

" — and never in its place at once. By all the gods, Clivus, thirty dinars for a single living soul — "

" — by the nameless god of Hermopolis, for a single living body," Clivus emended. "We are not a rich sect, Neoptolomus. Today most of our following is transient, with other interests than ours. It is simple need — necessity if you wish — that makes us bend the ways of chance as we do. Thirty dinars? Were it three thousand, then, indeed, you might call us barbaric. But I would say that thirty is quite reasonable. Easily it falls within the range of anyone considering, in this time and climate, the purchase of a hale and honest slave. A mere thirty, then? [. . .] Only you must promise that you will never reveal our secret — and terrify the poor youngster with the truth of the ritual that you have so generously, by your donation to the church, here, helped him escape."

"I do not find your irony amusing." I took my purse up from my hip and fingered free coins to that amount. "I would hope a young man like that need never know such appalling things are actually done anywhere in the world — and certainly not near *him!* Believe me, that will be an easy bargain to keep. What you have told me goes on in the cellars of this temple is so awful that I do not even want to think about it. Now, assure me, for this fee I will have this boy in the morning."

Clivus reached for the money. "You have my word — believe me." He smiled. "Compared to the one across the river, we are still a poor sect. Chance and necessity rule us, too, and all too surely. We can not afford to trifle with the truth."

Looking at his shaved pate, I sighed. "Clivus, I remember when your head was adorned with auburn ringlets. I remember, too, when you were first planning to give them up, and I wondered if you would be the same, happy-go-lucky, easy and loving youth you were." I gave him the coins. "Well, I think you lost something important when you came here and dropped your hair to the priests' shears."

Clivus smiled. "Were it to grow out now," he told me, gently, putting the coins in the pocket of his priestly robe, "what of it that is still there would be as white as is much of yours. Does it matter whether brass shears or an iron razor or simply the turnings of time take these things from us?"

"Another thing," I said, "that, at this point, I do not have the stomach to ponder."

Of course, as I followed the young acolyte Clivus had summoned to lead me down between the black, mossy stones in the close-set walls of the monastery's stairwell, down shallow steps to the corridor in which a wooden door opened onto my night's cell, I *did* ponder it — and pondered all the certainties harsh time had taken from me. I thought about them constantly, insistently, furiously. That so much of my life was now explained by what had happened here distressed me, for now I knew that my long-gone desert lover must have sat there, with the last High Priest, and had some similar conversation. Naïve women and crazed romantics believed in the full, the real, the material *phallos?* Well so, apparently, did these accursed priests! Though I have always had friends among the clergy — like Clivus — really, on any intellectual level, I had little use for organized religion. Here I decided that, after this, I had none at all.

In his cell, Neoptolomus tosses on his bed, till, from fourteen years back, the words of his desert lover return to him: *You cost me thirty silver dinars — and a night's sleep!* He hopes that, now in the temple of the nameless god itself, one of his dreams of sex with that impossible part human, part monster will come to usher him into slumber, as a prologue to his ownership of the black youth. But instead he can only mull on the past. For surely this, Neoptolomus decides, was the night his one-time desert lord had spoken of, so many years ago:

I had always remembered him fondly; but now I knew that I owed that scarred son of the sands my perilous and pointless life, my accidental cognizance as a living being; that he had saved my life as off-handedly as he had taken the lives of others.

Even as I considered my own disquiet, I must have drifted off. For suddenly, among the pitchy stones, dark as some sealed tomb, I awoke to the bleatings, raucous and pained, of a tortured animal. They rasped through the lithic walls, like the laughter of the nameless god. For hours — or, at any rate, three or four minutes — the bleatings continued. Then they grew weaker. Finally the death-cry stopped.

No, it was the *rest* of the night that was sleepless!

When, after what diuturnity, the susurrus of my breath alone for company, inky indigo touched the leafy edge of my stone window, then, over the next half hour, streaked the opening with cloud-striped teal, finally to overfill it with copper dawn, I was up, out my door, and into the temple courtyard. After perhaps twenty minutes, the priests and ruffians brought out, in chains, that stunned and stunning youth of midnight feature. Angrily I took him — though my anger was not at him — to lead him from that monstrous temple, back along the road, through the streets, and into the city. We returned to the inn where I had already taken a room. While out in the street the last of Thoth's celebrants passed, laughing and shaking their sistrums, for a moment, in my chamber, I was unsure whether to pull him to me or to release him. But he flung his arms around me (whether from lust or from fear I could not tell) and, with his head buried in my neck, blurted:

"But the *phallos* has been stolen — and you know where it is!" That halted me.

I told him, "Yes. That's true." Then I pulled him, with me, onto the bed — to take him as selfishly and angrily as I have ever taken another human being. When, once, he cowered away from me, blinking in something close to horror, roughly I dragged him back, growling: "You'd better be worth my thirty dinars — not to mention my night's sleep!" Somehow the fact that it had happened all before, that it only repeated an already-told tale, made it a ritual that, no matter how intense our coupling, nor how loud he or I groaned at his first, my second, or his third orgasm, only highlighted the luminous, pulsing emptiness at its core. [. . .] Indeed, for the next week, as we made our way across Egypt, each time I flung myself on him, it was with total selfishness. [. . .] Many times I tried to tell myself it was my anger at, or my fear of, what lay in the unseen temple cellars that fired me. A better explanation would have been, however, his divine comeliness, the god-like strength and grace of his body, and yes, the numinous marvel of his cock — for, indeed, though one had flesh of gold and one had skin of teak, aspects of it recalled that of the wonderfully-hung Bithynian, murdered in the streets ago these fourteen years, though just which (thickness, veining, odor, secretion, the looseness and length of prepuce) need not be detailed, for it is the category, not the specificities that admitted it to the category, in which desire inheres; for we fall in love with an identity, a thing no one possesses, though everyone approaches one, as we approach the form and behavior of others. [. . .] Over those few weeks, as selfish as I was, I saw that the fellow had learned, nevertheless, an astonishing amount about my own amatory mechanisms. Soon it was impossible not to feel how incredibly hard he worked to bring me to the pleasure that I tried only to rape from him.

One day — we had just disembarked from a ferry that left us at a port-side town in Samos — as we closed the door to our inn room, this time when I reached for him, suddenly and unexpectedly I found myself as tender and attentive as, before, I had been perfunctory, aggressive, and rude. Laboring upon him, as I knew I could, I made him come before me — I rolled him, then, on top of me, while, with his face against my chest, he took great gasping breaths. After moments, from the rim of sleep, I heard him say (it brought me awake; clearly he spoke with a smile on his full, black features that I could not see, though I heard it accent his words): "I knew it! I knew if I was good, that if I showed you long enough how much I loved you, if I tried to do everything you wanted of me, that finally I could release in you the better man I knew that, secretly, you must be!" It made me smile as well. It also made me wonder if he would ever believe it, if I told him, as moments ago in my drowsing I'd been intending to, that this monster of self-indulgence and aggression, which, for the last weeks, had made his midnight muscles quiver and spasm, and was all that he actually knew of me, was just not who I was.

I was silent a moment more.

Then I sat up on the bed's edge and made him sit also. "Truly it would be unthinkable," I told him, "to hold a youth of your breeding a common house slave — and even worse a catamite. Since we left Hermopolis, I know that you have been kind, obliging, and most generous to a very troubled man. But now, if you wish, you may go."

Quietly and to my astonishment, he began to cry. Through his tears he bit back the words: "I do not want to leave you — ever!" His tearful voice choked him like a man who wants above all things to appear brave and worthy. "Please, let me stay. I want to stay — stay with *you!*"

"And I . . ." Seeing him thus, I felt something within me build, block my throat, fill my body, blur my vision, weight my bowels and my tongue like rock, bind my chest as with a band so that my breath was stifled. A warrior who grasps a spear that has just transpierced his gut and, with one tug, wrenches it from his torso's thickness, would have had to exert the same effort it took me to get out: "Also — I want you . . . with *me!*" Then I seemed to tear apart around the iron within. And I realized I wanted to give him himself, not because of some idealized fetishization of freedom, a bright *phallos,* organizing the darkness, distant and near, into the known and the unknown, but rather because *he* was the most important thing *I* had — and I wanted that to be his.

Where he had cried quietly, I sobbed uncontrollably — so that the innkeeper came knocking, to ask outside the door were something wrong.

Ignoring him, Nivek held me, as I crouched over his lap, my wet face tearing against his black shoulder, one arm around his back, my other arm bent beneath me, my hand holding, yes, his penis, as between my thighs he held mine, our mutual grasps transforming them into the twin cables to any sane shore from the ocean of society's total madness (It had slavery! It had jealousy! It had poverty and wealth, conscientious sin and innocent suffering, ignorance and wisdom, sickness and health, freedom and domination! — and all the unfair boundaries and insane borders preserved between them, from which society constructed its self-iterating pattern!), as my body shook against his with the internal wreckage of my soul and I wept, not for the lacks in my own life nor what was missing in his, but for the great absences of love, compassion, generosity, and tenderness in the broad and booming world, in which, I had felt over those moments, we were at sea.

What changes did this incident bring? For one, our sex, always intense in level but monotonous in form, began to move, over the next weeks and miles of our journey, through new spectra, postures, pleasures, and timbres, till soon, first under Nivek's extraordinary curiosity, followed only shortly by mine, it opened up to include third and fourth persons — oft-times, orgies — a variety that marks it, I must tell you, twenty-five years on, even today.

Is there a lack at its center?

Let me say only that, with such variety, it becomes hard to hold onto where the lack lies, since that absent center moves about so: If I have learned anything in this time, it is that losing track of it, in such a secure relationship, is surely the closest we can come to filling it.

Thus, without abandoning any of its quality as absence, desire becomes a supplement to friendship, itself a supplement to the site and course of what, above their imbricated duality, is so easily called love, though — I must state it — rarely by Nivek or by me; for that was a word not to be soiled with the everyday of friendliness, sex, fret, fondness, enthusiasm, and reserve (so often called respect) on which the habits and conveniences of our joined lives were so soundly built.

What seems, at least now, a far lesser change — though many men would call it the greater — is that we traveled as two . . . no, not equals; for Nivek had just gambled with relative certainty from the meadows of youth in another land, while I wandered, unsure and pensive, through the local cities of maturity. But we were no longer slave and master. We were friend and friend, younger and older — and devotedly so.

Often I asked his advice in my business ventures. A sharp and observant man, his comments were always astute, and for him the giving of them was an honor. Confused now and then by the world around him, he could always find safe harbor in my arms — for which, whether with gentle observations to him on the workings of that world or simply silent support, I felt equally honored; because a man so strong, sensitive, and astute as Nivek, with all the things in the world he knew that I had never seen, could wish to attend me.

Full of dreams and drama, a hendecalogue of chapters now tells of sexual doings beside which much of what's come before pales. Business flourishes, and Neoptolomus and Nivek rent a villa in the Apennines, north of Rome, with eight servants used to Roman sexual ways, including as his chief steward the groundsman who had been friendly to Neoptolomus back at Lucius's Roman townhouse, whom Neoptolomus has run into again in Rome. At the villa a local shepherd boy, Cronin, spies on the Nubian whenever he goes in to relieve himself. He is fascinated by Nivek's blackness. Soon Cronin falls into a sexual relationship with Neoptolomus and Nivek. Shortly he is working at the villa for the two men — and sleeping with them.

That spring Nivek and Neoptolomus host a series of sex parties. Other characters enter their circle, of whom one, the other, or both become fond. One is a redheaded poet, Osudh, who has traveled from the druid-haunted hills of Britain and is now a favorite among the Roman aristocrats.

Another, Petros, is a black-bearded Macedonian, who has regular sex with his horse. Into this practice he initiates Nivek, Cronin, the villa's grooms, and some other goatherds — while Neoptolomus watches.

A third is a Christian priest, recently returned from a year of repeated fastings and prayers on the isle of Patmos, where the Christian mystic John suffered his revelations. "There, on that stony blister of rock and scrub, during the island's stark dawns and austere evenings, I could feel the very nearness of God," he tells Nivek and Neoptolomus.

"If he was *near*," Nivek remarks, "then he was not *there* — certainly the best place for gods: to watch, but not to interfere, easy to touch, but hard to grasp. That's where we kept them in my homeland, too. Let one of them make itself present, however, and there is always — how do you Christians put it? — hell to pay."

Startled by what he mistakes for Nivek's cynicism, if not blasphemy, the priest promises nevertheless to demean himself sexually in every way for them, if only they will reveal their secrets, which he can then use to benefit his church. But while masters, servants, even the steward — indeed, the whole household — use him sexually, no one is sure what secrets the priest wants. But each visitor has sought out Nivek and Neoptolomus because each believes they possess the *phallos*. ("Though all we had — which, yes, each mistook for its sign — was a certain pleasure in the world and one another, a pleasure our friends were sometimes rash enough to call 'happiness.'") On learning the truth, the priest hurries off the next morning before sunrise; Nivek is certain the Christian's talk of the *phallos* was only an excuse to indulge those pleasures his harsh religion forbids. Laughing, the Macedonian adventurer, Petros, lingers another week but finally rides his stallion on to further exploits. Only the poet Osudh retains her faith in their friendship, even as she is never fully convinced — though they tell her that her quest with them is futile.

When, of an evening, Osudh asks him finally to reveal the *phallos*'s whereabouts, if only so she can glimpse it for a moment and thus hymn it from firsthand knowledge in her elegies and odes, Neoptolomus sits with her on the villa deck, as the crickets burr in the sedge beyond, and explains to her what he knows. "So you see," he concludes, "it is nowhere and everywhere, a sign for the unlocatable desires of the other, that signification itself by which something else always molds us toward something better — or, sometimes, something worse — " for he is thinking of Maximin — "than what we already are."

But, over silver wine cups and sliced apple, as the smudge pots out on the flags drizzle smoke into the night and a tripod's fires flicker on the gold edges of her tortoiseshell combs, Osudh smiles: "Oh, no," she says. "Perhaps that's part of it. But I need to be in its presence, to see it, to hold it, to know it as I know you have. Maybe it's because I am a woman, that you do not consider me worthy of your trust . . . ?"

"Suppose I told you that a need such as yours, as it organizes the necessities and contingencies of your life, *is,* in fact, the *phallos?*"

"Were I a village boy, a simple sort who believed in myths or the ravings of sibyls, or perhaps a mystic trained to accept such high-sounding nonsense, I might be content with that. But I am a practical and hardheaded poet. I have seen more of the world than most: I have heard tales from too many people about your strivings and searchings for that node where power, wealth, creativity, and truth are welded into one — even as it has brought you and your black partner and young lover to your current and remarkable success. I know it must have a material basis. All the universe does. It's *got* to be less complicated than that . . . !"

After a winter of work in Sardis and Rome, which (with sexual adventures at each stop, involving peasants, princes, peons, senators, and centurions) takes them even to the forests of Gaul and farther south to North Africa, in Chapter Forty-four again Neoptolomus and Nivek repair to their mountain villa to host the next summer's sex parties.

A letter awaits them from one of the previous year's guests: Flavian has acquired a new servant with special tastes and talents. From a number of happenings at the orgies last year, he's opined his hosts and at least a few of their friends might appreciate his new man. "If you have facilities for him," Flavian writes, "say the word and I shall bring him."

"Please bring your man," intrigued Neoptolomus writes back. "He will be as welcome as yourself."

Meanwhile, having misunderstood a number of partially overheard conversations in the last season's orgies from the talk of Osudh, Petros, and the priest concerning the *phallos,* during the winter young Cronin has thoughtlessly told a ruffian in the town below the villa a garbled tale of his masters' relation to that fabled object. As Neoptolomus and Nivek prepare for the summer's gathering, the ruffian kidnaps Neoptolomus from his mountain estate with the help of some local prostitutes and their pimps. The kidnapper believes Neoptolomus's wealth is unlimited because it comes from his connection with the *phallos.* Neoptolomus spends three chaste days — and one depressed paragraph — tied in the man's shack (where Cronin sneaks him food, loosens his bonds, and is sincerely upset over the part he has played in the plot). With the help of redheaded Osudh, returning as a summer guest, Nivek, Cronin and a mercenary adventurer Nivek has hired to help them finally effect a rescue.

While, in the lightless cabin, the mercenary dispatches the kidnapper and two of the pimps (bullies who have terrorized the town and whom all are glad to see gone), Neoptolomus assumes it is the Macedonian Petros, but, when the lantern is lit, it's Lukey, older, heartier, and now with *two* teeth missing — as well as a notably larger gut than at the Chalice and the Forge. Having left the service of the Priestess of Bellona, Lukey travels throughout Italy, taking jobs from wealthy folk who require a smart, vigorous, and resourceful champion.

Neoptolomus could not be happier to see him.

"When, from your black friend, I discovered I would once again be laboring in the service of that elusive object — " Lukey winks at Neoptolomus — "how could I not take on the task?" Nivek and Neoptolomus invite Lukey to spend some time with them in the villa, at the sex party, which will now occur on schedule. Smiling, Lukey demurs. "I'm honored. But, no. My pleasures are still not — *quite* yet — yours. Pay me, and I shall amuse myself with these ladies here — " he means the town prostitutes — "then be off, looking for new mischiefs to untangle."

After paying Lukey, Nivek and Neoptolomus return to the villa with redheaded Osudh. The Celt is sad Lukey did not come back with them. Is she infatuated with their hero? wonders Nivek. But no, Osudh explains, back in the villa's gardens: Like Cronin, she has overheard exchanges between

Lukey and Neoptolomus, which have again convinced her that her friends are privy to knowledge they have not shared, even if it is not the source of their actual wealth.

Osudh also questions their keeping Cronin. "Why are you so kind to the boy," she wants to know, "when his silliness and stupidity betrayed you to the kidnappers?"

"Because it pleases me to be kind," Neoptolomus explains, "and because people have been kind to me. Besides, once, when I was *not* so kind to an-other boy, it made me unhappy." But he does not tell Osudh how closely her mistakes resemble Cronin's, even though, as a poet, she is interested in the *phallos*'s spiritual and esthetic potential, while Cronin has been impressed only by the wealth and power he suspects it involves — at least till now. Later, when they prepare for bed, Neoptolomus explains the similarity to Nivek.

"Well," the Nubian comments wryly, "her mistakes are more interesting than the boy's — and *surely* less catastrophic!"

Days later other guests come. The ten-day orgy is in full and joyous swing.

Osudh observes, writes her poems, and amuses herself with one of the villa's gay grooms. (At least he would appear gay. He's the one who had so eas-ily — and anally — accommodated Petros's horse the previous summer. But, then, Neoptolomus remembers Jason . . .) Flavian arrives with his new servant:

It is Otho, the giant Visigoth, whom Neoptolomus last enjoyed years back, on the boat to Greece!

The huge, good-hearted German is greatly pleased to see Neoptolomus. (Neoptolomus gets, yes, a messy kiss of recognition, whose description lasts a very funny three-quarters of a page.) Over the intervening years, however, Otho has learned all of Fronin's tricks — and then some. Neoptolomus has set aside a chamber in the barn, to which he, Nivek, Otho, Flavian, and a number of the older men retire — as well as three of the wilder young ones — along with a goat, four dogs, and a donkey.

The first of the following three chapters begins with Nivek and Cronin en-tering the barn, only to be urinated on by the naked German (who, from his spillage, seems to have a bladder as capacious as a camel's), already standing in the loft, and smeared and stinking with animal filth. Neoptolomus and the others watch and laugh — Nivek the loudest, for Neoptolomus's black lover, we now learn, is a born mud-puppy. ("The ability to regard as an honor and a joy what society has declared an insult and a defilement bespeaks an agile mind — often a mind that loves learning for its own sake. But I already knew this was Nivek.") The last of the three ends when, having climbed halfway up the ladder to the same loft, Nivek calls to the German, who turns, surprised, as, joined on the rungs by Cronin, Nivek urinates with a stream even fuller and broader, to hose away some of Nivek's feces, clotting the German, face, flank, and crotch; and laughing Otho pulls first Cronin, then Neoptolomus with him, into the Nubian's saffron saline flush . . .

I will describe little more of these matters, save only to say Otho has become a creative, even inspired, scat master. As well as the action, the language of these three chapters is the novel's most *outré,* employing puns, calligraphs, abstract and surrealist illustrations run in with the text, rhymes, riddles, Bester-like patterned and matrix-arranged prose, with internal and external monologues, and a *Shandy*-esque playfulness entailing a three-page description of the sensations between the first push and the actual expulsion of a turd, a two-and-a-half-page account of a single orgasm, and five pages devoted to the sensations accruing between the moment a man decides to release his bladder and the moment urine actually erupts from his foreskin-hooded head, among its accounts of bestiality, coprophilia, and worse (some dogs run in at one point and . . . well), in the author's unfailingly vivid prose. The punctuation — and lack of it — that, now and again, the author has played with for brief passages earlier on, here takes over.

This stylistic and typographical bravura suggests *Phallos* is surely a post-Joycean text, unless (again Binky's notion), Dujardin, Alphonse Allais, and the other surrealists of the yellow nineties and the Edwardian decade after them in France, Italy, and Scandinavia took directly from *Phallos* some techniques Joyce went on so inventively to appropriate.

Phyllis thinks, at this point, the author of *Phallos* has lost it and that, here, both in manner and matter (for her, *none* of this works), the book is deranged.

After we'd discussed the novel dozens of times over more than a decade, however, on a cold March Thursday Binky finally mentioned that these same chapters had always been his favorites. While the snow ticked my rented farmhouse's library panes and gold and ivory clouds piled above the pines and ice-laced slate on the mountainous horizon, Binky confessed he needed to borrow my copy to retype, as best he could, those pages' text, because by now, in his own, they'd grown worn, torn, stuck together, and unreadable.

These were the pages he returned to most often.

When the barn session with Otho and those who appreciate or enjoy participating in or observing his pleasures breaks up (and the prose becomes — somewhat — more normative), Neoptolomus asks Otho which he would do first: wash, rest, or eat?

"Food!" declares the Visigoth, who probably has no intention of washing — and, if his sexual appetite over the last ten hours is any indication, equally little of resting. Neoptolomus takes the towering, bronze-bearded Goliath into the main house through an entrance into a back hallway, planning to feed him in the pantry — where another guest, Staminius, encounters them.

Because of Neoptolomus and Otho's soiled and noxious state, Staminius neither realizes Otho is a guest nor does he recognize his host. Thinking rather they are a pair of naked sewer workers, he commands them, haughtily, to leave. Only when another visitor comes upon them does Staminius learn his mistake. He apologizes. Otho is not greatly upset. Neoptolomus realizes, however, that a certain egalitarianism he and Nivek had been hoping to maintain at the orgies they've mounted is more to be wished for than won.

He takes Otho on and, in a corner of the kitchen under the ceiling's heavy beams, as the servants prepare food around them, seats the giant on a bench by the heaped over table on the stone floor. He gives Otho a platter of roast pork, a square of paté, a loaf of oat bread, a red crock bowl of brined olives, and a ceramic flagon of wine. With massive fingers hooked over the table's edge, almost as if it is his thanks, Otho leans to the side and looses a flatulopetic eruption that, in the six seconds of its thunder, makes the kitchen workers glance over. Neoptolomus himself frowns at the tidal stench that rises through the scullery.

Otho grins. "I love to see you look like that," the rude giant declares, finishing with a rumbling eructation,[14] "because I remember how less than an

---

[14] "You might mention, Randy, that you've lifted many of the eccentric words for this section from the three chapters preceding. (I don't *believe* you knew what an "eructation" was without a swoop into the dictionary, if not a flip through *Mrs. Byrne's*. I didn't.) Also: Even after three evenings of Binky's and your disquisitioning on their interests, personal and poetic, I still think those three chapters are irrelevant, tedious, and nuts—as *well* as gross!" (Phyllis.)

hour ago you had your nose and your tongue back under my balls, trying to crawl up into me headfirst — and I know how in an hour you or your friends will have them there again!" The giant grasps his flagon to drink, and grabs up some meat to gnaw, while across from him Neoptolomus sits to keep him company, still distressed by the encounter with Staminius.

Later, as Neoptolomus and Cronin, who have assisted each other with scrubbing and toweling, come from the second-floor bath, Neoptolomus feels his lingering discomfort growing when, in the hall, Staminius confronts him with a confession: while Staminius thought them workmen, he'd spoken to Neoptolomus and Otho so haughtily only because he'd assumed them sexually unimaginative yokels. Secretly he'd found them exciting in their former befoulment but had been ashamed to acknowledge it, for fear they would laugh at him or even hurt him. Might Neoptolomus put in a word with the Visigoth and arrange a session between them all?

When, once more out in the barn, where Otho has returned with some of the other guests, Neoptolomus inquires of him on Staminius's behalf, Otho laughs. "Be sure of it — I'll hug him and roll with him, cuddle and coat him as I did you." He reaches under the donkey's tail to heft its hirsute and low-hanging testicles. "Let's see if we can get this furry fellow ready for your noble friend. Oh, yes, the Roman is a scared mouse, who wants the lion to play with him. But I'll do him, and have fun in the doing. That's how the proud ones always are! That's why I enjoy them so. I like the taunts they toss at me to make me grovel — and love even more when I can taunt them back, force them to lick the horse shit from under my toes and heels, and make them grovel in turn!" Only then does Neoptolomus feel relieved. "For," as Otho calls after him, as Neoptolomus starts out to find Staminius, "those are the games I *always* win, whether I come out above or below!"

That night, however, Neoptolomus has an unsettling dream. The reasons that keep me from detailing more of the day-time events in those columned halls, barns, balcony chambers, and outdoor pleasure-gardens are the ones that prevent me from recounting such night-time carryings-on. Basically, in the dream, however, Lukey sneaks into the villa and makes love to Osudh, then the town prostitutes (present in the dream, though not reality), and even Nivek, Cronin, and others, only to be stalked, encounter after encounter, by some beast.

Sometimes the creature is the black, horned, and wingéd god. Clouds shift under the moon outside the villa, however, and it transforms into something gigantic, resembling Otho, but with none of the giant's good nature, thrice as large as life, and clotted with his own filth. What Lukey begins with easy sensuality, the creature terminates with violence and sexual havoc. In the novel's most unsettling moment, the black/blond god/barbarian's vicious *phallos* erupts into a gold-and-black bladed flower that tries to swallow Nivek into its darkness.

Neoptolomus barely drags his lover free from the flailing knives, as they slash at his wrists, arms, and shoulders —

Neoptolomus wakes to the gasps, rustles, ruttings, and groans of his guests around him. Nivek has come to sleep up against him, back against his chest. Neoptolomus puts his arm around his black friend — who squeezes his hand. "I just finished with Cronin," Nivek whispers.

"Yes, I had him earlier, as well." Then Neoptolomus asks the back of Nivek's shoulder, "Did you enjoy it?"

"Oh, yes . . ." Nivek answers.

"And did he?"

Nivek turns to face and embrace his friend, his obsidian smile erupting through the inch of night between them. "Very much — for moments, I thought he would go wild!" Neoptolomus laughs with Nivek. While they kiss deeply, on a windowsill a dove wakes, flutters, and coos under the moon. "But —" Nivek says finally — "you know how intense the boy gets. *Almost as intense as you!*"

That they can share such pleasure, such knowledge, such time (thinks Neoptolomus) is as central to their happiness as the sex they give each other directly. With pleasurable sounds around them, as Neoptolomus holds Nivek, the black man's arms loosen and his breath slows in slumber.

Soon, Neoptolomus slumbers, too, without dreams.

Days later, Neoptolomus and Nivek say good-bye to Flavian, Staminius, Otho, and the dozen-and-a-half others. The visitors depart, and in the party's aftermath all relax — save Neoptolomus, who still mulls on his dream and some of the gathering's other occurrences.

"The social sharing of pleasure should bring those who indulge it closer,"

Neoptolomus tells Nivek and Osudh, as they walk back from the villa's gate, "and not encourage the arrogance and thoughtlessness already wedged between the classes — the fear of the power of the other, the fear of the *phallos*."

"But it did bring them together," Nivek reminds him, as a bird chirps among the pine trees, "and in ways it would not have, had they been in a less licentious home. It just took Staminius an hour or two longer."

That morning Cronin brings news up from the village. An outbreak of pox has been traced back to Lukey, who before leaving made love to three of the town prostitutes.

"Perhaps," Nivek suggests to Neoptolomus, "that's what your dream was about." As they breakfast on the villa's patio, Nivek tells Osudh: "If Lukey carried the pox, his declining our party was a gift, even a blessing from the nameless god. As the Greeks say, 'Be happy!'"

Neoptolomus decides to shut up the summer place early. Since the kidnapping, separately Nivek and Neoptolomus have each had sex with Cronin. That night, however, again the three go to bed together. It is wonderfully satisfactory, as Cronin — always eager to show off his virility — wants to make amends for having caused such trouble. (Comments Neoptolomus: "I have never seen a young man work so hard — and so successfully — to please others through pleasing himself.") If, during the dark hours, dozing, Neoptolomus has any dreams of the nameless god, they are benign and tender, humorous and contented.

I recall only that between his human and his feathered thigh, in the shadow of his taut wings — if he visited us at all — no *phallos* stood, no baetylus, but only a penis, now Cronin's, now Nivek's, now Otho's, now mine, and, serially, perhaps five or six others lifted from the sexual detritus of my life. I woke to what at first I thought far-off laughter.

Outside our window, filled with morning, high summer, and a breeze, sheep bleated below the barn, as one of Cronin's companions led his herd up the grass- and bramble-edged path to their cliff-side pasturage.

Waking between Nivek and Neoptolomus, Cronin yawns and sleepily mumbles about joining his friend to go off with the herd; but he stays for another two and a half hours in their bed — and five more orgasms among the three. Nivek is pleased. Neoptolomus takes that as sign he has made the proper decision to quit the villa.

After bread, juice, fruit, and cheese, with Cronin, Nivek, and Osudh in the villa's garden, Neoptolomus tells Cronin he will secure the boy a junior officer's position in the army, if he wishes. Cronin is old enough, now, to start his own adventures out in the world. Eagerly an excited Cronin agrees. Neoptolomus tells his steward to see to it — while Nivek and Osudh entreat the youth to remain pox-free till his regiment is far from Rome, where such unhappiness is less likely to mar the pleasures of women and men.

With Nivek and Osudh — who is returning to Rome at an invitation from a lady at court to lend her poetic talents to that elegant house — Neoptolomus returns to the eternal city, where the poet, on saying her good-byes, exhorts them, finally, if they will not tell them to her, to keep the secrets of the *phallos* from everyone. While, as he has done before, Nivek protests they know nothing, Neoptolomus only smiles.

On arriving, they receive news that Neoptolomus's Roman patron and employer has fallen ill and quit Rome for his summer estate on Syracuse: Nivek and Neoptolomus continue, now by boat, to the beautiful Mediterranean island.

The concluding narrative movement of *Phallos* — its final three chapters — begins:

Let me recount one more incident with my partner and lover, Nivek.

With bumpy wrists and elbows and the skeletal engines of knees and ankles pushing out his worn suede skin, perched on a piling at the Syracuse port, a bearded and tufty-haired codger waited for us as we strolled ashore. With broad fingers he tugged some parchment from under his leaked-in loin-rag. Left and right of it, hirsute flesh lapped from the cloth bound slackly between his stringy thighs, for his scrotum had bloated to the size of paired turnips. He held the packet up before breasts collapsed like a crone's, dugs as thick and as gnarled — and grinned over his one tooth, brown, pitted, and off-center.

I took the parchments and returned him a coin. For a moment he raised it to his gums — surely a habit left from when he'd had the teeth to dent gold. He and Nivek grinned at one another. Then the little man levered himself down to hobble barefooted, big-balled, and bowlegged up the boards.

Under that hot sky, as I broke the seal, Nivek looked around my shoulder, a black hand on my arm. "What is it?"

Days before, at his summer estate, Neoptolomus's Roman patron has died. While he has done nothing so rash as to make Neoptolomus his heir, nevertheless he has left him a sizable appreciation for his services from adolescence on. (In the letter, Yin — still his patron's secretary — has copied out the will's pertinent passages.) It came at a fine time for investments in some of the good lands around Neoptolomus's family farm — his patron's dying advice.

In a two-horse cart, our goods piled in behind, Nivek and I were passing within sight of Etna's fuming cone. Above the trees, the air was sulphurous and dim with the mountain's exhalations. Since the thunderous Titan was in such disapproval of mankind, I had no desire to mount its slope, or even to linger in the neighborhood. I hied the horses to a canter, and our wagon rumbled along the road.

Of a sudden I turned to Nivek, beside me on the bench. "I'm going to tell you something that I once promised I would not tell," I said. (Yes, I was thinking of the wall-eyed hare-lip and the old man who lived against that awful hill.) "You do not know the danger you were in the night I purchased you from the Hermopolis temple. Once you told me that you thought I knew the whereabouts of a stolen *phallos*. And I said that I did. Well, the *phallos* was stolen by the temple priests themselves — and hidden within their own cellars. Whatever they told you, it is not filigreed with gold and copper and set with jewels and jade. Neither within nor without will you find arcane lore or wondrous secrets. It is horrible and bladed and black with blood, an instrument of death and violence — and the night you slept there, drugged and oblivious to the horrid bleatings from their barbaric slaughter of some domestic scapebeast, you would have been dragged into their torture chamber and ritually impaled upon that lethal object, had I not intervened and purchased you for thirty pieces of silver."

Our cart racketed along — there was a flicker, then, three breaths later, a rumble above. It was not the hostile hill, however; only the approach of a summer storm.

After a moment's more silence, Nivek said: "I once promised to keep a secret till my death. But I will tell it to you, now. When I first came on my mission from the Chiefs of the Seven Great Tribes, I required a guide north across the desert. At a dune-side town I found an old man, who declared he'd once been a bandit chief and a brigand, a decade and a half before. He wore six rings in one ear — and the lobe of another was a fleshy loop from which, he told me, a grooved gold nugget had long since fallen and been lost. He wore rings too in his dugs, thick as the old fellow's back at the port. His extraordinarily fleshy foreskin had been stretched to inordinate length. His right cheek was deeply scarred, and he was blind in one eye. Yes, he had many times traveled from oasis to oasis through the desert and could take me into Egypt, to Memphis, where the giants of history had been turned to stone by time and the sands, to the city of Saïs, whose priests still teach their novices poetry and politics through tales of the Athenian Republic's long-vanished rival, great Atlantis, and even to Hermopolis, city of Thoth, the ibis god, on the fertile Nile.

"We set out.

"One night, when we'd made camp in the dunes and I was enthusing about my upcoming meeting and mission with the priests of the nameless god, usu-ally so silent, suddenly he began to talk. 'They are silly, stupid men,' he said, 'and they have made me do great evil. Better to be a student at Memphis or an adept of Saïs. Ever since the founding of the temple, the priests of the nameless god have yearned to be on the outskirts of a great city, for, apart from his consecrated town, Thoth — the god of death and writing — is a marginal god; and the nameless god — the god of erasure and absence, of silence, revision, and forgetting — is a god marginal to Thoth. But they have always believed that the nameless can never function fully without the named. Once the center of worship for Ramses II, Hir-wer only grew smaller and poorer, however, not greater and richer. Have the tales of Antinous and the Emperor Hadrian reached into the Ethiopian pampas? Well, if you have even heard their names, perhaps this story will mean something to you — though it is a secret history you must never tell another soul. Be glad you go in the autumn, for the temple rituals of that time of year, though horrible and inhuman, are easily circumvented with a little luck and money. The rituals of the spring, however, are much more virulent, far more powerful, and of a cruelty that dwarfs their autumn rehearsal. The Emperor Hadrian was a great student of the mysteries of the various and varied religions of his empire, and he wished to cement his lands by taking part in them all. In the spring, for a great fee, you can partake of the mysteries of the *phallos*. What they are in their totality and specificity, I do not know. But I know that part of the price is that you must supply a human victim, a young and comely man or woman — what is more, you must choose her or him at least a year before the sacrifice and, for that time, you must treat him or her as your king, queen, mistress, or master, acceding to all her or his wishes and whims, lavishing your wealth and material goods on her, making the last year of his life as close as you can to that of a true god or goddess. Only then, on the day of the vernal equinox, do you bring the victim to the temple, where you will watch him or her slaughtered in some awful and unnamed way in the temple's cellar crypt. As the nameless god takes from you the victim, whom, for a year, you have worked to supply with every possible pleasure, there you will learn the true and agonizing mystery of the *phallos* — for there you will face the dreadful absence, uncloaked and unmitigated, at the center of all and everything. Of course the victim chosen by Hadrian was Antinous — and, as you might imagine of such a humane emperor, when the vernal equinox arrived, when Antinous's year of pleasure was up, when they came to the temple, at the last moment Hadrian could not go through with it, for he had come to love the boy deeply he had so honored — and so the boy had come to love Hadrian. What was there to do? For the promises that bind an emperor, when indeed they bind, bind far more strongly than those that bind the likes of you and me.

"'In spring the adherents of the nameless god can no more forgo their victim, slaughtered on their terrible engine, than can the Bacchantes give up their annual Pentheus, torn apart in the furrows of a new-plowed field, or the early Christians their yearly Adonai, nailed to his tree. These are not like the mysteries of the autumn, which anyone can buy his way out of, an excuse for a harvest meal and some scary tales for children, a mere rehearsal for primaveral hideousness and horror.

"'The cult of the nameless god is still a marginal sect and greatly in need, and the emperor of Rome has an amount of wealth for his dispersal that ordinary men and women can not conceive. Antinous himself, of course, did not know what his marvelous treatment for the last year had meant — only that he and his lord had grown closer and closer in their love.

"'But finally for a fee many times that which he had paid to enroll himself in the mysteries, the emperor was able to purchase a six-month reprieve — and the promise of any easy autumn death for his young lover. As well, he had to promise once Antinous was dead, never to return to Hermopolis.

"'For the next six months, there in the Egyptian sands, their passion rose to new heights, new orgies were evolved, invented, and carried out. Only Antinous was unaware of the threat of death that impelled these new excesses — or perhaps he knew.

"'I was a bandit and assassin in those days — and I was chosen to deliver the death blow, swiftly, cleanly, and easily, to the boy. The emperor took my robe from me and wore it — since, as he said, he was the young man's true murderer.

"'And that is what I did.

"'Though you must promise me you will never tell anyone.

"'I stabbed him in the neck during a street brawl, manufactured to distract any passing witnesses, there in a Hermopolis alleyway — and took back my garment.

" 'The emperor had the boy's body taken across the water to Hir-wer — now the city of Antinopolis — because, though the mysteries forbade his return to Hermopolis, Hadrian wished to consecrate the place of the boy's death. For, you see, men in the emperor's employ had already fallen on the temple and stolen the *phallos* away — and for years the minions of the temple endeavored to wrest it back, while the emperor's forces moved it hither and yon, in an attempt — not always successful — to keep it out of their hands.' There in the desert the old fellow told me: 'Again and again the agents of the temple of the nameless god pretend to be far more powerful than they are, now luring the truly powerful to steal the *phallos* for them, then maneuvering the powerless to steal the *phallos* from *them* . . . When I am in Hermopolis, I still speak with the priests. I have heard that the *phallos* was finally thrown into the cone of the volcano atop Mount Etna, where a renegade hunchbacked priest older than I — a man who'd once purchased *me* from the temple, though he'd abandoned me even before we left Egypt — at one point led hundreds of adherents in the celebration of its destruction and *still* guards its secrets. But I cannot think so powerful an object could ever truly be destroyed. Isn't it odd?' Now he chuckled. 'Here I am, an old, one-eyed man guiding strangers across the sand. But once, with a single knife thrust in an alley on the Hermopolis waterfront, I ended the life of a beautiful boy — and raised a gold and marble city on the opposite shore.' After a silence, as darkness settled on the desert, within our shell of light the old man said: 'The religions that are popular with the people offer them generous, resplendent gods, who give and give and give. But the true god, the great god, the child of Muddle and Need who cannot be named, is a jealous and privative god, a god who only takes. Storing his plunder in the immense and inaccessible past, he takes and takes till there is nothing — *nothing* left!' Moments later, he added: 'In the autumn, when I was younger and the leader of a brigand band, practically every year at the temple I, too, would purchase myself some catamite — as once I had been purchased. It was easy. A mere thirty silver dinars. But they never stayed — nor could I ever keep them. Time, common decency, and the wanderings of my own heart — and perhaps some essential absence in me — or in them — finally took them away. As they were taken, that absence in me has grown to where even the ability to want, the god has purloined as well, so that now all that is left me is the desire for desire . . . and even that suffers its aphanasis.'"

"Though we tarried a season at Saïs," Nivek concludes, "and stopped by the statues of Memphis, at last he left me at Hermopolis, where I had already seen across the water that my mission to invest in Hir-wer was now sorely compromised; for Hir-wer was no more . . ."

When Nivek falls silent, Neoptolomus asks: "And did you lie with him to gain this knowledge?"

"No," answers Nivek, smiling. "I wanted to have sex with him — most heatedly. 'Since so much is to be taken from me,' I said, 'it behooves us to give one another all we can, while we can . . . ' 'By wanting me,' he explained, 'you have already satisfied what's left of my desire, little hedgehog. Have me, and you become just another young pest and more of a responsibility than you already are.' Then he laughed, told me to practice my coming privations . . . and go to sleep."

As they ride on, more slowly now and in silence, Neoptolomus wonders if Nivek realizes what a gift he has passed to his friend. ("How warming to hear that nickname after so many years, there on the road home.") He feels as though their dual betrayals have become affirmations and released them both from at least some of what is evil in religion.

Could the hallucinations in the cave on Etna have been prompted by the destruction — or some version of that destruction recounted by the old hermit — of the real and material *phallos?* Neoptolomus ponders the idea. But, then, that would have meant that there was no such engine any longer in the temple cellars, and the threat to Nivek was, itself, only ritual . . .

But what of the slaughtered scapebeast . . . ?

As the novel settles to its end, problems remain. A paragraph in the old Roman's will (which, while Nivek takes the reins, Neoptolomus unfolds and rereads aloud as they trundle along the road) still troubles Neoptolomus; for it, too, suggests that, from an autumn visit to Hermopolis in his own youth, when something unspeakable occurred that was nevertheless the start of his climb to wisdom and wealth (most of which he has left to the Shrine of Bellona in Rome), Neoptolomus's patron had long been aware of the desire of the priests of the nameless god to have a city raised on the site of Hir-wer, years before the birth, much less the death, of Antinous, in turn suggesting that his patron's involvement in the plot around the *phallos* of the nameless god had been far more extensive than, till now, Neoptolomus has believed.

In their cart, however, Nivek and Neoptolomus continue toward home. Etna drops behind.

A day or two later, after a night's orgy with several farmhands they've met en route, Nivek and Neoptolomus climb into their wagon before daylight, for an early start.

One of the farmhands to see them off is Aronk, a naked, barefoot little bull, furry as cub, with an eye missing like the adult Maximin, a hare-lip like the hermit's young servant, big work-hardened hands with fingers like Neoptolomus's desert lover's, equally hard testicles that have already started to enlarge like the geezer's at the port, and front teeth gone like Lukey's, a cock fatter than Nivek's — if not so long — a good-humored eagerness and enthusiasm about his sexual performance surpassing even Cronin's, and sexual tastes taking in most of Otho's, along with some others that, frankly, both Binky and I agree, are finally too much even for *us* — although, writes Neoptolomus, "to me he was as beautiful, after his twenty-four years of provincial labors at the lowest tasks, as Antinous alive." Both the men and women where he works have teased Aronk unmercifully, harassed him constantly, and even beaten him, for he masturbates all but constantly and often relieves himself like an animal on his own feet or down one or another of his muscular legs, wherever he happens to stand. Neoptolomus is surprised, then, when, as they are leaving, Nivek calls down to the fellow: "If you wish to work for us, and be released from your miseries here, we will be only three towns down the road. Just ask for the merchant Neoptolomus and the Nubian with him."

"Oh, yes!" declares the gap-tooth hare-lip. "What an offer! I will be with you in a week's time — count on it!"

But another hand who has taken part in the orgy tells them: "No, Aronk is all words — those you can understand in his bluster. The half-wit will never come. He's too used to the demons he knows to go running after devils like you, even were you to offer him a castle in the Christians' heaven!"

As their cart pulls way, Aronk protests he will definitely join them in a week. At least that's what he seems to be saying.

A morning storm is rising, however, even before the sun.

"Though I'm deeply pleased you did," Neoptolomus tells Nivek, "why did you do that?"

"Because I have been your lover for six years now, and I could see how much you liked him when you looked at him. Besides, I like him too."

As they ride on, Neoptolomus muses: "I wonder what pleasures, what confusions Aronk will bring us?"

"Just remember," Nivek declares, "if he does not come, at some point, even if he did, he would be taken from us, anyway. Thus without him we shall be no worse off than we would eventually be for the gamble. And, like provincial boys before their first visit to a local brothel, we have our anticipation to enjoy, and, from having sampled him and so many others, a good deal more knowledge of what he might bring than have most such untutored children. Besides — who knows, despite such preparatory qualifications for probable disappointments — he *might* come; and furthermore might please us."

Some half hour's distance from Neoptolomus's village, the two stop their cart on the road, just above the seashore, beneath the cliffs on which, as had Cronin with his sheep in the Apennines, Neoptolomus once herded goats. As it begins to rain, Neoptolomus bids Nivek dismount. Neoptolomus explains: "I want to show you where I fished as a child." Naked Nivek climbs down to the rain-peppered road. Standing in the wagon, Neoptolomus calls the black man to turn and look up.

As they smile at one another, lightning scrawls through the seaside clouds. In the flare, as Neoptolomus squats at the wagon's rim, Nivek turns marble white. Their hands grip one another's.

Helping Neoptolomus down, Nivek tells him: "There, with the lightning behind you, for moments you were as black as if you'd been born my natural brother."

"In the same flash — " Neoptolomus gains the ground — "you grew as pale as mine," though he is thinking of death and the profusion, the abundance, the superfluity of life, of which death is the center, the ever-shifting organizer, and the surround; and wondering what the moment has evoked in his friend. At once, beside the creaking cart and the nervous horses, like a leap across whatever gulf between them, the men embrace ("our faces pressed one another's necks. The *Da, Da, Da* of the talking thunder rose to overcome the ocean. What a good, fine man Nivek was! What a good, fine man he made me feel I should, I could, and I would be! Chest to chest, knee to knee, Nivek's foot over my foot on the earth, Nivek's hand behind my head, mine spreading the small of his back, we gripped each other. His heavy penis lifted under mine, and thunder crumbled away among the waves"), till, finally, holding hands in the summer rain and warm wind, they descend to the sea edge ("night and light and water and sea air all a-stir with ocean storm"), to contemplate nature's raging ("which, someday, will be taken from us both, as — someday — we shall be taken from one another").

"I wonder which it will be — " Nivek muses, "Cronin, Osudh, Aronk, all, none, or possibly some woman or man we do not know as yet — whom we shall eventually send on our behalf to the temple at Hermopolis." Together, they walk out on a stone outcrop, where, below them, as the warm Sicilian rain increases, Neoptolomus points to a branch that has fallen into the swollen waters, a few twigs and leaves still on it, some dead, some green, afloat in the ocean's roll and rush.

The novel closes:

Slurring its susurrus about the foam-menaced rock, throughout its resounding surround, its slough and slosh, its many-voiced boisterousness over wet chaos, storm-bloated dark listed away, singing of drenched depths, dimensions, the recurrent currents supportive and silent beneath, the monsters that finned and glimmered within. Its wet leaves turning under, then lifting and dripping over, the branch drifted — finally to be taken — while, below weaving water, between its ebb and neap, primordial liquefaction raged and roared, briefly, against dawn.

A serene, thundering, and finally troubling finale, it's as satisfactory as it is full of questions.

EVEN A SYNOPSIS AS DETAILED as this must omit much. Rereading my account I realize it makes no mention of Clivus's extraordinary (certainly in such a book) midnight peroration in defense of celibacy.[15, 16] (It opens Chapter Thirty-nine.) Nor have I described Neoptolomus's equally astonishing — and, while rhetorically as extravagant as any sexual passage in the volume, quite beyond this reader's ability to untangle in its details — analysis of evil (it closes Chapter Twenty-eight), as he stands in the chill mountains at sunrise, gazing down among the cloud-cloaked Pyrenees — like Caspar David Friedrich's *Traveler Looking Over the Sea of Fog* — which, as far as I can make out, en-

---

[15] Binky writes: "Come on, Randy. A *defense* of celibacy? The three-page letter awaiting Neoptolomus at the Syracuse port from Clivus, which, on the midnight beach, unable to sleep, Neoptolomus reads by moonlight, says in effect that the problems of deciding, now with one lover, now with another, when the laws of singular possession and jealousy should obtain and when the egalitarian laws of friendship that allow shared and multiple partners should be assumed have *driven* Clivus to celibacy; that, indeed, the reign of jealousy has turned men and men (who represent teacher and student, friend and friend, and radical differences respected as a field not of nominal equality but rather of compensatory privileges, rights, and obligations to produce actual equality and thus *respected* by one another) into men and women (who represent owner and property, master and slave, the enforcement and compulsory internalization of power differentials in order to survive the complimentary needs *exploited* by one another). Until men and women, women and women, can maneuver the social forces about them so they can stabilize the paths along which they must travel if they are to become such radically different equals as homosexuality *sometimes* allows men and men to be, Clivus writes, the range of humanity, including *all* the genders and their possible combinatories, will not be able to throw off *completely* the tyranny of the sexual jealousies, in their several forms. Clivus praises Neoptolomus for how well he has succeeded in his attempt to negotiate the field of inequities from which Clivus himself has withdrawn into religion. It's not a defense, Randy. It's a lament!"

[16] Phyllis writes: "Other than reminding you that, in *Phallos,* what Binky calls 'respect' is one with 'reserve' (i.e., cutting the other some slack)—yeah, Randy—I was going to call you on that one, too. It works the way Fraud's famous (infamous?) comment in *Three Essays on the Theory of Sexuality* does (Basic Books, p. 85), that "libido is invariably and necessarily of a masculine nature, whether it occurs in men or women and irrespective of whether its object is a man or a woman," where his 1915 footnote explains, in effect, he is using "masculine" only as a synonym for "active"—and nothing more, however unhappy subsequent readers, many of us women (I include myself), have been with the rhetorical choices available at the time.

tails fixing the concept of absence at a rigid center, rather than allowing it to roam through, play freely with, and rearrange all and sundry it passes among, along its various trajectories and progressions, then declaring that positioned and circled absence itself transcendent, numinous, and holy — and thus and incidentally a positive justification for any and every thoughtlessness, inattention, barbarousness, or cruelty. But (" . . . in the accepting throes of light and the denied mists of an eternal temperance, an enchaining and enchanting ring a-quiver before that gleam — tawdry, luminous, embracing — as much from the mica beneath me as from the reflections a tear sheeting a lover's eye makes in some memory I refuse, yes, refuse even to recall, what can we grasp, here, now, of this dawn, that has not already spectacularly and disdainfully vanished even before the most impoverished, the most filigreed of prophetic abnegations, the richest, the most inarticulate of proprioceptive defections . . .") it's *got* to be less complicated than that.

Rereading my own account, I become aware how, by giving so much of the "story," I have suppressed, in fact, almost all of the sexuality, the affect, the sheer *feel* of the book. *In synopsis,* the disappointments of sex seem a great, gloomy theme. *In situ,* amidst such cascades, eruptions, tides of achieved pleasure, their mentions function as *en passant* reminders, rather, that sex *can* be — sometimes — less than satisfactory. An argument that omits — that, indeed, represses — all passages of direct sexual description suggests that *Phallos* is somehow stark, Apollonian, and parabolic, when it is rich, Dionysian, and hyperbolic in the extreme. The reading experience is virtually drenched in insights and proprioceptive pleasures that any sexually active gay man must recognize again and again — insights and pleasures that, again and again, sound the gamelan of truth. Easily, however, I can envision a different synopsis, quite as detailed as this, and at the same time wholly other, in which the passage of the years and the progress from social stratum to social stratum we so cavalierly call "plot" were elided and the sexual alone were foregrounded — one, say, that concentrated on the sexual dreamings that dominate the book more and more, until, by the final chapters, present Nivek has become all but one with the nameless god of Neoptolomus's dreams (as once did absent Maximin), so that it is sometimes difficult to distinguish, at least in the text's final third, where dream ends and reality recommences — in which the effect would be that of tumbling, glorious, sensual wonder and confusion. Finally, however, until *Phallos* becomes more widely available, my readers must make due with such chrestomathies as this, such moments and spot quotations, always partial, never exhaustive, aping its plot while ignoring its structure, through such inadequate shards and fragments.

THE AUTHORSHIP QUESTIONS around *Phallos* are much vexed. Having mentioned them there at our beginnings, we return to them here at our ends.

Presuming the book was written in the middle or late 1960s, I've found no printed references to any known writer, although, in the handful of essays that now and again have appeared on it, especially since its second edition from Avon in 1982, guesses at its author have included Thomas M. Disch, Coleman Dowell, L. Timmel Duchamp, Vin Packer, Michael Perkins, Joanna Russ, Darieck Scott, Gore Vidal, and Edmund White. At the time of the Avon reprint, a tale that circulated in those circles concerned with such things was that the book had been penned by a black southern writer, currently living in New York City. But at the risk of sounding hopelessly racist, *Phallos* just does not seem the sort of book I would imagine from a black man (or woman). Though many of the main characters are, indeed, black — arguably, given his lineage, even Neoptolomus himself — the string of unsatisfactory lovers (all except the last) makes it closer in feel to, say, *Sentimental Education* or something by Jean Rhys than to *Invisible Man, Iceberg Slim, Beloved,* or *Roots.*[17] Finally, then, this is as unconfirmed as any statement about the book

---

[17] Binky adds this note: "The first two times I read your synopsis, Randy, I thought you'd done an admirable job. *Most* of the things I was afraid you'd do, you didn't. Still, someone who reads only what's written here would never know Nivek succeeds in his mission to invest in Hir-wer (Antinopolis), though it takes him a few extra years—that, indeed, Nivek, fundamentally unconcerned with the *phallos,* is ultimately successful in his mission for the 'Chiefs of the Seven Great Tribes of Ethiopia.' Remember, the wealth that Nivek's exploits allow them to bring back from Africa is the money that finally secures them their Apennine villa—which, despite the non-phallic or anti-phallic ground of their relationship back on Samos, contributes toward making him an ideal figure for Neoptolomus, nevertheless. Neoptolomus would appear, by contrast, to have failed his generous patron. That's the whole point of the last half of Chapter Forty-one, Chapter Forty-two, and the first half of Chapter Forty-three. *You* omit all mention of 'the ebony orgy,' with the Arabian slavers, the black tribal slavers, and their black slaves, which attends all that North African hugger-mugger, where the two white men involved are so shockingly slaughtered and Neoptolomus escapes only because Nivek convinces the

in its suspect "Introduction." *I* suspect that it was a rumor started for much the same reasons as those other false assertions; I give it as much credence.

Books in Print lists a forthcoming edition from Kasak Books, to appear sometime next autumn. But while I have called that company several times, making a nuisance of myself with everyone from publicist to publisher and spending much too much on long-distance calls to do so, the entire staff seems to take personal delight in protecting the writer's identity — unless most of them simply and truly don't know it.

(Phyllis has urged me strongly to stop. After all, she says, it's *only* pornography [18] . . .)

Binky phoned last night, however: He cannot wait. He asked if I might get him a Xerox copy of the entire text, which he promises to take better care of than he has his dog-eared, decade-old, second-hand mass-market.

(Will mass-market paperbacks endure, I wonder, twenty, even fifteen, more years?)

It's a favor I've done a dozen readers over time, but I discontinued the practice eighteen months ago, Binky knows, when the manager of our lo-

---

Ivory Chief that Neoptolomus is his personal property (along with his veiled references to the *phallos*, which Nivek first makes, thinking they are jokes). You omit the whole chapter, with its African de-bauches (and what Neoptolomus learns of his lover's feelings living under Rome as a black man), that falls between the first and second set of summer orgies at the Apennine villa! Surely *that's* the sexual high point of the book for readers of a certain persuasion. But you just drop it. My third time through, however, I realized you had pretty much elided *all* the cleverly worked-out details of the novel's ac-tual plot. (Were you worried about 'spoilers' . . . ?) Because I'm so familiar with them, at first I hadn't missed them. But you omit all references to the hostilities between Bellona and Thoth in Hermopolis, as well as the virtual *denouement* that Lucius's father provides for Neoptolomus, when he shows up in the North African chapter, just mentioned, in a futile attempt to save his two doomed emissaries, and finally takes Neoptolomus and Nivek back to Rome instead . . . Trying to trace out the *actual* plot from your synopsis is as impossible as trying to locate the *phallos* itself!"

Mmm—I confess, all those s&m jungle bunnies bouncing about, buggering and being blown, no matter how eloquent, passionate, or poetic, hit me as hopelessly racist. (The fatal castration of the two other white men working for Lucius's father may be inverse racism; but it's racism nevertheless.) In a document whose main purpose is advocacy, I saw no reason to stress it. And why should I give away the *actual* plot of a book I hope people will eventually read for themselves?

[18] Phyllis remarks: "The five times in six years I've read *Phallos*, I've always thought I ought to iden-tity with Osudh. (We both write poems. Clearly we're both attracted to gay men—fag-hags, if you like. We both enjoy travel. We both have red hair—though I'm sure I weigh twice as much as she does.) But I don't. When she starts in on why they shouldn't be so kind to miserable, repentant Cronin, I want to smack her! The ones I identify with are the sad-eyed, abandoned boys: Maximin, Egon, and, oh, yes— *my* favorite—Moises, the witty and well-hung Jewish soldier—another one you mention only in pass-

cal copy shop read a page — just one, he swore — and stopped the job. At eleven in the morning he phoned to tell me that I had exactly an hour to get it out of his place or it would be shredder time in Moscow. I got into my blue Chevy pickup, drove by split-rail fences and through that piny 'scape, under those tall, tall clouds, and retrieved it. Fortunately I'd left him the set of masters on heavy laser paper I'd made specifically for reproduction. I'll loan them to Binky, who, since he was granted his doctorate — *Influences from the Age of Johnson on the Prose of Jane and Thomas Carlyle,* his dissertation: *Phhht!* — has spent every spare minute at the gym and has had three different garage mechanic jobs. (The *academic* market is simply non-extant!) He can copy them by hand on some self-service machine or brave the cheaper rates of an overnight job on his own.

— October 14, 1994
[New York, Philadelphia, 1996–2006]

ing but tell us nothing of his chapter traveling with Neoptolomus." Since she completed *Silence: Pierre de Ronsard and Jean Dorat at the Collège de Coqueret,* Phyllis has had two secretary jobs in two different roofing and demolition companies, at the most recent of which they say they love her and couldn't run the place without her. In October she has an interview, though, at an Iowa community college.

Two weeks after I posted this synopsis (she says the interview did not go well: Does that color what she writes here?), Phyllis sent me the following: "Randy: Finally, though, I'm not as sanguine about your synopsis as our tattooed, well-muscled, and multiply-pierced friend. You might guess: My questions—as have so many of mine to you of late—concern my 'bloody feminism,' as you styled it the night Binky dragged us in your pickup over to John's Alley, down on Sixth, that tipsy evening last March. It would be naïve for any reader to expect a novel such as *Phallos* to present an egalitarian portrait of such a patriarchal world as the Adriatic Mediterranean, much less to divide attention equally between genders.

"And yet . . .

"Yet the second time I read it, I was struck with how rich a picture Neoptolomus gives of the social world around and throughout his luminous presentations of gay male sex. Indeed, once he reaches adulthood, Neoptolomus's travel method appears to be that, whenever he arrives in a new location (on both his first and his second visits, Hermopolis and Rome are the exceptions), first off he engages some local in conversation, to learn something of where he's arrived.

"Neoptolomus admits (in Chapter Four) that, because of his sexual appetites and interests, he is shyer about approaching men than women, even when the man is not his particular type.

"My second time through the book, in search of a readerly pleasure experienced but only vaguely understood during my first, this richness of social portraiture struck me enough so that, on my third, I made notes. By count, during that third reading, I found eleven of these strangers (in Ephesus the serving girl at the café beside the Library of Artemis; in Byzantium the three matrons waiting for their husbands at the docks; in Alexandria the lame women among the beggars; at the Piraeus the barmaid who suggests he try another inn; in Athens the children's nurse in the park; in Barcelona the sharp-tongued laundress he retains; in Lemnos the scatterbrained woman servant shopping for housewares in the market; in the Pyrenees village the frightened woman who stares out at him from her back door, whom he eventually engages in conversation; in Tyre the acrobat's daughter, who discovers Neoptolomus masturbating behind the fair tent and laughs at him, and whose brother he beds and loses half his purse to; in Marseilles the dancing girl the lawyer flirts with at the inn while she tries futilely to seduce Neoptolomus; and in the North African port the—yes, Binky—black jewelry-maker who first delivers the centurion's message, hidden in her wares, and from whom, just before they leave, he buys the neck chains for himself and Nivek) were women—older, younger, bourgeois, working-class, or slave. Three times Neoptolomus approaches men or boys (in Corinth the young leper, in Cumae the old woods-man, and, on the morning of his departure from Byzantium, the crippled boy who tells him at which dock he'll find his boat). But with none of these, male or female, does Neoptolomus have sex.

"In each of these tertiary encounters, however, we get a remarkably full character portrait, now a third of a page, now three-quarters of a page, and, in the case of a secondary character such as the under-clerk at the temple of Artemis Nana, in Chapter Twenty-eight, a page-and-a-half description of her and her butch little friend (whom Neoptolomus initially mistakes for a man lurking in the col-umns' shadows. I always assumed they were a young lesbian couple. By secondary, I mean someone who has something to say about the *phallos* or the plot around it. By tertiary I mean someone who appears only once). But in all the cases I've mentioned, secondary or tertiary, we find out who the father was, who the mother was, or both, where each came from, what she (or he) likes and doesn't like in her (or his) current life—and with four we learn their favorite foods and where, in their respec-tive towns, they prefer to eat!

"In your synopsis, however, the only characters whose history we learn in anything near such detail are Jason, Neoptolomus's Roman carpenter friend, Lukey, and perhaps Maximin, while in the book we get such information about more than two dozen characters, many, if not most, women.

"*You* don't even mention that the temple under-clerk *is* a woman, much less that her father was 'a surveyor from Corinth's central mountain ridge' or that she had 'grown up on her mother's farm till bad management lost her the land'—not to mention that, off in Britain, Osudh was raised by a cousin, a blacksmith married to a midwife: 'The rhythms that first controlled my life and poems came from the mallet's repeated fall upon the anvil's back,' or that once she 'began to lurk about the boys studying with the druids,' who so regularly tried to shoo her away, eventually she 'learned Greek from a sailor with sea-grime caked beneath his nails,' finally to run off south with another young woman apprentice of a local woman ollave and thus, with her woman friend (Adara, "whose dry wit kept me sane over five months, tramping through rainy forests and hiking over hot hills and marshy meadows, until, at a three-day stop in some Gaulic town where the peasants praised her songs, suddenly she decided to stay—and, as far as I know, still chants her beautiful paeans there to those basically simple people, pos-sibly leading a better life than I, who finally went on to") continue her travels and education . . .

"Sure, you had to cut something. But whether it's the aging Spanish prostitute who recognizes Neoptolomus as 'one of those gentlemen more interested in his own sex than in mine,' who goes on to buy Neoptolomus dinner and who jokes about her many clients as she drinks with him all evening on his first—and, later, his last—night in Lutetia, or the young girl disguised as a boy in the market café in Tyre, fleeing her blind tyrannical uncle, who's demanded she choose between 'a shallow lout and an aging widower,' purely for their money (you *knew* I'd mention that one), with said uncle coming in with his men to drag her away in the midst of their conversation, they enrich the social portraiture immeasurably. Still, the egalitarian gender *attention* (God knows, the women don't have it well in the novel: Take the 'long-faced' fifteen-year-old prostitute, among those Lukey infects with 'pox,' whose four sisters, Cronin tells Neoptolomus and Nivek, have put her out on the road to beg), with its skew-ing toward the *female* on this contingent tertiary level, makes me, at any rate, trust the primary level's skewing toward the *male* in a way that I don't when I read your account. Also, the handling of those gratuitous characters is what most gives the book the feel of a text from the eighteenth century or before—*pogoing* aside.

"For me, the women present in the rest of the novel, *with* their histories, make the women absent—or, all tits and *no* histories, if Saul and Costas's comments are to be trusted, the sexually objectified, endlessly unattainable (i.e., phallic) women—in that male heterosexual enclave, Hebe's Chalice in Part Two (Saul: "Where do they come from? Where do they go?" Costas: "They simply enter, linger, touch their thighs without a thought, and are beautiful—to make us suffer!"), register with such critical, even satiric, weight: Compare them to the most voluble of the three matrons, commenting to her friends on the Byzantine docks about the handsome sailors around them, or the raunchy dinner-time tales of the aforementioned prostitute (the first 'heavy-breasted'; the second with 'her breasts shaking in their loose silks'), i.e., with sexuality *and* history (a family wealthier than her husband's in Persia; a childhood on the streets of Barcelona).

"Since I first read *Phallos,* I've felt the writer was working against the grain of modern fiction and somehow against the forces that made you rush to excise that same cascade of mini-portraits. This is social and historical, not sexual or even psychological. Certainly you are no 'gayer' than he. I don't for a second believe *Phallos* was written by a woman. (But then . . .)

"I miss them greatly. (As I miss the dozen passing anecdotes of Nivek's tribal childhood and adolescence you elide—three, to the length of four pages, from your pages 95 and 96 alone—particularly the charming one about what people in his tribe do when they come across a couple in the high grass making love: squatting just out of sight and rocking back and forth, holding their genitals, until they have an orgasm on their own.) It was a real lesson to find how sharply your excisions changed the book's affect. Finally, I'm drawn to a statement, which I hope isn't too harsh. Perhaps, however, it's unavoidable. The anonymous author of *Phallos* wrote a novel about a historical world in which, however oppressed and constrained women were, women and men existed in more or less equal numbers. The narrator is simply more interested sexually in the men—an interest any basically heterosexual female, such as myself, easily identifies with. But your synopsis presents a book where, despite the High Priestess, Ihelva, and Osudh, somehow *most* of the women have vanished! I suppose I'm only locating another level at which, for all its pornographic thrust, *Phallos* displays the novelist's art—a level that, as much as the racial skewing Binky cites, must be betrayed, or at any rate made to leap up and cast a shadow, at least in memory, by such, dare I call it, castration."

CRITICAL ESSAYS

AFTERWORD

ROBERT F. REID-PHARR

Nobody loves a genius child.
Can you love an eagle,
Tame or wild?
Wild or tame,
Can you love a monster
Of frightening name?
Nobody loves a genius child.
Kill him—and let his soul run wild!

Langston Hughes, "Genius Child"

"Haven't you learned yet that quests such as yours can never be fulfilled?"

Samuel R. Delany, *Phallos*

ONE OF THE CLEAREST MARKERS OF GENIUS, one of the signs that a creative intellectual has unveiled some mode of thought or action that is at once elegant, productive, disruptive, and dangerous is the presence of an abundance of generosity. Refusing to maintain the fictions of the so-called commonsense, his practice is both deconstructive and pedagogical. Like a magician who reveals the card tucked up his sleeve or the rabbit hidden inside an old-fashioned hat's secret compartments, the genius is first and foremost an iconoclast. His work is to force us to recognize that even our most cherished structures might be (must be?) dismantled. This is why when we encounter such individuals we are often so quick to either dismiss or ridicule them. In their efforts to disclose profound insights and novel techniques they strip away the "invisibility" of established forms and practices. Their high-wire acts demonstrate that our own stumbling about is never effected on stable ground. On the contrary, our most well-cherished technologies are temporary and ephemeral, always in the process of becoming laughably outmoded. It is difficult then for even the most self-assured and flexible among us to choke back hostility and derision when we encounter the work—and generosity—of such individuals; difficult to squelch the assumption that they have short-circuited our hopes, spoiled our comforts. The child who announces the emperor's nakedness may be correct, but he nonetheless interrupts the "innocent" pleasure one feels when watching a well-orchestrated procession.

Samuel Delany is a genius. In the fifty years since the publication of his first novel, he has consistently struggled not only to demonstrate the discursive and ideological contours of the various worlds that we inhabit, but also to make plain that these discourses, ideologies, and worlds are of our own making. In novels, short stories, essays, and comics, Delany pushes against both the limits of what an author might properly treat as well as the equally stultifying conceptual limits surrounding how readers can and should be hailed. To feel the weight of Delany's writing in one's hands is to relinquish hold on the notion that one might escape with one's innocence intact. His genius and his generosity turn on his willingness to disrupt his readers' normative conceptions of identity and culture as well as their commonsensical beliefs regarding the "proper" place of literature in society. Instead, having spent much of his career working in extra-literary forms, particularly science fiction, Delany leaves his often adoring public(s) painfully aware of how fragile our own discursive and ideological structures actually are.

A four-time recipient of the Nebula Award and two-time recipient of the Hugo award, Delany is the author of some forty books of fiction and criticism, including the classic science fiction novels, *Nova* (1968), *Dhalgren* (1975), *Triton* (1976), *Stars in My Pocket Like Grains of Sand* (1984), and the Return to Nevèrÿon series (1979, 1983, 1985, 1987). He has also published many finely wrought short stories, some of which were gathered together in the collections, *Driftglass* (1971) and *Aye, and Gomorrah, and Other Stories* (2003). His autobiography, *The Motion of Light in Water: Sex and Science Fiction in the East Village, 1960–1965* (1988), is one of the finest treatments of the literary and cultural scene in and around New York City's East Village ever written.

Of particular significance for readers of *Phallos* are Delany's difficult and often quite raunchy works, *The Mad Man* (1994) and *Hogg* (1995), which combine Delany's intricate and razor-sharp writing with explicitly sexual themes and a hardnosed concern with complex matters of philosophy and criticism. Delany sets his plow against similar ground in both his 2007 novel, *Dark Reflections*, for which he won the 2008 Stonewall Book Award, as well as his 1999 nonfiction treatment of the "redevelopment" of Times Square from a (largely gay) "red-light district" into a "family focused" tourist destination, *Times Square Red, Times Square Blue*. All these texts demonstrate Delany's interest in what one might call the beastliness of human sexuality, the ways that our sexual desires and practices represent not only our need for affection and companionship but also an unquenchable fascination with violence and degradation.

This hopefully gives you some insight into the nature of the complications that Delany imbeds within *Phallos*. The work is in Delany's words "the tale of a tale"; a sex-filled story set in the ancient world (Egypt to Syracuse, Rome to Paris to Athens and back again) in which the orphaned protagonist, Neoptolomus, searches for the "stolen" jewel encrusted *phallos* of an unnamed god. The presumed value of the *phallos* is that, hidden within it, are secrets of science and society that will inevitably lead to power, knowledge, and wealth. Of course, in proper Lacanian fashion there is nothing (but desire?) inside the vessel. And more distressing still, Delany even refuses to allow his readers to settle into the conceit that what they are reading is a fantasy—prurient or otherwise—of "Western" antiquity. Instead Delany draws attention to the ways that *Phallos* continues many of the dominant themes and forms of his oeuvre while also (generously) disallowing "easy" reading practices.

Let me borrow Steven Shaviro's concise account of the novel's outermost frame.

In a brief preface we are told about a young African American man, Adrian Rome, who is looking for an anonymous pornographic novel called *Phallos*, which is out of print and difficult to find. Adrian stumbles across a copy of the book several times, but each time loses it again before he has had a chance to read it. In the course of his search for the book, he meets his life partner, Shoat Rumblin—the eponymous protagonist of another (as yet unpublished) novel by

Delany. "But the closest [Adrian] ever comes to reading *Phallos* is a synopsis he discovers on the Internet." That synopsis, by one Randy Pedarson, of Moscow, Idaho, makes up the main body of Delany's novel.

Moreover, even this transcription has been expunged, in order to protect potential readers from the many naughty sexual interludes that the work presumably describes.

Thus both the antiquity and the sexual libertinage that *Phallos* represents are presented to us via means both modern and unstable. It is a text that flaunts its status as fiction. The images of the ancient world that it offers are perhaps nothing more than the reiteration of modern fantasies of *pre*-modern licentiousness. Its central character, Neoptolomus, "born" on the island of Syracuse (today Sicily), is a figure who lacks solidity. He is at best a hybrid, a half-breed, carrying with him both the pretensions of Greece given to him by his father and the unvanquished sensibilities of Africa passed down by his part-Egyptian mother. He is continually in transit, continually learning to recalibrate his assumptions and "instincts" for new—and always dynamic— situations. He is, therefore, necessarily a diligent student of language and culture whose first action in the novel is to learn three hundred words or so in the "foreign" Greek tongue:

> fire, river, resin, rust, life, copper, fish, bread, wine, site, salt, garlic, honey, song, vision, rain, bird, history, drinkable, discourse, barley, poet, laughter, belief, now, undrinkable, then, gods, treaty, nation, change, grain, cricket, necessity, mountain, astonish, commander, beauty, thunder, all, hear, steersman, nothing, love, freeman, pain, water, good, wet, weep, slave, night, tomorrow, suffer, justice, moon, rest, sorrow, up, down, no, yes, sun, tree, branch, head, hand, clitoris, earth, body, jar, breast, bad, wisdom, city, road, root, cattle, common, dawn, tomb, none, day, when, urine, measure, gold, horse, create, deathless, shit, experience, laughter, destroy, eternal, opposite, blade, on-the-one-hand, shield, on-the-other, wasp, finger, penis, people, eye, peace, battle, journey, pleasure, exchange, strife, star, foot, sleep, sand, rectum, remain, mud, and death

I would invite you to recognize *Phallos* as a text that is fully self-conscious about what one might call its three-dimensional status. It faces both backwards and forwards: backwards toward ancient traditions of thought and literature (Greek, Roman, Egyptian), and forwards toward the not fully known or understood "traditions" that presumably will arise out of the possibilities inherent in the various textualities that have been—and will be—produced by and through new modes of communication, including the Internet. At the same time, the work is bounded on all sides by (fictional) readers and critics: Adrian Rome, Randy Pedarson, and Randy's friends Binky and Phyllis, who labor to place the text within discursive structures that might be accessed by modern audiences.

Thus what we resist in this edition of *Phallos* is the sense of closure that attends many scholarly editions. Unlike other reprints of underappreciated works by prominent writers, the book that you hold before you does not represent an attempt to settle questions of canon or tradition. On the contrary, we remain self-conscious here about the "necessity" of adding yet another level of discursive complexity—and uncertainty—to the novel by appending not only this afterword, but also three additional critical essays written by a remarkably accomplished group of critics: Ken James, Steven Shaviro, and Darieck Scott. In doing so we hope not only to expand upon the "joke" of the work in a manner that is certain to delight Delany's many fans, particularly those with interests in his more recent fiction, but also to continue its infinitely expansive conceits. We work to show the ways that *Phallos* demonstrates the "absent center" from which desire is produced, while also suggesting that this absence, this space of nothingness, is hardly fixed. It moves. It travels through space and time. Its "presence" is noted and reiterated in a variety of cultural and linguistic contexts. Thus that generosity that Delany—and the authors who accompany him—demonstrate is based in their willingness to allow that *Phallos* continues to be unfinished. It is a work that provides no solace to its readers. Instead it asks that they actively participate in explicating the text, in opening it up. Delany, James, Shaviro, and Scott are most eager to spark the creativity of their readers, to present to them the methods by which secrets and mysteries (*narratives*, some might call them; *discourses*, others might object) are maintained.

In Kenneth James's essay, "Discourse and Desire, Muddle and Need: Radical Reading In and Around *Phallos*," he carefully notes *Phallos*'s dialogical relationship to the rest of Delany's body of work. Cleverly reminding the reader that Lacanian arguments around narrative ought to be read alongside a longer tradition of thinking about the "tricks" that are part of the novelist's trade, James argues that Walter Pater, Jacques Lacan, Gayle Rubin, Samuel Delany, and many others have continually struggled both to utilize and make sense of the fact that the "realities" that are announced in novels are never there for readers to sample. Instead the very pleasure that we take in reading texts is that they speak to our desires without corralling them, they allow for structured articulations of phobias and fantasies while nonetheless conceding the fact that "the phobic" and "the fantastic" can never be fully encompassed within narrative, no matter the gifts of the individual writer. Delany's careful attention to this reality is one of the reasons that a short novel like *Phallos* seems so complete to its readers. It is a text that insists that its readers participate, that they work shoulder to shoulder with Delany in order to push forward into the infinite expanse of words and images that are the most basic elements of fiction.

Continuing this line of thought, Steven Shaviro's essay, "Ars Vitae: Delany's Philosophical Fable," both celebrates and bemoans the coyness of *Phallos*, noting that though the novel promises its readers a wealth of graphic representations of the most naughty forms of sex, it tends to treat such matters "off stage," thereby forcing the reader to confront his or her own expectations and desires in relation to Delany's oeuvre. Or as Shaviro notes, *Phallos* is a novel established through "regimes of misrepresentations and indirections" that work to "keep sexual desire moving." As a consequence desire remains excessive and undomesticated, a "surplus" in Shaviro's language. Yet Shaviro does not simply name the mechanics of the work. Instead he boldly argues for the way that it remains essentially a pedagogical text, one that focuses most directly on the "ethics of the everyday."

Completing this distinguished trio, Darieck Scott argues in "I Can See Atlantis from My House: Sex, Fantasy, and *Phallos*" that, as with the many narratives that bunch around the "lost" city of Atlantis, *Phallos* is a work that is concerned first and foremost with those things that are missing, or that perhaps never existed, those absences that structure so much within modern discourse. As with Shaviro, he takes his lead from Lacan, noting and explicating the essentially productive nature of the "absent center." At the same time, however, Scott's essay presses forcefully on the idea that Delany's ability to structure a delicious tale that focuses on "nowhere" and "nothing" allows his readers to recognize that their own efforts as readers—and writers—place them within "an immortal company." It allows them to project themselves both backwards and forwards in time thereby resisting the sense of fixity and isolation that is so much a part of the human condition. Indeed Scott goes so far as to suggest that this ability leads readers to an awareness that language allows one to exist in worlds limited by neither space nor time. This is, in fact, "the novelist's art," the thing that keeps us returning to difficult and generous works like Delany's time and again.

What you will undoubtedly have come to understand already in your discursive and erotic journeys with Delany, Shaviro, Scott, James, Adrian, Randy, Phyllis, Binky, and Neoptolomus is that *Phallos*, for all of its "thinness," is hardly an easy novel. You have chosen to bring a wild and monstrous thing into the comfortable environs of your home. At once pleasing and irritating, it threatens and soothes, delights and frightens. Indeed I would say again that like Delany himself, *Phallos* is profoundly generous. It educates its readers; requires of them that they self-consciously and steadfastly engage with the narrative arts. It asks us to note, engage, and re-order the structures that hold together this "tale within a tale." It is in this sense that Delany has created yet another work of genius, one that eschews escapism for the more fulfilling—and rigorous—pleasures of self-aware and engaged reading.

DISCOURSE AND DESIRE, MUDDLE AND NEED

RADICAL READING IN AND AROUND *PHALLOS*

KENNETH R. JAMES

I

The fictive events of the inner narrative of *Phallos* — a historical fantasy recounting the sexual and philosophical adventures of the young merchant Neoptolomus as he traverses the Roman empire — occur on the margins of an actual historical incident: the emperor Hadrian's establishment of a cult devoted to his deceased male lover, Antinous. By Hadrian's decree, temples to Antinous really were constructed throughout the empire, as the inner tale indicates. Subsequent commentary on this extraordinary moment in the history of homosexuality — commentary dominated, in the centuries to follow, by the discourse of ascendant Christianity — is rife with conflicting interpretations of Antinous's death. Was it part of a ritual sacrifice, an emblem of Hadrian's fascination with the cults of his empire? Was it a mark of excess, of some limit transgressed — in short, a punishment for sin? Or was it sheer accident? The events of the inner story — conveyed in synopsis by one Randy Pedarson, a character in the outer narrative, and based on episodes from an anonymously penned pornographic novel, first published in 1969 and also entitled *Phallos* — occur in the shadow of this contested history.

Meanwhile, the episodes of the outer narrative echo those of the inner story as well as the scholarly commentary on the historical events that provide its mise-en-scène. Neoptolomus's quest, both for the jeweled *phallos* belonging to the image of the nameless god of an obscure mystery cult and for an understanding of its significance, mirrors the search by the outer tale's three contemporary scholars — Randy, Binky, and Phyllis — for the identity of the novel's elusive author. (Both these quests resonate in turn with the outermost narrative, an authorial foreword synopsizing the story of Adrian Rome, whose quest to find a copy of the novel eventually leads him to Randy's own synopsis — which thus stands revealed as an excerpt or extract, the only *non-synoptic* part of Adrian's tale we're given.) In turn, the exegetical debates of the three scholars over the book's authorship and dates of composition, the credibility of the historical apparatus accompanying it, and, increasingly, the reliability of Randy's editorial criteria, mirror the debates over the story of Hadrian and Antinous. Taken together, then, the two major narrative layers or strata of *Phallos* present us with an allegory of interpretation, of reading. But what kind of reading?

The home city of the cult of the nameless god is Hermopolis, located across the Nile from Antinopolis, founded by Hadrian in the name of his deceased lover's apotheosis. Hermopolis, the center for the worship of Thoth, the Egyptian god of writing, was named for the messenger god Hermes, whom the Greeks identified with Thoth. "Hermes" is thought to form the basis for the word "hermeneutics" — the art of interpretation, specifically the interpretation of texts, more specifically the exegesis of Christian scripture (Mueller-Vollmer 1–2). It is the methodology of understanding a text rightly, of "getting the message" — particularly a message received from an historical, cultural, or linguistic remove. In *Phallos,* the cult of the nameless god is located on the edge of the city of Thoth, suggesting that the ideas of interpretation to be found in this novel bear a marginal relation to entrenched assumptions about hermeneutics. Some of these assumptions might include: the unity of communicative intention at the message's origin, the coherence of reception at its arrival, the hidden meaning that interpretation reveals, the unbroken (or at least reconstructable) continuity of the message's transit, and, once interpretation is complete, the unification of interpretive horizons between sender and receiver. (These last two notions underpin the concept of interpretation advanced by Hans-Georg Gadamer, a major theoretician of modern hermeneutics.) And indeed, the action of *Phallos* undermines just these assumptions. But this undermining does not register as a dark negation of all possibility of interpretation: it has positive, or at least precise, implications — implications which resonate throughout Delany's fiction and criticism.

From the beginning of his career, Delany's stories have consistently taken the form of hermeneutic quests. *The Jewels of Aptor* (1962) turns on the interpretation of ancient verses in a post-holocaust landscape, *The Ballad of Beta-2* (1965) concerns a graduate student's analysis of a folk song originating on a generation starship, the Nebula-winning *Babel-17* (1966) pivots around an attempt to translate an artificial language, and *Empire Star* (1966) traces the transit of a message from the periphery of an interstellar empire to its center. In Delany's experimental SF and fantasy of the '70s and '80s, this hermeneutic concern is massively elaborated. The protagonist of *Dhalgren* (1975) comes into possession of a notebook whose contents haunt him over the novel's considerable length — eventually overtaking the text of the novel and presenting its mysteries directly to the reader, who, to navigate to the novel's ambiguous end (and beyond), must become its active exegete. A key passage in *Stars in My Pocket Like Grains of Sand* (1984) presents a tour-de-force description of a technologically augmented experience of speed-reading. The fictive premise of the Nevèrÿon quartet is that the tales contained within it have been inspired by the translation of a single, nine-hundred-word ancient text, and most of these tales themselves turn on interpretive quests; see especially the parallel narratives of the smuggler and the Master in *Flight from Nevèrÿon* (1985). Finally, *The Mad Man* (1996) concerns the researches of yet another graduate student into the enigmatic life, death, and surviving fragmented writings of a gay philosopher of language. Even the stories that do not turn directly on textual interpretation can be taken as allegories of successful or unsuccessful reading — with the text, in these cases, being a social or sexual landscape.

In his criticism, too, Delany has placed the notion of reading as such — reading as a structured act — on center stage. The essays with which Delany first made his name in SF criticism approached the genre not as a cluster of thematic concerns, but rather as a set of reading protocols by which sense could be made of a given SF text. This focus on sense-making has remained a baseline concern, around which Delany has deployed ideas from analytic philosophy, feminism, structuralism, Marxism, psychoanalysis, and — crucially for his criticism of the '90s and after — Foucauldian discourse analysis. The result has been the creation of a critical corpus of astonishing range and startling incisiveness; for all Delany's erudition, his is a supremely undistracted intellect. And I would suggest that a major source of this critical precision has been Delany's sustained focused on the question of reading.

What ways of reading structure *Phallos?* We can begin to answer this by separating the two major narrative strata of *Phallos* and holding them apart, in order to foreground elements within them that can be aligned with the larger continuum of Delany's writing and with broader fields of theoretical endeavor. What makes this operation more than an ordinary thematic analysis is the tightness with which Delany has contrived to laminate the two strata. They "want" to collapse back together, and how and why this is so, as we will see, is directly relevant to the ways of reading in question. What I hope to demonstrate about the structure of *Phallos* is captured by appropriating and recasting a remark Delany makes about Shoshana Felman's psychoanalytic reading of Henry James's "The Turn of the Screw": namely, that Felman reads James's text as "an allegorical anticipation of the critical dialogue grown up about it" (*Silent Interviews* 215). I submit that the hermeneutic dramas of the two narrative layers of *Phallos* can each be aligned with an historical "reading event" relating to the theorization of the sexual margins. Structuring the inner story is the feminist — or more precisely, socialist-feminist — reading of Lacanian psychoanalysis, while structuring the outer story is Delany's own reading of Walter Pater through a Foucauldian lens. I submit further that, when placed in interplay, the narrative layers in *Phallos* can be read as an allegory for a particular vision of the hermeneutic drama — the possibility for interpretive challenge, danger, and triumph — of reading queerness, and of queer reading.

II

The inner story of Neoptolomus presents the reader with an itinerary of ideas about meaning as embodied by the *phallos*. In Alexandria, Neoptolomus is told that the *phallos* is a container, hidden inside which are ancient papyruses filled with "philosophical, mathematical, and astrological wonders" (38). Later, in Cumae, Neoptolomus is told by the sibyl Hirophilia that "the secrets of the *phallos* are not deep within it but rather blatantly on its surface for all to read" (61). Later still, the High Priestess of Bellona claims that the *phallos* is "a simulacrum, an image . . . It holds no secrets, no wisdom — either of magic or of history" (77) — leading Neoptolomus to infer that "there *is* no original: Any of its imitations is, in fact, as real, actual, and authentic as any other" (78). Meanwhile, regardless of the claims made about it, for Neoptolomus what increasingly seems to characterize the *phallos* — or, more accurately, its rumored presence, absence, and movement — is its capacity, Maltese Falcon–like, to set schemes in motion. It mobilizes spontaneous attempts at petty theft, and more organized, orchestrated capers (41, 101), provides the occasion for attempts at seduction (39), becomes the privileged game piece in the rivalry between the temple of the nameless god and that of the goddess Bellona, and repeatedly reveals the shape of the longings of the people into whose sphere it enters (cf. Neoptolomus's discussion with Osudh on the subject [99–100]). In short, the inner narrative of *Phallos* elaborates an idea of signification shaped not by a structure of surfaces and depths, concealment and revelation, but rather inflected by the presence of intention, expectation, and desire.

In his lecture "The Rhetoric of Sex / The Discourse of Desire," Delany has commented that desire is "a very scary notion. Its mark is absence. Accordingly, a positivistic culture frequently finds itself at a loss to explore it or elaborate its workings" (RS 15). He goes on to discuss Freudian and Lacanian formulations about desire, while acknowledging that these formulations are imbricated with the discourse of patriarchy (RS 20–21). (Delany vividly dramatizes the vexed relationship between psychoanalysis and patriarchy — and normalizing discourses generally — in what is arguably the climactic emotional encounter of *Dhalgren,* the psychoanalytic session between Kid and Madame Brown. I have long suspected that this scene was conceived as a response to Theodore Sturgeon's classic SF novella "Baby Is Three," whose story unfolds within the framework of a psychoanalytic session that, in its rapid progress from revelation to revelation, its ideally lucid communication between analyst and patient, is itself something of a wish-fulfillment dream. *Dhalgren,* by contrast, presents a session that is a farrago of misreadings and miscommunications, shot through with sex, gender, race, and class tensions [762–76].) Among Delany's critical essays I count a good half-dozen in which Lacan's work takes center stage or provides a supporting role, and in virtually all his fiction after *Dhalgren,* Lacan either functions as a major subtextual presence or — owing to Delany's democratic attitude toward source citation — is directly named: see, for instance, the epigraphs and appendices of *Trouble on Triton* and the Nevèrÿon books, not to mention references in the main bodies of those texts. (For a justification for this democratic attitude, see also Delany's discussion, in "Shadow and Ash," of the poetry of Ron Silliman [172].) *Phallos,* as a novel that is simultaneously its own commentary, follows in this vein.

Key elements of the inner narrative of *Phallos* closely track the major terms of Lacan's seminar on Poe's story "The Purloined Letter," starting, of course, with the *phallos* itself. As it circulates, or appears to circulate, from owner to owner, its value, like that of Poe's letter and Lacan's signifier, is shown to derive from its position within the circuit it both traces and gathers around itself. Eventually Neoptolomus comes to recognize that this circuit, like Lacan's, is an intersubjective one driven by absence and lack; after dissembling to the would-be thieves Blutus and Egon about a rumored treasure being held in a warehouse, and, later, declining to confess his fabrication, Neoptolomus speculates: "In holding my silence as much as I had till then, perhaps I was also actually holding the *phallos*" (65). Moreover, the particular rumor Neoptolomus invents — that "a gang of Nubians, all of them black as the night itself, with a young Greek among them," intend to steal the treasure (64) — returns to him the next day as gossip about a successful theft carried out on the previous night by a "gang of Greek thieves" led by a "handsome young Nubian" (66): a circumstance where, in the words of Lacan's seminar, "the sender . . . receives from the receiver his own message in reverse form" (52–53). Finally, beyond these structural correspondences — and consistent with Delany's deployment of critical sources — the editor/redactor Randy directly states that in its portrayal of the *phallos* the narrative is "[r]eflecting Freud and anticipating Lacan" (55). The notion that the novel pre-dates Lacan, of course, reflects Randy's presuppositions about the novel's origins; nevertheless, whatever its status within the fictive situation, *some* relation to Lacan has been made explicit.

But as Delany has remarked — while discussing extratextual influences on fellow sf writer Joanna Russ — "a *critical* relation is what, finally, any aesthetic influence worth the name must be, so that the differences are as much a part of the influence as the similarities" (507, my emphasis). Regarding possible sources for a critical reading of Lacan in *Phallos,* we have, again, direct claims from Delany, who has stated his interest in feminist interpretations of Lacan by Shoshana Felman and Jane Gallop (*Silent Interviews* 242). However, we do not, at this point in our argument, address specific influences, because our aim is to draw attention to an entire discursive surround — a *way* of reading, marked by a characteristic set of concerns, parameters, terms, and procedures. As an exemplar of this way of reading — that is, as a metonym for a whole field of critical endeavor, established by countless feminist writers — we choose Gayle Rubin's classic study, "The Traffic in Women." We suggest that in the terms it deploys, the modes of reading it engages, the way it engages them and, finally, the way it fits into a continuum of subsequent readings, some by Rubin herself, "The Traffic of Women" provides a useful itinerary for a reading of the structure of *Phallos.* In making this claim we do not suggest that all that is feminist in *Phallos* is reducible to this earlier moment in the history of feminist reading, or that this earlier moment is reducible to Rubin's text. And while Delany has remarked, again on Russ, that reading a text in relation to the psychoanalytic unconscious "does not require a finding of intentional borrowing" (507), we emphasize that we make no claim here for direct appropriation of Rubin, intentional or otherwise. Rather, we wish to show how Delany's text inhabits a field of discourse established by an earlier reading event, or more specifically, how it can be read as an allegory of the historical circumstance that, in the words of Annamarie Jagose, contemporary queer reading "developed out of — and continues to be understandable in terms of — feminist knowledges" (119).

In her study, Rubin notes the tendency of Marxist critics to read sex and gender oppression as an epiphenomenon of a more primary structural inequality (TW 166). According to Rubin, this way of reading is challenged by the accumulating historical and ethnographic evidence pointing to women's subordination in pre-capitalist and tribal societies, suggesting a system of sex/gender oppression that is relatively autonomous from class exploitation (TW 163). To enable that system to articulate itself in relation to the Marxist framework that has tended to elide it, Rubin turns her attention to psychoanalysis and structuralism, performing what she calls an "exegetical reading" of Freud and Lévi-Strauss (TW 159). By means of this exegesis, Rubin is able to extract what is potentially radical in all three theories but has been suppressed by an ideological overlay.

Rubin claims she is examining Freud and Lévi-Strauss through what she calls a Lacanian "lens"; after all, it was Lacan who, in his own act of radical reading, had first folded Freud and Lévi-Strauss together, importing the structuralist model of human cognition into the Freudian unconscious (TW 159). But for just this reason I would suggest that the true object of Rubin's exegesis is Lacan. By disentangling Freud and Lévi-Strauss from their tight meshing in Lacan, she allows the ethnographic aspects of Lévi-Strauss to stand out once again in their autonomy — and thus to re-coordinate in specific ways with the ethnographic data that has motivated her project. Thus Rubin performs a double exegesis: to disarticulate sex/gender from class, she must disarticulate Lévi-Strauss from Lacan. The resulting reading redounds as much upon Lacan's system as on the others.

According to that system, the "phallus" is the signifier that inhabits the pivotal position in the intra-psychic economy where sexual difference, infantile desire, and social interdiction converge. In the extra-psychic realm, the phallus has a precise structural double: acknowledging Lévi-Strauss, Lacan notes that women function "as objects for the exchanges required by the elementary structures of kinship . . . while what is transmitted in a parallel way in the symbolic order is the phallus" (*Ecrits* 207). However, in the cross-cultural context foregrounded by Rubin's exegesis, the phallus begins to appear suspect in its role as the privileged symbol of sexual difference. Rubin avoids an explicit critique of Lacan on this point, though her argument implies one; other readers have been more direct. Elizabeth Grosz indicates that the phallus's signification of the presence/absence of the male organ cannot be read as "arbitrary" in the Saussurean sense — as a purely formal binarism — but rather as a mark of patriarchal apologetics smuggled back into the system: "it is surely arbitrary, in the sense of social or conventional, that the continuum of differences between gradations of sexual difference along a continuum is divided into categories only according to the presence or absence of the one, male, organ" (124–25). The imposition of binary categories on a continuum of differences, as Rubin indicates, just *is* the operation of gender (TW 178–80). But in the pluralistic context Rubin's reading foregrounds, the concept of "appropriate/inappropriate sexual liaisons" — which provides the foundation for the structures of both kinship and the unconscious — begins to ramify beyond anything that could be cleanly modeled with a simple male/female dyad:

> For instance, some marriage systems have a rule of obligatory cross-cousin marriage. A person in such a system is not only heterosexual, but "cross-cousin-sexual." If the rule of marriage further specifies matrilineal cross-cousin marriage, then a man will be "mother's-brother's-daughter-sexual" and a woman will be "father's-sister's-son-sexual." (TW 181)

In short, once it has been repositioned within a multicultural space, the locus of the privileged signifier of difference and desire begins to be set in motion, to circulate — to elude the control-structure of the discourse that produced it.

Rubin's re-articulation of theoretical systems in terms of the ethnographic data has implications that reverberate in many directions. For instance, her proposal of the term "sex-gender system" itself responds to the recognition that in an ethnographic context, the term "patriarchy," so important for feminist critique, has less than universal applicability: "the power of males in these groups is not founded on their roles as fathers or patriarchs, but on their collective adult maleness, embodied in secret cults, men's houses, warfare, exchange networks, ritual knowledge, and various initiation procedures" (TW 168). Contrariwise, bringing the ethnographic data under a feminist lens highlights the differences between exchange circuits involving women and men: "Men of course are also trafficked — but as slaves, hustlers, athletic stars, serfs, or as some other catastrophic social status, rather than as men. Women are trafficked as slaves, serfs, and prostitutes, but also as women" (TW 176). Furthermore, Rubin notes that while the traffic in women relies on a tacit obligatory heterosexuality in order to function as an exchange circuit, numerous kinship arrangements create a functional space for homosexual liaisons (TW 181). In relation to prior discourses, then — psychoanalysis, structuralism, feminism — Rubin's reading re-inflects key terms and relations.

Having established this reconfigured critical field, Rubin then performs her most bracing move: she re-joins it with Marxist discourse, generating a veritable explosion of questions that can be asked of any society that traffics in women:

> Is the woman traded for a woman, or is there an equivalent? Is this equivalent only for women, or can it be turned into something else? If it can be turned into something else, is it turned into political power or wealth? On the other hand, can bridewealth be obtained only in marital exchange, or can it be obtained from elsewhere? Can women be accumulated from amassing wealth? Can wealth be accumulated by disposing of women? Is a marriage system part of a system of stratification? (TW 207)

Questions like these enable Rubin to speculate about how the exchange of women might be implicated in "large-scale political processes like state-making," through, for example, "the accumulation of wealth and the maintenance of differential access to political and economic resources; in the building of alliances; in the consolidation of high-ranking persons into a single closed strata of endogamous kin" (TW 209). Thus, through a meticulous exegetical extraction — Lévi-Strauss from Lacan, sex-gender from class — the terms and parameters of a vast scholarly and political project are delineated.

Reviewing that project, we recognize that its terms provide a lexicon for major elements of the inner tale of *Phallos* that is more precise and extensive than that which might be provided by a strictly psychoanalytic reading, even a Lacanian one. We recognize the priesthood of the *phallos* as a non-patriarchal yet male-centered mystery cult fitting Rubin's formulation. We recognize the cult's "ownership" of the *phallos*, coupled with its form of extortion through the morally coerced purchasing of slaves, as a means to accumulate both social capital and material wealth. We also recognize in this scheme a situation in which men are indeed trafficked as men: within this circuit Neoptolomus himself becomes a catamite, and later, briefly, a physical embodiment of the *phallos*. In this scheme, moreover, the homosocial circuit of the *phallos* preserves a functional space for homosexual liaisons, which in turn tug on its operations like a tidal force. Further, the appropriation of the *phallos* by the Bellona priestesses is readily interpretable as a feminist appropriation of the tools, as it were, of the master's house. Finally, the Marxist inflection of Rubin's project enables us to read Neoptolomus's steady accumulation of wealth as central to the story in a way that a reading without that inflection might not; as the narrative progresses, increasingly we register that commercial transactions, land acquisitions, and disparities of wealth quietly but profoundly structure the action.

But at the same time, the reconfigured terms of a psychoanalytic model of signification refracted through Marxist and feminist lenses do not cancel the direct explanatory force of psychoanalysis in relation to the question of reading in Neoptolomus's story. When Randy notes, for instance, that his synopsis elides the sexual content of the original novel in favor of "[t]he progress from social level to social level we so cavalierly call 'plot'" (93), we note in turn that psychoanalysis implies a shift in the value that ordinarily accrues to "plot" so described — a shift the inner story of *Phallos* appears to acknowledge, since Neoptolomus's rise to wealth and fame never figures in his story as a focus of intention, decision, or action. For Neoptolomus himself, his social progress is peripheral to the steady drift of his desire.

Still, that success *does* come to Neoptolomus suggests some structural similarity between the intersubjective economy dramatized in Poe and theorized in Lacan, and Neoptolomus's own material situation. We never learn just what commodity Neoptolomus traffics in; perhaps, like the signifier, the phallus (and the *phallos*), what matters isn't so much its intrinsic value as Neoptolomus's structural relation to it. (Anthony Wilden reminds us that the phallus "represents the advent of exchange value in the family itself" [269].) If this is so, we might ask whether, for example, Neoptolomus's feelings of personal guilt in relation to the impoverishment of Maximin are misplaced, or rather, understood in a muddled way: whether his worldly success may arise less from an intention — from a self that knows, that plans, that acts — than from a persistent inhabiting of a certain position in relation to the structures of exchange of his world. I would argue that it is the socialist-feminist appropriation of Lacan, understood as a whole field of discourse and method, that enables such a question to be asked of the story — that, indeed, enables such a story to be told.

III

═══

The outer narrative of *Phallos* tells a story of the reception of the fictive *Phallos* which doubles that imaginary novel's moves — like the doubling Lacan observes in Poe, but with the act of textual exegesis itself playing a major narrative role. Readers familiar with theoretical debates in Lacanian psychoanalysis will recognize in this repetition-through-interpretation an image not just of Lacan on Poe, but of the debate on Lacan's seminar engaged in by Jacques Derrida and Barbara Johnson, among others. Certainly this debate, particularly Johnson's highlighting of the aporias revealed by reading Lacan and Derrida against each other, informs the outer narrative. I want to make the case, however, that the primary reading act structuring that narrative is Delany's own, and is best described as a queer reading, concerned with what Delany calls the "social policing" of texts with sexual content. In his lecture "Aversion/Perversion/Diversion," Delany relates this policing both to psychoanalysis and to exegesis:

> It is often hard for those of us who are historians of texts and documents to realize that there are many things that are directly important for understanding hard-edged events of history, that have simply never made it *into* texts or documents — not because of unconscious repression but because a great many people *did not want them to be known.* And this is particularly true about almost all areas of sex. (140)

The particular way this insight plays out in the structure of *Phallos* can be approached through an examination of Delany's critical response to, or radical reading of, the aestheticism of Walter Pater — who, like Lacan, is an important presence in the novel.

We readily recognize Neoptolomus's adventure as a kind of desublimated version of Pater's *Marius the Epicurean,* the story of another philosophical quest in ancient Rome. Once again, the novel makes no secret of this: Phyllis comments that "Pater is all over *Phallos*" (10), and Binky associates the novel's frequent images of oceanic flux with Pater's considerations of Heraclitus in *Plato and Platonism* — a work Delany has referenced in more recent writing (*Conversations* 115). But in Delany's work in general, we recognize a longstanding attitude that aligns with Pater's aestheticism. We find it in the concern with Rimbaud's "derangement of the senses" that structures *Babel-17* and *Nova,* as well as in the celebration of the opening toward experience in *Dhalgren, Stars in My Pocket Like Grains of Sand,* and *The Mad Man.* Contrariwise, we find dramatizations of the tragedy and self-betrayal of the foreclosure of experience in *Trouble on Triton* (1976) and *Dark Reflections* (2007). Implicit and explicit in these affirmations and laments is a recognition of the nurturing of the senses as conundrum and challenge. The narrator of *Empire Star* concludes the story with this enjoinder to the reader: "It's a beginning. It's an end. I leave to you the problem of ordering your perceptions and making the journey from one to the other" (92). And in *Dhalgren,* the street preacher Reverend Amy Taylor proclaims the "need" for "an analytics of attention, which renders form on the indifferent and undifferentiated pleroma" (472).

But we find evidence of a specifically *critical* appropriation of Pater's aestheticism in a comment by Delany, in *Times Square Red, Times Square Blue,* on Foucault's concept of discourse: "in general, discourse constitutes and is constituted by what Walter Pater called, in the conclusion to *The Renaissance,* 'a roughness of the eye'" (191). We can infer what Delany is getting at by examining the passage from Pater: "In a sense it might be said that our failure is to form habits: for, after all, habit is relative to a stereotyped world, and meantime it is only the roughness of the eye that makes any two persons, things, situations, seem alike" (197). By Delany's characterization, then, discourse operates through conflation, superimposition, emphasis and de-emphasis, the tightening of perceptual focus here by its loosening over there. In Delany's fiction, the play of superimpositions, doublings, and undecidables is an important aesthetic device. It makes its first major appearance in *Dhalgren,* with its innumerable interference patterns and temporal overlays. A similar confounding of situations and chronologies structures the action of the Nevèrÿon stories and *The Mad Man.* The tragic arc of *Trouble on Triton* is shaped by the protagonist's insistent conflating or "typing" of those around him in self-serving terms. (One of the chapters in *Trouble on Triton* is headed with an epigraph from G. Spencer Brown's treatise on mathematical logic, *Laws of Form,* which might serve as an epigraph to Delany's entire oeuvre: "We note in these experiments the sign '=' may stand for the words 'is confused with'" [LF 57].) And there are still more examples, as we will indicate later.

One significant effect of discursive conflation, according to Delany, is an increase in the ambiguity of historical data. In "The Rhetoric of Sex," Delany mentions an anomaly found in an anatomical sketch by Leonardo da Vinci, which represents a human uterus as spherical rather than pear-shaped. Delany describes this anomaly in discursive terms:

> There was, of course, a Renaissance discourse in place that spoke of the womb as the center and sun of the body, that talked of its necessary perfection in terms of the perfect geometrical form, the sphere. Did da Vinci just draw from an uncharacteristically spherical womb? Or did he see the pear shape but dismiss it as an anomaly of his particular cadaver and silently correct it in his picture? Or did he know the pear shape as well as Fallopius would come to but simply pandered to current prejudices? Or did the womb look round? We don't know. That is precisely the knowledge that the discourse itself excludes.
>
> That is what discourse does: it excludes — information, distinctions, differences . . . and similarities.
>
> That is its precise and frightening power — the mark, the trace, of its one-time presence. (28)

Thus, it is not simply that discourse suppresses some kinds of information and favors others; it also multiplies the possible import of the information that does appear. In relation to the AIDS epidemic, Delany has repeatedly called attention to a kind of biopolitical sleight-of-eye in which popular belief and operationalized science are superimposed upon — conflated with — one another, with the effect of obliterating clear empirical distinctions in the field of sexual health (RS 38). As Delany insists, "that is what discursive exclusions *do*" (RS 34). The larger point is that in the study of sexuality generally, and marginalized sexuality in particular, the likelihood of encountering such historical anomalies and undecidables is high, due to numerous discursive pressures.

Delany's conception of discourse obviously bears a relation to his earlier notion of the reading protocol: like protocols, discourses "lodge inchoately in the processes by which we make a text make sense — by which we register a text well-formed or ill-formed" (RS 8). But the field of operation of discourse is far wider. Discourse contains the notion of the reading protocol — the production of right reading — within itself, but also encompasses the mechanisms and institutions for the formation of right texts, right readers, and right authors. Discourse is not simply a structure of cognitive abstraction, understood at the level of individual perception (RS 26–28); rather, its arena is social, the conception of the subject underlying it dispersed, materialist, and post-Cartesian.

This subject-of-discourse is the critical linchpin of Delany's appropriation of Pater's aestheticism. If, speculatively, we read Pater's aestheticism or latter-day Epicureanism as a nineteenth-century attempt to construct a kind of Foucauldian ethic-without-a-norm, it is tempting to speculate further that part of what lay him open to charges of immorality after publishing *The Renaissance* — beyond any other Victorian norms — was the lack of a well-formed theory of discourse. Without it, the refinement of the senses considered as an end in itself does indeed resemble, as Harold Bloom says, "an index of the remoteness in the self's relationship with others," an expression of "the near solipsism of the isolated sensibility" (35). But recast in terms of the subject of discourse, Pater's "roughness of the eye" becomes an object of the situation, the context: the refinement of the senses becomes an act that is social and material in its origins, trajectories, and effects. And it is this re-inflected conception of the subject that enables us to discern the structure of correspondences between the outer narrative of *Phallos* and the inner, Lacanian one.

Critical assessments of the "cautious" aspects of Pater's life and art often read them as expressing sexual sublimations, if not "profound repressions." Here is a not atypical example from Graham Hough in 1947: "Remembering too the continual evidences of homosexual feeling in Pater's life and writing, one almost inevitably begins to form a composite picture of a kind of temperament in which more or less suppressed erotic fantasy, combined perhaps with the frustration or diversion of normal sexuality . . . play a major part" (27). But Hough also acknowledges the presence of the well-policed conventions of the Victorian cultural environment; it was as a conscious response to such policing that Pater revised his "Conclusion" to *The Renaissance* in later editions (Bloom 13). The doubled status of the textual elisions in Pater recalls Delany's remark at this section's opening, and suggests a basic truth regarding biographies of queer subjects: the presence of discourses controlling the expression of homosexuality make it possible to read an elision in a text on sexual matters as expressing *either* a mark of unconscious repression *or* an intentional adaptation to the presence of power. This situation directly expresses the reading conundrum with which *Phallos* confronts us. The redactions that create the basic comic conceit of the book — that it presents a pornographic novel without the sex scenes — may, as Randy's editorial remarks suggest, express his own personal aversions, which might be describable in psychoanalytic terms. But since, as Randy himself reminds us, the synopsis is intended as a work of "advocacy" for the novel, the redactions may also be strategic, the fussy persona a pose — a *knowing* response to power's demands (117 [note 17]). The undecidable status of the redactions is what marks the presence of a discourse.

If, following the methodological lead of Rubin's essay, we now fold the two narrative layers of *Phallos* back together, we find that material originally readable as a dramatization of Lacan on Poe can also be read as a dramatization of Pater through Foucault. When Neoptolomus's narrative about the theft of the treasure returns to him in inverted form, the event is now readable as both a metaphor for the circuit of the Lacanian signifier, and a literal representation of the public distortions of discourse (49). Earlier in the narrative, contemplating the machinations of the competing cults, Neoptolomus feels panic at the clockwork necessities of "Need" that seem to govern the *phallos*. (The term "Need" recalls the primordial deity whose counterpart is "Muddle" — both mentioned by Hadrian near the novel's opening.) But Neoptolomus then asks: "Or was this all only the work of Muddle mistaken — in some muddled way — for the plottings and plannings of Need?" (44). Again, actions explainable in terms of the inescapable forces of desire now carry a second valence as an uncoordinated cluster of events that have been discursively conflated. But here the aporias begin to multiply. "Muddle" itself could signify either unconscious condensation or discursive conflation, and "Need" could signify either unconscious desire or material lack. Furthermore, the other twin terms that appear in the novel in relation to the unfolding of events — "chance" and "necessity" — are themselves multivalent. Is the "necessity" by which the cult of the *phallos* justifies its actions merely greed (or Need), understood in a muddled way? (But which kind of muddle?) Is the "chance" which governs the fall of Maximin and the rise of Neoptolomus actually a muddled understanding of necessity, given the organization of wealth in the empire?

Here it would appear we really do stand on a Derridean abyss of undecidables. But I want to insist that the aporias confronting us are Foucauldian, and that it's the overlay of Neoptolomus and Randy's narratives that renders the Foucauldian mise-en-scène visible. Some small details relating to the warehouse sequence provide a case in point. When Neoptolomus hears his own prevarication echo back to him as gossip about a successful theft, part of the evidence offered in the gossip is the scuffling of footprints outside the warehouse, which — the text implies, but does not assert — Neoptolomus reads as a "muddled account" of the footprints of Blutus and Egon, to whom Neoptolomus had first conveyed his false rumor (49). (This misreading of ambiguous evidence, a misreading itself presented ambiguously, resonates with the botched chronological inferences that permeate Delany's work, from the rumored events that swirl around the riot of Bellona in *Dhalgren*, to those around the trashing of Timothy Hassler's apartment in *The Mad Man*.) Moreover, the gossip has also likely incorporated, by conflation, Blutus and Egon's own report that the treasure had already been stolen. Here's a portion of Blutus and Egon's account of the episode, synopsized by Randy:

They tell Neoptolomus that, yes, at the warehouse the door had been left unlocked, but when they'd gone within, someone had beaten them to it. Nothing had been left in the inner treasure room, and when Blutus thought he'd heard a sound without, Egon had urged him to flee — and they'd run away empty-handed. (The fact that the treasure has been usurped convinces Neoptolomus for just a moment it *must* have been the *phallos* they were trying to steal — although, as he points out, no one has mentioned it directly.) (48)

Let us isolate a seemingly unexceptional clause from the above passage: "someone had beaten them to it." Although the inference is attributed to Blutus and Egon, the actual speaker here is Randy. Because of this, we have no access to additional information about the account that might have been conveyed, tonally or otherwise, by the voices of Blutus, Egon, or the narrator Neoptolomus himself in the source-text. The flat, un-inflected phrasing of Randy's synopsis encourages the reader to take the statement at face value, and Neoptolomus's subsequent reflections reinforce that reading. However, an alert reader might suspect that all the players, including Randy, could be wrong (indeed, may have been duped) in assuming any item was there to be "usurped" in the first place. But again, any information from the original passage that might further clarify the situation has fallen out in its transition to synopsis. Later in his account of the novel, Randy reports that after further attempts to seize the *phallos* fail, Neoptolomus makes an observation similar to that in the earlier episode, but with a qualification: "Someone else has beaten him to it — if it was ever there to begin with" (60). And once again, because the voice here is Randy's, we cannot discern whether this qualification represents Neoptolomus's growing comprehension of the possibilities or a development in Randy's own interpretation. One voice has been laid over another, generating an interpretive impasse. But to recognize the ambiguity contained in this single qualifying phrase, as in the earlier clause, is to recognize that, due to its double-voiced structure, such ambiguity permeates the novel from beginning to end. To re-read *Phallos* in light of this recognition is to experience every moment within it as shimmering with doubt — and possibility.

We find similar structures throughout Delany's fiction: in the conflicting voices that weave through *Dhalgren*, the monologues that punctuate *Trouble on Triton* and structure the Nevèrÿon books, and the moments of heightened experience which, at their points of greatest intensity, are delivered to us in the voice of someone present in the scene, as with the Mummer's "Amnewor" monologue in *Flight from Nevèrÿon*, with Hart Crane's monologue on the

Brooklyn Bridge in "Atlantis: Model 1924," or the "voice of the ship" describing the appearance of the red giant of the Aurigae system at the close of *Stars in My Pocket Like Grains of Sand.* In such sequences, in which one voice, one account, appears to overtake and over-write another, we are not sure what information has been elided — if, echoing the ambiguously voiced claim of *Phallos,* it was there to begin with. But our ability even to begin to discern the undecidables of such texts — a discernment encouraged by that very same intricate doubling of voices — is just what makes *Phallos,* and the entirety of Delany's work, such an indispensable lesson in reading.

IV

In this double-tale of a hermeneutic quest under the aegis of Muddle and Need, the reader is presented with a drama structured by the history of the labor of reading the sexual margins. The relation between desire and discourse implied by this structure is succinctly captured in Delany's passing comment on psychoanalysis and language, once again in relation to the work of Joanna Russ: "Today the most salvageable lessons from Freud tell us that the unconscious part of the mind works by maneuvering the signifier rather than the signified (and discourse controls what might be considered the signified excess)" (507). The possibilities for reading implied by this model of signification are complex and troubling. They suggest a particular application of Quine's notion, present in much of Delany's work since *Dhalgren,* that investigation and interpretation will tend to converge not on "the" truth but on limit-cases in which "countless alternative theories would be tied for first place" (23). On the one hand, a rigorous psychoanalytic reading alone must include the possibility of the experience of meaning, in Shoshana Felman's words, "as a loss and as a flight" (153). But the way of reading implied by *Phallos* implies a whole additional coordinate space through which the trajectory of that flight might also be traced. Such a way of reading would deliver not monovalent knowledge about claims regarding sex and desire, but rather a rigorous way of recognizing the form and parameters of the impasses we're confronted with, a precise delineation of the shape of our own confusion.

But in a more optimistic vein, it would also indicate where additional data is needed and more investigation can be done. *Phallos* closes with an affirmation of this attitude toward empirical investigation, an affirmation the more resounding when read in dialogue with the conclusion of Pater's *Marius the Epicurean*. There, surrounded by Christian worshippers, in dubious affirmation of their faith and care, Marius dies (265–67). Contrariwise, the inner narrative of *Phallos* ends with Neoptolomus's rejection of the moral conflations of organized religion, and leaves Neoptolomus and his partner Nivek contemplating the Heraclitean flux of the universe, the certainty of loss, and the utter unknowability of the future — which is to say, the certainty of its novelty: the certainty of the arrival, even in the midst of loss, of new persons, new stories, new data (114–117). And the outer narrative of *Phallos* ends with an image of Randy, Binky, and Phyllis patiently and persistently endeavoring, in the absence of institutional support and reward characteristic of research into the marginal fields, to produce such new data (117–121). It was, after all, the accumulation of new data, coupled with rigorous critical reading, that enabled Gayle Rubin to articulate her conception of the sex-gender system. And as Rubin has recently indicated in a consideration of the development of her own work, it was just such unsupported and unrewarded empirical investigation both within and in relation to the lesbian and gay community which generated the data that made it both possible and necessary for her, again, to separate out two concepts conflated in her first study — sex and gender — and consider sex in its autonomy: thus leading to the writing of "Thinking Sex," a foundational text for lesbian and gay studies (308–9; "Blood Under the Bridge" 17–19).

The immediate precedent in Delany's work for the fictive situation that closes *Phallos* is certainly *The Mad Man,* in which the slow temporalities of knowledge production and the cumulative creation of new readings and reading constituencies — specifically in relation to queer subjects — mark the forward motion of the narrative. But in the inner tale of *Phallos,* the process of knowledge production and constituency creation also has a non-exegetical counterpart. For what the suppression of the sex scenes in that tale also helps to foreground, to bring into sharp relief, is the gradual development of partnerships and community, the cumulative formation of possibilities of ethics and sociality, around that sex. This is a development within the narrative that our own focus on reading in and around *Phallos* has elided: the accumulating force of, and prospects for, such a sociality.

In the notion of a god who is the child of Muddle and Need, some readers may hear hints of a critical reading — an appropriation with a difference — of a passage from Plato's *Symposium,* in which the philosopher Diotima considers the qualities of Eros, the son of Resource and Need. In the transformation, in *Phallos,* of Resource to Muddle, we may perhaps recognize an attitude toward intention and process that finds ample support in the novel. But consider Diotima's characterization of Eros as "a master of device and artifice — at once desirous and full of wisdom, a lifelong seeker after truth, an adept at sorcery, enchantment, and seduction" (556). Certainly we recognize here the presence of something like intention and craft — if not craftiness. (Note that in this passage we hear not Diotima herself, but a synopsis of her words by Socrates — and, in turn, not Socrates himself, but the persona created by Plato.) Perhaps, then, given the parameters of the discursive fields we have examined, which would seem to call both for a certain reticence in relation to claims of intention and a recognition of the collaborative context of literary production, what we can properly say we honor here with our critical labor is an exemplary instantiation of a way of reading — paraphrasing Barthes, a "performance of the discourse" (36) — which now stands as a resource for subsequent performances, subsequent readings.

BIBLIOGRAPHY

Barthes, Roland. *Sade, Fourier, Loyola.* Berkeley: University of California Press, 1976. Print.

Bloom, Harold. "Introduction" and "The Place of Pater." In *Walter Pater: Modern Critical Views.* New York: Chelsea House Publishers, 1985. Print.

Bowie, Malcolm. *Lacan.* Cambridge, Mass.: Harvard University Press, 1991. Print.

Chiesa, Lorenzo. "Le ressort de l'amour." *Angelaki* 11.3 (2006): 61–81. Print.

Delany, Samuel R. *The Jewels of Aptor.* 1962. New York: Bantam Books, 1982. Print.

———. *The Ballad of Beta-2.* 1965. New York: Bantam Books, 1982. Print.

———. *Babel-17.* 1966. New York: Vintage Books, 1994. Print.

———. *Empire Star.* 1966. New York: Vintage Books, 1994. Print.

———. *Dhalgren.* 1974. New York: Vintage Books, 2001. Print.

———. *Trouble on Triton*. 1976. Middletown, Conn.: Wesleyan University Press, 1996. Print.

———. *Stars in My Pocket Like Grains of Sand*. 1984. Middletown, Conn.: Wesleyan University Press, 2004. Print.

———. "Russ." In *Starboard Wine*. Pleasantville, N.Y.: Dragon Press, 1984.

———. *Flight from Nevèrÿon*. 1985. Middletown, Conn.: Wesleyan University Press, 1994. Print.

———. *Silent Interviews*. Middletown, Conn.: Wesleyan University Press, 1994. Print.

———. "Atlantis: Model 1924." In *Atlantis: Three Tales*. Middletown, Conn.: Wesleyan University Press, 1995. Print.

———. *The Mad Man*. 1994. Rutherford, N.J.: Voyant Publishing, 2002. Print.

———. "Aversion/Perversion/Diversion." In *Longer Views*. 1996. Middletown, Conn.: Wesleyan University Press, 1999. Print.

———. "Shadow and Ash." In *Longer Views*. 1996. Middletown, Conn.: Wesleyan University Press, 1999. Print.

———. "The Rhetoric of Sex / The Discourse of Desire." In *Shorter Views*. Middletown, Conn.: Wesleyan University Press, 1999. Print. (Referred to as RS in the text.)

———. "Street Talk / Straight Talk." In *Shorter Views*. Middletown, Conn.: Wesleyan University Press, 1999. Print.

———. *Phallos*. Whitmore Lake, Mich.: Bamberger Books, 2004. Print.

———. *Dark Reflections*. New York: Carroll & Graf, 2007. Print.

———. *Conversations with Samuel R. Delany*. Ed. Carl Freedman. Jackson, Miss.: University Press of Mississippi, 2009.

Felman, Shoshana. *Jacques Lacan and the Adventure of Insight*. Cambridge, Mass.: Harvard University Press, 1987. Print.

Gadamer, Hans-Georg. *Truth and Method*. 1975. New York: Continuum Publishing Group, 2004.

Grosz, Elizabeth. *Jacques Lacan: A Feminist Introduction*. New York: Routledge, 1990. Print.

Hough, Graham. "The Paterian Temperament." In Harold Bloom, ed., *Walter Pater: Modern Critical Views*. New York: Chelsea House Publishers, 1985. Print.

Jagose, Annamarie. *Queer Theory: An Introduction*. New York: New York University Press, 1996.

Lacan, Jacques. *Ecrits: A Selection*. Trans. Alan Sheridan. New York: W. W. Norton & Company, 1977. Print.

———. "Seminar on 'The Purloined Letter.'" In *The Purloined Poe*. Muller and Richardson, eds. Baltimore: Johns Hopkins University Press, 1988. Print.

Mueller-Vollmer, Kurt (ed). *The Hermeneutics Reader*. New York: Continuum Publishing Company, 1985.

Muller, John P., and William J. Richardson (eds). *The Purloined Poe*. Baltimore: Johns Hopkins University Press, 1988. Print.

Pater, Walter. *The Renaissance.* 1873. New York: Random House, 1963.

———. *Marius the Epicurean: His Sensations and Ideas.* 1885. New York: Oxford University Press, 1986.

———. *Plato and Platonism.* 1893. New York: Greenwood Press, 1969.

Plato. *Plato: The Collected Dialogues.* 1961. Ed. Edith Hamilton and Huntington Cairns. Princeton, N.J.: Princeton University Press, 1982. Print.

Quine, Willard van Orman. *Word and Object.* Cambridge, Mass.: MIT Press, 1996. Print.

Rubin, Gayle. "The Traffic in Women." In *Toward an Anthropology of Women.* New York: Monthly Review Press, 1975. Print. (Cited as TW in the text.)

———. "Thinking Sex: Notes for a Radical Theory of a Politics of Sexuality." In *Pleasure and Danger.* Ed. Carole S. Vance. 1984. London: Pandora Press, 1992. Print.

———. "Blood Under the Bridge: Reflections on 'Thinking Sex.'" In *GLQ: A Journal of Lesbian and Gay Studies* 17.1 (2011): 15–48. Print.

Spencer-Brown, George. *Laws of Form.* 1969. Leipzig: Bohmeier Verlag, 2009. Print.

ARS VITAE

DELANY'S PHILOSOPHICAL FABLE

STEVEN SHAVIRO

"BUT THEN, IN THE PROFLIGACY OF EGGS laid by fowl or fish or spider, in the amount, the intensity, the variety of the sexual instincts themselves, we know that most of life is a riotous superfluity." One might expect to find a sentence like this, perhaps, in Bruce Bagemihl's *Biological Exuberance: Animal Homosexuality and Natural Diversity* (1999), a massive book that demonstrates, with encyclopedic breadth and in overwhelming detail, the prevalence of nonprocreative sexual acts, and particularly of same-sex couplings, throughout the animal kingdom. But in fact this sentence is spoken by Hadrian, emperor of Rome (76–138 CE; emperor from 117–38 CE), in the novel-within-the-novel that is at the center of Samuel R. Delany's novel *Phallos*. Hadrian goes on to praise human same-sex lust and attachment as the source of all that is highest and most precious in civilization and culture; his words here are reminiscent of early and middle twentieth-century (i.e., long pre-Stonewall) "homophile" discourse. Hadrian ends his speech, however, by stating that "the only gods truly great are that rambunctious pair, Muddle and Need"; the novel later translates this pair into the more philosophically reputable terms of Chance and Necessity.

But the chain of associations in Delany's book goes further than this. Both Muddle or Chance, and Need or Necessity, are themselves subsequently associated, in the course of the novel, with Desire. Neoptolomus, the protagonist of the novel-within-the-novel, is at one point exhorted to "follow your *own* desires — as much as desire can be said to be 'owned' by anyone, or that anyone can own what chains us all, one to another . . . For lust is never fixed. Its variety is as glorious as its superfluity. But do not treat it as a scarcity, fixing it within the straits of convention and law." Here Desire is Need or Necessity, in that it drives us so imperiously that it might well be said to "own" us, rather than we "possess" it. Desire limits individual autonomy, as it "chains us . . . one to another." But Desire is also Muddle or Chance, in that it is never fixed, but seems to wobble aimlessly and unpredictably, now favoring one particular person or thing, and now another.

In this speech, Neoptolomus is being given the rather good advice that he should stop trying to mimic the feelings and actions of the normatively heterosexual (and extremely misogynistic) men with whom he has been hanging out recently; instead, he ought to stay true to his own desires, which are oriented almost exclusively towards other men. But these homoerotic desires of his are themselves "never fixed"; they do not constitute an essence to which he could, even in theory, stay faithful. Desire overwhelms Neoptolomus with its excessiveness and changefulness, which can never be regulated by any law, or doled out parsimoniously according to some economic calculus. We know, in fact, that societies do develop laws and conventions, which endeavor to regulate and manage sexual desires. And often this regulation comes in the form of an imposed scarcity: desires are given prices on the market, or rationed in accordance with norms of "proper" heterosexuality, or with ideals of chastity and monogamy. But these impositions are never really effective: laws, conventions, and imposed scarcities always generate their own counter-movements and transgressions. What else could be the case, given the actual plenitude of sexual possibilities available in a cosmopolitan metropolis like ancient Rome, or modern New York City? And this brings us back to the glorious "superfluity" of life with which my own tracing of links began.

Phallos is a short book, of well under two hundred pages. But it contains depths — or perhaps I should rather say *breadths* — since its movement is always a lateral, ramifying one, rather than a digging down to ultimate foundations. There is no grounding for desire (or anything else) in this book; no metaphysical conclusion, no unimpeachable certainty, no Final Theory of Everything. Instead, the novel takes the form, on several levels, of a quest whose goal is never reached, but that instead lures the quester on endlessly. In a brief preface we are told about a young African American man, Adrian

Rome, who is looking for an anonymous pornographic novel called *Phallos*, which is out of print and difficult to find. Adrian stumbles across a copy of this book several times, but each time loses it again before he has had a chance to read it. In the course of his search for the book, he meets his life partner, Shoat Rumblin — the eponymous protagonist of another (as yet unpublished) novel by Delany. But "the closest [Adrian] ever comes to reading *Phallos* is a synopsis he discovers on the Internet." That synopsis, by one Randy Pedarson, of Moscow, Idaho, makes up the main body of Delany's novel.

In Randy's synopsis, we get a summary of the plot of the anonymous gay porn novel *Phallos*, together with commentary on its aesthetic qualities (with additional comments, in the footnotes, by Randy's friends Binky and Phyllis), and some discussion of the book's provenance. The novel-within-the-novel is set in the second-century Roman Empire, and narrated in the first person by its protagonist Neoptolomus. The published volume contains an introduction claiming that the text was a cult favorite among such eighteenth-, nineteenth-, and early twentieth-century aesthetes as Winckelmann, Walter Pater, Lionel Johnson, Arthur Symons, and Frederick Rolfe. This list of names reminds us of how pervasively aestheticism has been a privileged mode of expression for gay male eroticism in the modern West. Within Delany's fiction, however, Randy concludes that this history of the pornographic novel *Phallos* is probably a fabrication. The book was most likely written in the 1960s (its first commercial publication dates from 1969); Randy says that it is an excellent example of the "literate pornography," both "straight and gay," that abounded in that decade.

Who, then, is the anonymous author of the novel-within-the-novel *Phallos*? Adrian Rome believes that he is in reality "an elderly black man of letters." For his part, Randy offers a list of contemporary American writers (many of them in actuality friends of Delany) as possible authors. However, Randy also argues — on deeply questionable grounds — that "*Phallos* just does not seem the sort of book I would imagine from a black man (or woman)"; despite the presence of many black characters in the novel, he says, he finds it "closer in feel to, say, *Sentimental Education* or something by Jean Rhys than to *Invisible Man, Iceberg Slim, Beloved,* or *Roots.*" Now, the novel-within-the-novel does indeed contain a direct evocation of *Sentimental Education*, when Neoptolomus's life partner Nivek, speaking of another man whom they have invited to an orgy, says that "like provincial boys before their first visit to a local brothel, we have our anticipation to enjoy." This echoes the famous closing lines of Flaubert's novel, in which the protagonists conclude that their moment of anticipation, as teenagers, before their first visit to a brothel was the happiest moment of their lives — everything afterwards has been a disappointment. This seems to chime with Randy's own sense that the novel largely recounts the story of a "string of unsatisfactory lovers" encountered by Neoptolomus.

But in the passage from the novel-within-the-novel that I have just cited, Nivek immediately distances himself from this Flaubertian resonance, by adding that "from having sampled [this prospective lover] and so many others, [we have] a good deal more knowledge of what he might bring than have most such untutored children." This suggests an emotional tone, and a horizon of expectations, that are quite distant from those of Flaubert's relentlessly disillusioning portrait of petit bourgeois male-heterosexual mediocrity. Neoptolomus and Nivek are cosmopolitan travelers, who revel in the variety, profligacy, and superfluity of what the world has to offer them. You cannot, by definition, accurately anticipate the unexpected; but you can remain open to adventure and surprise, as the characters of the novel-within-the-novel do, and as Flaubert's characters do not. Towards the end of his summary, Randy himself confesses that "by giving so much of the 'story,' I have suppressed, in fact, almost all of the sexuality, the affect, the sheer *feel* of the book . . . The reading experience is virtually drenched in insights and proprioceptive pleasures that any sexually active gay man must recognize again and again."

Randy's own concession in these lines suggests to us that his overall aesthetic take on the novel — which he sees largely as a narrative of erotic disappointment — may well be as curiously askew as his assumptions about what sorts of things black people might and might not feel, and write, are indubitably (if unconsciously) racist. However, our only access to the novel-within-the-novel is through Randy's own synopsis. In consequence, we have to take him pretty much at his word both when he describes "the passage of the years and the progress from social stratum to social stratum" (his own half-ironic definition of what "we so cavalierly call 'plot'" — which would almost make *Phallos*, not altogether wrongly, into a social realist novel), and when he hints at the text's evocation of "tumbling, glorious, sensual wonder and confusion." In short, we are faced with an unreliable narrator giving us a dubious, second-hand account of a book that is itself fictional. Delany's *Phallos* might therefore be regarded as meta-pornography, or as a Borgesian self-reflexive fable. And yet, it retains more than a hint of those "proprioceptive pleasures" that actual pornography can give us, but that are not present in Borges, nor in any of the erudite, self-referential games that are generally held to typify "postmodern" fiction. There's a tension here, between what's explicit and what's implicit, or between expression and content, or between canonical literature and what Delany has often called *paraliterature*.

One crucial way in which this tension manifests itself in the course of Delany's *Phallos* is that Randy's summary of the novel-within-the-novel skips over all the explicitly sexual or pornographic passages that make up the greatest part of its bulk, and that are presumably its rationale. Where many of Delany's other novels present sexual activity in quite dense and explicit detail, here we only get the briefest of indications, due to Randy's anxiety about posting sexually explicit material online — and on a university website, no less. A comparison can help to make this clear. One of the most memorable passages in *The Mad Man*, for instance, is the one containing a thick description of "golden showers" night at a gay club in Manhattan in the 1980s: a rhapsodic set piece which goes on for something like fifty epic pages. In contrast to this, Randy's summary of the novel-within-the-novel in *Phallos* simply notes, at one point, that the narrative moves "to take in sadomasochism, urine, group sex, and more"; and at another point, that it contains "five pages devoted to the sensations accruing between the moment one decides to release one's bladder and the moment urine actually erupts from the foreskin-hooded head." This last phrase that I have quoted is quite lovely in its own right. But in the context of the book as a whole, it works as something of a tease. I would love to read such a five-page passage, after all; and Delany is the one author who would conceivably be able to write it!

All in all, the cautious and never-quite-obscene phrasing of Randy's synopsis works to convey his (sincere, but slightly fussy and literal-minded) character. Randy's own literary style tellingly differs from the heightened, Paterian style of the passages from the novel-within-the-novel that he does bring himself to quote directly, from time to time (provided that they are non-pornographic in content). Consider this, for instance: "Tugging up its heave and slosh, pushing them down, spindrift wind swung and swirled above continuous discontinuity, flux, and swell, scumbled with foam and nudged by evening's slant-light through all the colors of glass." There is indeed a close attention here to "proprioceptive pleasures," as well as an insistence on the inherently transitory nature of existence, which an elegant prose may capture in its tiniest nuances, just as it passes. I cannot help thinking of Walter Pater's determination to intensify and particularize perception, and thereby to "pass most swiftly from point to point, and be present always at the focus where the greatest number of vital forces unite in their purest energy." Here intensity (born of Need) and transience (born of Muddle) go together. Erotic pleasure is fleeting, but indefinitely renewable under new guises and in new arrangements.

Delany's novel as a whole, with its multiple levels, its different styles, and its extensive paraphrases and periphrases, creates an overall effect of swirling indirection. The novel is replete with associations, references, and similitudes — such as the ones that I have been tracking in this essay. But such bits and pieces do not add up to some master code or ultimate revelation. There is no secret to discover in the course of the novel; nothing is hidden. All these associations, references, and similitudes exist only to keep things moving: to keep the narrative moving, to keep our reading experience moving, and (within the text) to keep sexual desire moving. Such indirection is, of course, the very point of Delany's novel, as well as of the novel-within-the-novel. Who reads a pornographic novel just for its plot, after all? Not to mention the fact that Randy's friends Binky and Phyllis suggest, in their interpolated footnotes, that he has overlooked some of the novel's most important points. But again, such a regime of misrepresentations and indirections is precisely what Delany is trying to convey. And this is a point that remains beyond the grasp of any of the book's protagonists, on any of its narrative levels.

To explain this indirection and misrepresentation as clearly as possible — if that is not too oxymoronic a way of stating things — we may say that Delany's *Phallos* is a book about the phallus of Freudian/Lacanian theory, the signifier of desire, and of erotic (and masculine) potency, but which (as a mere signifier) is always absent, or continually other than itself. Indeed, the most important point to be derived from Lacan's own indirections on the topic is that the phallus is always an imposture. No one ever truly possesses it. In Delany's *Phallos,* the phallus is — on one level — the unavailable, and only indirectly narrated, pornographic narrative itself. But also — within the frame of that distanced, non-present narrative — the phallus is, quite literally, a *phallos,* meaning a physical rendering or representation of the male genital organ. In the novel-within-the-novel, the *phallos* is the missing male organ of an obscure, nameless god; that is to say, it is the missing portion of a statue or idol of this god. Early in the story, as he attends a ceremony in an Egyptian temple, Neoptolomus learns of the apparent theft of the temple deity's "golden *phallos,* encrusted with jade, jewels, and copper." He spends most of the novel-within-the-novel hearing rumors of this object's presence in one place or another, and searching after it in response to these rumors. In this sense, the phallus/*phallos* is something like what Hitchcock called the MacGuffin.

In any case, the search for the *phallos* is a fool's errand. Neoptolomus never definitively learns whether this object even exists; and if it does, whether it is an object of supreme pleasure, or rather a torture device for inflicting pain, "horrible and bladed and black with blood, an instrument of death and violence." It is also impossible for Neoptolomus to determine whether the *phallos* is valuable for its sculpture and its jewels, or for the precious written papers supposedly contained within its interior — or whether, rather, it is "merely a hollow dildo of plate and paste." This means, in effect, that the *phallos* is valuable precisely, and only, because people believe it to be of value; and they only thus consider it valuable because they believe that it belongs to somebody else. Such is the slender thread upon which sexual desire moves. The absence of the *phallos,* its indeterminacy or its quality of being-missing, circulates through the narrative of the novel-within-the-novel, and works as the "absent cause" of its picaresque repetitions, permutations, and deviations.

In Lacanian theory, the phallus is always associated with Lack. This means, all at once, a fundamental lack of being, and the felt lack of a particular desired object, and (most importantly, perhaps) the lack resulting from the fact that every desired object is itself only a substitute for a primordial lost object that can only ever be missing, because it is a retrospective construction of fantasy that never actually existed in the first place. In the novel-within-the-novel in *Phallos*, we get a certain sense of this when Neoptolomus reflects that "the *phallos* is simply a set of multiple imitations and distractions, of markers in a plot of plottings that web together the material world, an extraordinary fiction disseminated over the land to net a host of other fictions of power." This further implies that "there *is* no original" phallus/*phallos*; rather, "any of its imitations is, in fact, as real, as actual, and as authentic as any other." Neoptolomus is momentarily tempted to think that his very knowledge of this situation might allow him to, in effect, wield phallic power, which is to say, "the power to seize [the *phallos*] from its endless circulations." But of course, the reader (both the reader of Randy's summary on the Internet, and the reader of Delany's novel) is well aware by this point that such an impulse is only another fiction that puts the *phallos*/phallus into even more frenzied circulation.

The way this all plays out in Delany's *Phallos*, however, implies something more than just a metaphysics of Lack. The absence of the phallus/*phallos* — or better, the absence that the phallus/*phallos* itself *is* — is associated, in the novel, both with a deficit and with a surplus. The always-missing phallus implies the absence of finality, the impossibility of definitive accomplishment, the failure ever to attain a final state of peace. But it also points to an overfullness, an excess of possibilities, an ongoing "continuous discontinuity, flux, and swell," offering opportunities whose stock will never be depleted — even though my own ability to take up such offers will ultimately come to a halt with the brutal fact of my death. The phallus/*phallos* offers us (as I have already suggested) a "superfluity" — with the double meaning this word has of something that is on the one hand plentiful even to excess, and on the other hand unnecessary or redundant. (I leave open the question of whether the phallus already has this double significance, as both excess and lack, in Lacan.)

One obvious way that Delany's novel is different from a psychoanalytic treatise is that, in the former, the experience of the phallus/*phallos* is played out overtly in the lives of its characters. Neoptolomus's desire is never sated by total satisfaction. But for this very reason, he always finds that, after a period of satiety, or one of danger and harm, his desire is awakened again. Neoptolomus learns the hard lesson that the object of his quest is unattainable, for there is no such thing as "an actual, graspable, material *phallos*." But in consequence, he learns that there are no fixed limits to his desire, or to that of his prospective partners. "Desire is as endlessly unquenchable as it is repeatable": its very non-satisfaction implies its endless renewal. The phallus/*phallos*, in its very absence, always throws us back upon change and becoming.

And so, as Neoptolomus muses towards the end of the novel-within-the-novel, the phallus/*phallos* "is nowhere and everywhere, a sign for the unlocatable desires of the other, that signification itself by which something else always molds us toward something better — or sometimes, something worse . . . than what we already are." We are mortal; and even before we die, life necessarily implies a certain degree of loss, disappointment, and unfulfillment. There is no guarantee that any given change will be for the better. But *Phallos* acknowledges this finitude and contingency in a way that is defiantly non-tragic. There is indeed a "lack" at the center of desire; but this "lack" is also the source and the impetus of (sexual) variety, which is literally the spice of a life of (often gratified) desire. No matter how jaded or satiated we may think that we have become, there is always "something else" to entice us, and to "mold us" into something different from whatever we were before. There is always lack; but, as Neoptolomus himself puts it: "with such variety [of sexual experiences and pleasures] it becomes hard to hold on to where that lack lies, since that absent center moves about so: If I have learned anything in this time, it is that losing track of it, in such a secure relationship [as that he has with Nivek], is surely the closest we can come to filling it."

It is clear, by the end of the novel-within-the-novel, that Neoptolomus and Nivek have led what can rightfully be described as largely fulfilled and virtuous lives. (As is appropriate for a narrative set in ancient times, I am using the word "virtuous" here in an Aristotelian sense: meaning something like a quality, or a state of character, that is fully engaged in — and devoted above all other things to — the process or the art of living well.) Neoptolomus and Nivek have established a safe and secure home for themselves; but they have also traveled widely, and engaged in all sorts of strange and wonderful adventures. They have prospered, economically and materially, to the extent that such a thing is possible for people of humble birth in a society as stratified and tyrannical as that of the second-century Roman Empire. And they have even attained, in their lives with one another — if not in regard to the larger society of which they are a part — a situation of equality and mutual respect. That is to say, they have "become such radically different equals as homosexuality *sometimes* allows men and men to be" — which is a rare and admirable achievement in any historical age.

If a wide range of visitors have continually "sought out Nivek and Neoptolomus," we are told, this is "because each [visitor] believes they possess the *phallos.*" Such a belief is of course an illusion, as is demonstrated time and again throughout the novel-within-the-novel. But Neoptolomus accounts for this belief — and extracts from it, one might even say, its "rational kernel" — when he remarks that "all we had — which, yes, each mistook for its [the *phallos*'s] sign — was a certain pleasure in the world and one another, a pleasure our friends were sometimes rash enough to call 'happiness.'" What does it mean to be able to take such pleasure, and to be able to sustain it, or reawaken it, for a prolonged time, and through the varied twists and turns of Muddle and Need? Such a capacity has nothing to do with possessing the phallus/*phallos* — it has nothing to do with what we would conventionally think of as power, mastery, authority, or superior, enlightened knowledge. But this pleasure does imply, perhaps, that Nivek and Neoptolomus possess — and more, that they are actually able to live by — a certain sort of worldly wisdom.

Phallos gives voice to this wisdom. Delany's novel is many things, but most importantly it is a book about how to live. It proposes an ethics of the everyday, in much the way that Stoic and Epicurean texts of the period in which the novel-within-the-novel is set propose ethical systems or ways to live. Alternatively, we may say that *Phallos* is a philosophical fable, in the manner of such eighteenth-century texts as Voltaire's *Candide,* Diderot's *Les bijoux indiscrets* and Dr. Johnson's *Rasselas.* In either case, the novel is both a discourse upon, and an exemplification of, the way to achieve what we might be "sometimes rash enough to call 'happiness.'" *Phallos* is a book about *Ars Vitae,* the Art of Life. It provides us with a vision, not just of what it means to live, but also of what it might mean (in the words of Alfred North Whitehead) to "live well" and to "live better."

It is in this context, I think, that we can best understand the sexual extremity, even to the point of a brush or flirtation with death, that is so major a topic in *Phallos* — and indeed in many of Delany's books. In *Phallos*, of course, such sexual representation is locked within the inaccessible text of the novel-within-the-novel; as I have already noted, Randy's synopsis only alludes to it, or presents it to us indirectly. Nonetheless, the sexual encounters and orgies seem to pile on in a prolonged crescendo; Randy even tells us that "the novel's final third . . . in defiance of Nabokov's observation about the serious literature of sex, turns out to be the book's *most* sex-drenched section." It's in the final pages of Randy's summary that we are apprised of scenes involving "accounts of bestiality, coprophilia, and worse" — scenes which the self-described "fag-hag" Phyllis finds both "gross" and "deranged." Beyond this, Randy alludes to a scene, near the end of the novel-within-the-novel, involving the expression of "sexual tastes . . . that, frankly, both Binky and I agree, are finally too much even for *us*." Of course, this is yet another instance of Delany teasing the reader — in this case, by leaving a blank that, in its obscene suggestiveness, is more disturbing than anything concrete that might actually serve to fill it in.

But Delany is also making a serious and important point here. His vision of the good life quite unequivocally involves a wide range and great frequency of sexual encounters and pleasures, with a large number of partners. There are good ethico-political reasons for this, as well as hedonistic ones. Concerted and extreme sexual practices tend to break down — or at least to interfere with — "the enforcement and compulsory internalization of [the] power differentials" through which people are "*exploited* by one another." Such exploitation is generally the case under the regime of hegemonic and compulsory heterosexuality, with its frequent coercion and its "laws of singular possession and jealousy." In contrast, wide-ranging sexual experiences, not restricted to procreative heterosexual norms, at least open the *possibility* of "radical differences respected as a field not of nominal equality but rather of compensatory privileges, rights, and obligations to produce actual equality," in such a way that people may truly be "*respected* by one another" outside of pre-given hierarchies. Neoptolomus and Nivek seek to maintain "a certain egalitarianism" in the orgies they organize, although they realize that such a state "is more to be wished for than won."

In any case, the ethical principle behind the sexual acts that are indirectly but so insistently narrated throughout the course of *Phallos* is that "the social sharing of pleasure should bring those who indulge it closer." Rather than being a war of all against all, the orgy is a situation in which each man "works . . . hard . . . to please others through pleasing himself." (This sentence is phrased carefully by Delany in order to indicate two things. First, the hedonistic release of the orgy is not opposed to work, but is itself produced through a kind of work — unalienated labor, we might say. Second, this is something that, for the moment, can only happen between men. Such will remain the case "until men and women, women and women, can maneuver the social forces about them" into less oppressive forms.) In this way, Delany presents even the most "extreme" sexual practices as forms of civility and community, no less than as forms of ecstasy. Ethics merges with aesthetics, and community with individual singularity. In the absence of such sexual practices, life is impoverished, and it is delivered over to oppression. Delany presents unbridled sexuality as an adornment of life, an embrace of its superfluity. But in this way — since adornment and superfluity are themselves, as it were, essential — an enhanced sexuality becomes a vital and necessary part of the art of living well, and of living better.

Let me restate this point in another, more overtly theoretical way, by contrasting Delany's sexual vision with that of the great early and middle twentieth-century meta-pornographer Georges Bataille. Both writers present "visions of excess" in which sexual extremity, waste, and superfluity are affirmed, but also shown to be shadowed by death. Yet Delany's sexual writing has little or nothing to do with the theme of *transgression* that was such a major concern for Bataille, and indeed for much of twentieth-century modernism. This distance from any sense of transgression is perhaps the most radical thing about Delany as a writer. Delany, no less than Bataille, is concerned with expressing, articulating, and enacting a range of desires and deeds that escape the "economy" of the bourgeois family, and of capitalist exchange and representation. But Delany's vision of expenditure beyond exchange-value does not have any of the Bataillean connotations of sin, unnaturalness, "perversion," and guilt. For Delany, even excess to the point of exhaustion, and even the most outrageous and extreme sexual acts (from eating shit to incest), have nothing to do with the old dialectic of law and its transgression.

This leads to an important difference in the way that these two writers conceive subjectivity. Bataille always seeks after the shattering of the ego, in the exasperation and extremity of desire. He insists that laws and norms and limits and taboos need to exist, precisely in order to fuel the erotic *frisson* that comes from negating or violating them. For Delany, in contrast, sexual extremity is conceived not as a rupturing of the self, but as its continual metamorphosis — or better (to use a word from Gilbert Simondon and Bernard Stiegler) as its *transindividuation,* its becoming-with-others. For Delany, sex is a continual, and never-to-be-concluded, exploration of the intensities and extensities of the flesh. Sexual acts involve a whole range and series of bodily pleasures, and an activation of the body's previously unknown potentialities. These actions, and the potentialities they unleash, connect people more intensely to one another, and to the world as a whole. Far from involving a shattering of the ego, these actions help to define, and also to change, the contours of an evanescent "self" that does not pre-exist them: a self that has certain persisting efforts and obsessions, to be sure, but that is also open to the warmth and openness of contact with others, as well as to the vagaries of time and chance and Muddle.

Bataille was both the most lucid, and yet the most helplessly ensnared, witness to — and visionary prophet of — the hopes and horrors of the twentieth century. Delany, for the last thirty-five years or more, has already been looking forward to a possible new articulation of desire — and civility and compassion, and excess and extremity — that might be more suitable for the twenty-first. Of course, we are unlikely to realize anything close to the hopes and feelings that a book like *Phallos* gives voice to, without radical changes in our social, political, economic, and environmental conditions. In this way, the book is a utopian or imaginary one, in which "it is sometimes difficult to distinguish . . . where dream ends and reality recommences." But as a discourse on how to live well, and how to live better, *Phallos* remains instructive, as well as alluringly seductive. With its dazzling multiplications and indirections, it leads us, alongside Neoptolomus, to reflect upon "death and the profusion, the abundance, the superfluity of life, of which death is the center, the ever-shifting organizer, and the surround." There is no evading the finality of death; but in the meantime we can learn to cultivate *ars vitae,* the art of life, the better to explore and enjoy the world in its riotous superfluity.

I CAN SEE ATLANTIS FROM MY HOUSE

SEX, FANTASY, AND *PHALLOS*

DARIECK SCOTT

THE NOVELLA *PHALLOS* MIGHT BE HISTORICAL or philosophical fiction, an affectionate parody or satire of both kinds of fiction or of the kind of literary geekdom, high and low, that generates crazes for *The Name of the Rose* at one end of the continuum and *The Da Vinci Code* on the other. It might be a mystery, an adventure story, or simply what it claims to be, a synopsis of pornography — and certainly we could preface each of these genre descriptions with a *meta-*. But when I enter its pages, and when I exit them, febrile, the delight of *Phallos* is that I read it as a fantasy, an imaginatively rich, avowedly homoerotic version of the sword-and-sorcery genre, where lusty and laconic muscle-bound world travelers stride out of the likes of Fritz Leiber's and Robert E. Howard's imaginations into the taverns of dusty ancient cities and vine-shuttered temple ruins to cross swords with grotesque monsters and dying gods.[1] The genre of fantasy generally serves up elaborate dreams of *could-be-but-wasn't/isn't/won't-be/couldn't-be* satisfactions. In *Phallos*, though the characters' sandaled feet seem at first only to tread the dust of our "real" world and history, the novella performs a magician's trick, a literary sleight whereby we shift by degrees into a strange couldn't-be world: and suddenly here there be gods and monsters (or at least the drugged visions of them). But the surprise, and perhaps the greatest of this parallel world's delights, is that the novella sprinkles its enchantment by seducing us to dream in the hyperbolic way of the fantasy genre about what might otherwise be dismissed as prosaic or unworthy: *Phallos* makes us dream about sex; or rather, Sex (explanation of the distinction to follow).

Part of the pleasure of the work credited with establishing the genre of modern fantasy, J.R.R. Tolkien's *The Lord of the Rings* is, as Tolkien puts it, the suggestion of matters "higher or deeper or darker" beyond the adventure plot on the page,[2] how reading it produces a frisson of yearning toward what is not fully articulated. These matters feel "high and deep" insofar as their very vagueness (a strange place-name you can't find even on the map of Middle-Earth...), their presence as only adumbrations, imparts to them the glow of possible existences and histories that tantalize us as wildly different or better than the world we read or the world we know, and which makes them fertile ground for the imagination of "secret wisdom," as the Umberto Eco epigraph Delany selects to open the novella phrases it. This effect — the summoning up as out-of-reach specters of lost civilizations and supplementary worlds that make us yearn for a repletion we could never experience on the page or in life — is an effect on the reader of Tolkien not unlike the effect of the *phallos* on the characters in the summary-of-a-novel, who, upon learning that the *phallos* exists but that it is missing, imagine that the secrets of power or wealth or eternal youth or great knowledge might be theirs if they could recover it. Delany drafts Eco to warn us of the fool's gold that is this secret wisdom we dream of; but the warning of course cannot escape the standard pink-elephant effect, and thus our appetite is whetted.

Phallos is a novella about a novel that does not exist (unless Delany, like Tolkien or like the musician-composer Prince, has been keeping the "real" *Phallos* locked away from us in a vault, as the priestesses of Bellona or the priests in Hermopolis may or may not have kept the *phallos* itself under guard and key), and thus a story gone missing about a missing piece. Much is missing, lost, and mysterious in the novella, and we see these items — or rather we do not see them, but take note that they are not there — strewn about the story like so many glassy sand-kernels catching sunlight on a beach: you stoop down, drawn towards the luminosity of what appears to be a jewel, but come up empty-handed. One of the greatest of Roman emperors meets Neoptolomus disguised as a beggar and, never directly revealing his identity (Hadrian), arrives on the scene having set in motion the murder (but perhaps not fully intended) of one of Neoptolomus's anonymous lovers, later revealed to be Antinous, and shortly seems to have also set in motion, in ways likely mysterious even to him, Neoptolomus's sale as a catamite — thus tethering *Phallos*'s story to the forever-unsolved historical mystery of Antinous's death. Hadrian also passes on to Neoptolomus a nugget of philosophical insight — life involves tacking the "straits" between a pair of gods, "that rambunctious pair, Muddle and Need" (hitherto unknown, and thus divinities of a wisdom possessed only by initiates) — wisdom which is a riddle, and that Neoptolomus is to spend the novel resolving. This is a minor but significant episode in the story; several other mysteries and lost items from history and legend appear in passing. Another emperor, less great in the estimates of conventional historians and far less available than Hadrian to historical account, Elagabalus, victim of another murder, has little or nothing to do with the story, but his probably-gossip-and-certainly-legendary history appears by way of a long footnote, as the background that speculatively decodes a reference to a black flower in Neoptolomus's account. When Neoptolomus is sold by his bandit master he becomes briefly the slave of a scholar "at work editing the texts from Pergamum to replace Alexandria's library, long-ago destroyed by Caesar." During his travels, Neoptolomus joins an artists' colony at the Pillars of Hercules, where "elder sages believe that, with the right weather, across the ocean they can glimpse the ruins of risen Atlantis." The *phallos,* in at least one of that talisman's rumored iterations, is supposed to house the secrets of Atlantis — Atlantis, the Ur-myth or near-Ur-myth in the Western world of what is lost or missing conceived as a *place* and a geography and culture, i.e., as an alternate world.

The lost library of Alexandria is just one of several collections of texts gone missing from our historical record to which *Phallos* points. Neoptolomus learns Greek — one of the two common tongues of the ancient Mediterranean world, along with Latin — by being taught "the first of the three sections . . . of Heraclitus's great treatise." Heraclitus, one of the pre-Socratic pioneers of Western philosophy, lived in the sixth and fifth centuries BCE, and Neoptolomus some six hundred years later has access to only a part of his great work; but this is far more than we have evidence to know exists, since Heraclitus's philosophy survives, as one of the footnotes informs us, in some 120 or so fragments, usually composed of only short prose sentences of such dense ambiguity, similar to the pronouncements of oracles, that Aristotle — who provides one of the testimonies that there ever *was* a "great treatise" by Heraclitus — complained of the difficulty of unraveling their meaning. It is from this Obscure Philosopher, avatar of a knowledge that tantalizes but frustrates his readers as they grasp to fully possess the meaning of his teachings, that Neoptolomus learns his first words in Greek: not just the words, but "the ocean of ideas and sounds from which the learning of the language itself lifted." The reference to Heraclitus thus doubly suggests a source of knowledge concealed from the reader, but knowable if only the complete text could be read and completely understood: secret wisdom.

In the salon of his wealthy Roman patron in Syracuse, where Neoptolomus receives further cultural education, among a list of poets and philosophers whose work Neoptolomus hears recited, including Euripides, Horace, Plato, and Homer, is Diotima. But Diotima as best we know is an invention of Plato in his *Symposium,* a female philosopher who appears solely in the mouth of Socrates as Plato reports (and/or invents) what Socrates said: she is a lost philosopher, possessor of lost knowledge, to whom the character Neoptolomus has access, but we the readers do not. In this same period of learning, Neoptolomus meets an "elegant woman visitor" who owns a copy of all the volumes of the *Satyricon* by Petronius, though she has brought to Syracuse only a portion of them. The *Satyricon* is well known as a bawdy work, perhaps even proto-pornography as it is a proto-novel, and thus a kind of model within the story for Neoptolomus's supposed composition of the novel *Phallos;* but as another missing text, it is also particularly resonant in our reading of the novella *Phallos.* Steven Moore writes in *The Novel: An Alternative History,* "When classicists bewail all the lost works from ancient Greece and Rome, they cite the hundreds of vanished plays by Aeschylus, Sophocles, and Euripides, the poems of Sappho, Ovid's *Medea,* or the missing books from Tacitus's *Annals.* For me, the greatest loss is the complete *Satyricon.* The 150 pages or so that survive represent only a fraction of the whole, and are so tantalizing that the mind boggles at what the entire work must have been like."[3] Delany's use of this historical tease is elaborate, since though Neoptolomus is tantalized with access to this "very valuable" and entertaining fiction, he like us never hears or reads all of it; the elegant woman promises to return once she has "the whole of it" copied, and to read more of the *Satyricon* at the salon, reports Neoptolomus, "But, alas, she never returned while I was at the villa." The *Satyricon* is a fiction recognized by the characters in the story as precious in part because of the pleasures reading its contents produces (pleasures entangled with erotic pleasures, some of which are homoerotic), but also because it has been censored by the official or officious silence of the powerful whom the work offends: the parallel with the imaginary novel *Phallos* and with our novella is clear.

Directly after mentioning the *Satyricon*, Neoptolomus describes how Pericles's "full funeral oration" (known to us via Thucydides's "shorthand") is recited "that same day." But what same day? The day of the woman's visit? The sequence is ambiguous — as though "that same day" is the day (which could never really be a day) that the unnamed woman "never returned." Neoptolomus then has an epiphany:

> Later in bed, my patron shocked me explaining that Nero had been emperor of Rome not a decade back . . . but a whole *century* before — and that it was the cutting quality of his humor and rhetoric alone, which kept Petronius's work still dangerous. Pericles had addressed his troops . . . in the words I had listened to only hours ago, even hundreds of years before that! For all these fine remarks and expressions were from men and women dead fifty, three hundred, six hundred, even eight hundred years. And for the first of many times I began to feel myself, there in my patron's summer home, somehow part of an immortal company.

Here time becomes so elastic that Neoptolomus feels "immortal," not through writing or reciting these works himself, but in hearing them, in reading them. This revelation occurs on a day of uncertain temporal location, which is only the first of many times Neoptolomus enters this immortal company. And this experience has as its foundation what his patron tells him in bed, so that it is an education Neoptolomus receives within the context of an erotic connection. The combination of erotic connection and the intimation of "whole" or "full" texts or performances of texts that remain beyond full hearing or reading (an intimation which is itself a form of seduction), and texts which do not, in the moment of encounter with them, locate themselves solidly or clearly in the time of their provenance, is the gateway to "immortality" — that is, reading/hearing texts and studying and reflecting upon them (learning from his patron when the texts were composed) — interpreting them — shifts Neoptolomus into a new perception of what it is to be alive (signified by the contrast between an idealized immortality and everyday mortal existence).

This is not only epiphanic for Neoptolomus; it is also a model or map of the possible way our own experience of reading *Phallos* can shift our perception — a shift that for us also depends upon the eroticized context of our reading and interpreting the novella.

In the cases of Heraclitus, Diotima, and Petronius, "the whole of it" is both there and not there, flagged as available within the novel only available to us as a synopsis, but thereby irrevocably lost, always over the horizon, the knowledge we might glean from it incomplete. Significantly, too, "the whole" of Petronius and Diotima (who in Socrates's mouth proposes a philosophy of Love) is at least not unconnected, if not directly associated, with eroticism, so that epistemological and erotic practice are twinned in the novella (such a twinning is, as Steven Shaviro notes in "Ars Vitae," very much in the vein of Walter Pater, one of the tutelary spirits of the novella).

These mysteries major and minor, these evocations of lost texts and historical lacunae, are not themselves the missing pieces the characters seek in the guise of the *phallos*. The *phallos* is likely best understood, as Shaviro discusses, as Lacanian Lack, in the terms that the Pillars of Hercules sculptor who can see Atlantis the way Sarah Palin could see Russia provides, when he points out to Neoptolomus "the absence at the center of your being." But these mysteries and lost texts are analogues of that central absence, emblems in *Phallos* for one of the novella's most trenchant themes, missing-ness and lost-ness and — *less*-ness, the things we search and yearn for which will "complete" or "solve" either us or a question vital to us. They provide little amusement-park trapdoors we can fall through, into what — maybe surprisingly — is the sweetness, the pleasure, of a fruitless search, the ecstatic vertigo as we fall of being able to imagine that at the bottom, there *might be* . . .

The *might be* of *Phallos* is centrally an erotic speculation. For above all what is missing as much as any other absent element in the novella is the sex with which the non-existent novel is, according to its summary, replete: the explicit sex in what is presented as the writer Randy Pedarson's favorite pornographic novel. In this sense, we can read the novella *Phallos* itself as a hollowed-out shell not unlike the paste-and-fake-gem *phallos*: a porn novel in which the porn is evacuated.

This absence of explicit sexuality in a nominally pornographic story is at the heart (and therefore, definitively, a missing heart) of the magic of the novella. That we are barred from, and thus must fantasize about and are prodded to yearn for, *accounts* or *stories* of sex — which is to say smut, porn, and their pleasures — means that within the reading of the novella, sex, because it remains not-described even within the very discursive form which is, alas, almost all that we have by way of representing it in language (pornography), becomes idealized: it becomes textualized in the curious form of an *anticipated, imagined* text, as (the-account-of-)Sex(-we-cannot-have). Sex provides the gesture towards, the adumbration of, what in our shared life-world it is not *really* (we cannot have the account of Neoptolomus's sex, nor can we actually experience the kind of sex the withholding of that account comes to represent as idealized in our imagination) and what Neoptolomus, imbibing Lacanian lessons, learns it cannot be for him: *jouissance,* which for present purposes I will just translate as full enjoyment: or which within the terms of the fantasy genre might also be the full comprehension of matters high and deep.

"Yet there is always something . . . missing, I suppose," speculates Antinous, "at the core of even the most ardent love — something making those of us with a certain restlessness of soul seek further, want more, yearn to explore beyond all we are given." Antinous's narration of his sexual biography gives Neoptolomus the language for, and possibly instigates, Neoptolomus's own beginning quest for sexual variety. For Antinous, and for Neoptolomus after him, this quest, the very plot of the purportedly pornographic novel, is a restless searching for a "core" — for a completion, for a solution to a mystery, a missing piece that could be restored — and sex is the mode of this searching. This is, from a psychoanalytic point of view, a standard misfire of sexuality, questing through it for a wholeness you will never achieve because to be you is to have arisen into being with a loss, a "missing" piece. Later we learn that the sexual restlessness Antinous narrates as a search prompted by the hollow core of love might well have been, instead or in addition, the prescribed performance of elements of religious ritual choreographed by Hadrian, so that Antinous's formative account is inflected with the possibility that it was based upon a lie (and thus his perception of love's emptiness might be hollow at *its* core). Neoptolomus ultimately demurs somewhat from Antinous's account of the absence at the core of love, when, reflecting on his relationship with

Nivek near the end of the story, he asks himself whether "lack" is at the center of the love between him and Nivek. "Let me say only that, with such [sexual] variety, it becomes hard to hold onto where the lack lies, since that absent center moves about so: If I have learned anything in this time, it is that losing track of it, in such a secure relationship, is surely the closest we can come to filling it." At the level of the tale where Neoptolomus is pursuing what he misses, this realization caps even if it does not solve the mystery for him, and it does so in suitably equivocal fashion, with our hero drawing "close" to "filling" the lack, but not deluded he will ever really do so.

At the same time, however, that Neoptolomus searches for something he cannot grasp, we the readers are directed to consider what we do not get to read — what we do not enjoy, what is in fact foreclosed from our enjoyment because presumably it does not exist at all, not at least as a public, published document — which is the "Technicolor" sexual intensity of Neoptolomus's encounters. Of the Neoptolomus-Antinous pairing we read:

> In these eight pages all five senses are appealed to half-a-dozen times. Here are the differing heats of palm, genital flesh, inner arm, and nape, the second finger's slip across the rucked foreskin, wet with excitement's pre-leakage, the straw's roar when you throw the side of your face onto it, how the passing tongue flexes, pressed to a thumb knuckle, the feel, the odor, the tastes of two male bodies, the hammering heart behind someone else's ribs during orgasm, hammering yours; times, hefts, shifts in weight and tautness, the slap of bellies slicked with sweat and rain, a dithyramb of rising and resonating intensities.

This is one of the key passages of the novella, for the perception of absence at the core of an experience or a relationship which Neoptolomus narrates is perforce given to us as readers: an absence is hollowed out in the core of the novella, and that absence is filled — but only prospectively and imaginatively, beyond the page — by the sex we don't see. Just a few pages later when Hadrian meets Neoptolomus disguised as a beggar and describes watching Antinous have sex with a variety of partners, their conversation is delivered to us in "full," but this fullness is deceptive, as footnote 7 tells us, "Phyllis has suggested I quote this passage [the Hadrian conversation] because, beyond Chapter One, it is the longest section of prose in the book where the sexual carryings-on are indirectly, rather than directly, described; and thus, unlike the warehouse tryst, for which it functions as a kind of rhetorical recovery, it can be reprinted without lapsing into rank explicitness." Thus the section is complete and not reduced to synopsis largely because it already functions as a reductive, sanitized synopsis — of sex (and again, all of this is of course the novella's conceit, since the "full" text of *Phallos* only exists as a synopsis).

The moments of highlighted sexual omission accrue from there. During the first encounter with the bandit who ransoms Neoptolomus: "As with the passage describing his love-making with Antinous, I cannot quote it," our synopsis author gravely says, "But . . . it is possibly even more vivid and intense; and is quite a sexual set piece." Of Neoptolomus and Maximin's first coupling: "I wish I could let you read it. It's another of the novel's choice sexual set pieces — and so different in feel from the others." Great swathes of sexual debauch and thrill disappear — but are tantalizingly noted as having been disappeared — from Neoptolomus's sojourn in Byzantium. The final third of the novel *Phallos*, we are told, "turns out to be the books *most* sex-drenched section — which means, alas, it's the one about which I can say the least," so that the denouement of Neoptolomus's adventures, the conclusion which we would expect to "tie up loose ends," bring closure to the narrative, and give it its *meaning*, is the most withheld from us as readers.

Randy the synopsis author describes the principles of his editorial technique:

> Observational obsession by the author of *Phallos* is at once the source both
> of the text's poetry and of its prurience . . . , which, besides the fact that, in
> full context, they would result in this website's being struck by our university
> monitors, I have excised because, I suspect, along with most modern editors,
> such cascades of detail finally slow the reader . . . As well, many such minor
> incidents simply flesh out an atmosphere of sensuality without advancing the
> story in any way I can discern.

Randy's elaboration of the novella's playful conceit thus claims that the sanitizing of explicit sexuality in the synopsis is also a diminution of its poetry — which is to suggest that in an effort to please censors (strictly imaginary, but plausibly reflective enough of cultural rules governing what's speak-able), much of what constitutes the literary merit of the novel has also been excised: again tossing a ball of value for the reader beyond reach, again creating a ghost of fullness to haunt the reading of the novella — a point underlined by footnoted lines from Phyllis, remarking on the bowdlerizing done by the synopsis: "I'm only locating another level at which, for all its pornographic thrust, *Phallos* displays the novelist's art — a level that . . . must be betrayed, or at any rate made to leap up and cast a shadow, at least in memory, by such, dare I call it, castration."

What is significant here is that these layers of absence are *marked* repeatedly: that the novella is a synopsis of the book means the "real" "text" is absent, but at the same time the novel *Phallos,* insofar as it exists at all, is present in the synopsis; in the same way the textual accounts of the sex are absent, but present, too, illuminated in high relief — with broadly winking irony, as Binky notes that "you can't describe" what he's in fact partially described — by a list of descriptive bits which claim to be reductions of fuller descriptions, a list claiming to restore at least by way of suggestion what has supposedly been left out, and illustrating the truncation of a "full" text. We are thus cajoled to imagine a full text even as we are only given its outlines and fragments. Even the descriptive list in the long quotation above is a list of body *parts,* by and large. Absent-present sex in *Phallos* operates as an illustration of that aspect of synecdoche — the species of metaphor in which the part evokes the whole, as in "Shakespeare" stands for "the plays of Shakespeare" — which is frustratingly unsatisfying (it does not give you the whole, only a part), but which is also tantalizing and pleasurable precisely in doing so, in that manner Oscar Wilde uses Lord Henry Wotton to ventriloquize, speaking of a cigarette as "the perfect type of a perfect pleasure. It is exquisite, and it leaves one unsatisfied."[4]

Censored, only briefly described, or mostly retreated-from sex is a missing piece for us as readers, just as the *phallos* is for the characters of the imaginary novel *Phallos.* What the High Priestess of Bellona says about the *phallos* might be said of sex in the novella as well: "[E]veryone knows it is a fake, an imitation . . . still the wheedling rumor that it might be the real, the true, the authentic — full, rich, and replete with its treasure — always precedes it, always accompanies it, always follows it, always makes its way about and around it . . . "

This aligns with the way the supposed mystery of who has authored the novel *Phallos* is a missing piece for the characters supposedly writing the synopsis and commenting on the story (Randy, Binky, and Phyllis). Both censored sexuality and mysterious textual provenance hover around, above, behind and below the novella, functioning through Delany's teasing refusal to explicitly name them as paradoxical evocations of idealized plenitude just beyond reach. The effect created is this: if Randy et al. could just "have" the name of the author (like having the *phallos*) or we as readers could "have" the full text and its reportedly Technicolor, poetic, and explicit sexuality — if we could have the complete text-of-sex, or the Sex — then the present-absence, the lack structuring love, life, and desire that Antinous describes to Neoptolomus and that Lacanian theory insists upon, would be solved, the empty space filled.

The characters of the imagined novel want the *phallos,* which is a symbol and perhaps the iteration par excellence of the symbolic; Randy, Binky, and Phyllis want the author's name, which is an operation, mode, or instance of symbolic activity; I want the full account of sexual adventures. Early in his story, Neoptolomus articulates what is common in these desires and suggests how they might possibly be fulfilled. In this passage, Neoptolomus wants something he's not getting (though what he is getting is incandescent) in his sex with Antinous: "to more-than-touch: to grasp, hold, or even *determine the outline of what it was that had so far seemed absent* in our encounter" (emphasis added). Sketching an outline to mark the absence "so far" not only intimates that you may yet fill in the contents of the outer lines, but it puts something there to see, however flimsy and hard to hold. The symbols and names-as-symbols these three layers of desire aim toward are absent, and not named explicitly, but they are symbolically present both within the story of the imagined novel *Phallos,* and within the contexts and experiences of reading the novella *Phallos:* they are *outlined.*

Here I must bring in once more a body of theory far more voluminous and complete but nearly as recondite as Heraclitus and his ghostly treatises, Lacan — but I bring him in within the leaky bubble-walls of a bracket, to show that Delany is using Lacanian precepts in order to imagine a literary context which, to a degree, flouts Lacanian conclusions, as Shaviro observes. I think

Delany is working in *Phallos* with the difficult, complex notion of jouissance in Lacanian psychoanalytic theory. In Lacan, all humans become speaking subjects by suffering an alienation and self-division: we become ourselves through the imposition and acquisition of language (that is, through the operation of discourse, of the Other). A loss — a loss we can discern in the lack of complete correspondence between the symbolic name of a thing in the world and the thing itself, and thus between the language that constitutes our speaking of ourselves and "full" selves — instantiates human being. One cannot be a subject without this self-division, but *desire* — which in operating as the mode of a recognition of division between subject and object (*I want that*) also enacts this constitutive subjective self-alienation — can discursively posit a subject position without such division, which has full access to ideal or unlimited enjoyment (an aspect of what is meant by the term *jouissance*). This position without the self-alienation constitutive of subjectivity is a non-existent, mythic figure, and it *has* jouissance. According to Lacan interlocutor Tim Dean, "In Freudian theory, the father of the primal horde and the phallic mother are both conceived as all-enjoying and lacking nothing. In Lacanian theory, The [backslash] Woman and the *père-jouissant* occupy this position of plenitude . . . As their mythic status suggests, . . . none of these figures actually exists. But this fact of nonexistence does nothing to diminish the effectiveness of their functioning."[5]

Sex in (and around) the novella *Phallos* — sex as it is invoked and evoked through its being both limned and withheld — does seem to have or provide access to jouissance. Lacan would warn us that to ascribe to sex access to jouissance is to fundamentally be misled. (Dean again: "As a consequence of life in the symbolic order — that is, subjectivity as such — my own excess *jouissance* resides in the Other, forever alienated and inaccessible. But misrecognizing the Other in my partner promotes the fantasy that *jouissance* may be regained through sexual relations . . . What is promiscuity if not the constantly thwarted attempt to access the *jouissance* from which I'm separated as the price of symbolic existence?")[6] Delany's playful but deep-trawling use of Lacan in the novella may mean he would agree with Lacan and Dean, but only to a point. The novella is an imaginative exercise, a fantasy that sex *could be* such an access to the jouissance of the Other. Although the characters cannot access jouissance via sex (just as we cannot) and Neoptolomus learns he cannot fill or evade that Lack but only seek to move it from site to site, the way that sex both marks as absent and suggestively fills through outlining something missing at the core of the reading of the story gives us the reading experience that sex is, at least for purposes of this novella, that access: sex becomes Sex, capitalized for us as those forces-made-divine Muddle and Need are for Hadrian and Neoptolomus.

The novella's imagination of the relationship between a subject-constituting loss and the solace provided by sexuality we can see playing out in the repeated transactions at the temple of the nameless god, which propel much of the action of the story. Neoptolomus is sold as a catamite to the desert bandit, a man of "power, wealth, and wisdom," to save him from being sacrificed and "in exchange for his [the bandit's] commitment to return the *phallos* to its right and proper place." This exchange echoes in Neoptolomus's own purchase of Nivek years later, and in the many stories the old Roman patron, Nivek, Clivus, and the desert bandit later tell about similar exchanges. The way that the *phallos* is valued in these exchanges is through the establishment of a position of catamite, which necessitates and implies a master — which is then to say a *relation* of one man as a sex slave or sexual subordinate to another. The trope of this exchange (meager amount of money plus master-slave sexual relationship) is significant in Delany's work; it also plays a central role in *The Mad Man* (which, as Shaviro notes, is by contrast not in the least coy in its representation of sexuality). The logic of substituting one thing for another is of course the logic that governs the various characters' near-worship of the *phallos,* and this logic is of paramount importance in Lacan. Heraclitus, synecdochic author of one of the novella's lost texts, and, notes Binky, perhaps "the guiding thinker for *Phallos,*" also makes exchange a central component of his conception of the cosmos, in ways that are illuminating for the novella. Heraclitus implies (and Aristotle later understands him to have argued) that "the mind of God" (which is the *logos* or the divine law governing the universe) is "fiery," or that the cosmos itself is in truth fire. James Warren translates Heraclitus's fragment of observation thus: "This ordering (*kosmos*), the same for all, no god or human made, but was and is and will be always, fire everlasting, kindling in measures and going out in measures." Warren explains that Heraclitus is describing, "a regular and regulated system of elemental exchange . . . The simile . . . suggest [*sic*] that, just as when I buy a loaf of bread for 70 pence, an exchange takes place and the loaf I take away is worth but not composed of 70 pence, so when fire becomes, for example, sea, . . . sea is somehow worth or equivalent to a certain amount of fire but is not itself made of fire."[7] In the world of *Phallos,* the coin of exchange for the replacement of the *phallos* — which is both the object and the representation of a fruitless pursuit of secret wisdom and power, wealth, etc. — and for the potentially sacrificed youth's life, is a catamite-master sexual relation; and perhaps by implication, too, the constituent component which underlies and gives structure (or meaning) to the activities and relations of the novel is *this kind of relation.* This exchange is thus the coin of the cosmos, as it were. It figures a central aspect of the entry into subjectivity — which is being made by discourse, being its object and product, and in the process losing what discourse does not symbolize (jouissance); we are subjected under the world-making, cosmos-steering (insofar as the cosmos is a human cosmos) power of discourse and rendered subjects by our abjection to it. We are told that, "the nameless god is an old, old god, with an old, old thirst that must be slaked." This demand for a sacrifice is a playing out of the loss that entry into the symbolic requires — it so happens, though, that an entry such as the nameless god demands would also be a final exit (you'd be shredded by the blades of the *phallos*), and so the catamite-master relation substitutes for it, so that what is lost is freedom — for a time, actual physical freedom — but then this loss becomes ceremonial and ritual, ritual and ceremony through which one's original abjection is recognized.

At one point the ritual replaying of this constitutive loss summons the presence of divinity — which, recall, is (at least) an altered perception of the everyday: Nivek, when Neoptolomus buys and saves him, suddenly becomes godlike, possessed of "divine comeliness, . . . god-like strength and grace . . . and the numinous marvel of his cock." This kind of hallucinatory-effect-slash-theophany highlights the way that the exchange and the catamite-master relation repeat in microcosmic ritual form the macrocosmic magic of the creation of subjectivities in a symbolic universe, or, in Heraclitean terms, of the fiery *logos* steering the world. These theoretical predicates help clarify the joy in being sexually mastered that we observe in both Neoptolomus with his desert bandit and Nivek with Neoptolomus. Both urgently desire to be connected with their lovers in the mode of a master-slave relation, but this is not some willful servility or self-abnegation on their part; it is because the catamite-master pairing provides sexual redress of self-division. The master is, for the catamite, a living image of the complete self (though he could not function so without the catamite there to project this image), *an* other as *the* Other in possession of jouissance. In other words, the master is for the catamite the substitute for the nameless god, and he acts like a god, which is to say he *possesses* (as the divine can be said to possess, or take over, the mortal) the catamite, thus making him, for a moment, able to *play* at being complete. Neoptolomus, when circumstances put him in the role of playing the master, revels in deceiving himself that Nivek is, at least during sex, an abject vessel for his dominance, but also sees that the master part he plays is as much a chimerical monster as the nameless god is, and that he is of course void of what his catamite projects on to him. Nevertheless, this process of mutual projection on voids is pleasurable; the emptiness Neoptolomus finds is not the cold death one expects of voids, but is described as "luminous, pulsing." We can read the paradox of an emptiness that is living and light-filled this way: the emptiness is luminous in that the characters' sexual role-play momentarily makes legible for Neoptolomus what is otherwise evanescent and inaccessible. The "pulsing" quality of this empty core implies that it has some form of life, that it is generative, that in this emptiness lies magic — the ability to create (or to imagine) something out of nothing.

By setting up the mysterious author and explicit, pornographic sexuality as though they were mythic figures within the tale, Delany makes the two gateways to the dangled but tangible possibility of full enjoyment, and suggests that although, according to Lacan, the ideal jouissance cannot be taken up in human experience, and indeed these two textual elements remain unrepresented or only suggestively rendered in the novella, their prosaic existence somewhere, even if in experiences that the novella will not allow to be shown, allows us to get *close enough* to full enjoyment in meaningful ways.

This is a gift of Delany's fantasy: the story enables us to imagine, to pretend, to feel in the tension of our minds inhabiting our bodies as we read, an ardor being stoked for the imagined ideality of sex — and we, like the nameless god, sprout horns which are the marks of our coming into our "animal" lust but also mark our constitutive cuckoldry. We like the nameless god have been constitutively violated; there is always-already *someone else somewhere* having the sex we would otherwise be having with *our* partners, someone therefore *possessing* what we wish to possess, someone *enjoying*. (The magic of *might be* and its cuckoldry effect stings with special sweetness for me: I've always *wanted* to write or to read an epic-adventure Tolkienesque story that would take place in the ancient Mediterranean world, and would involve lots of rough sex with lots of rough Mediterranean men. Lo and behold, Randy et al. list my name among the possible authors of the novel *Phallos,* in a company I could never qualify to join. Delany's character "Darieck Scott" might have written it: but I still haven't really read the text, only its summary.)

At our hollow core we are dispossessed, but the novella emphasizes how we are *sexually* dispossessed, which narrows the scope of our violation and makes feasible its redress. And delightfully, *Phallos* makes us feel that just getting the sexual accounts — just getting nothing more than mere smut: something we know we can get, even if we cannot get *this* smut, because it is not there and does not exist — would give us what we imagine the secret wisdom of Atlantis and the complete works of Heraclitus, Diotima, and Petronius would give us: full enjoyment, freedom from subjective alienation, access *to* the inaccessible, jouissance, the answer, complete knowledge, the full text.

NOTES

1 Delany's Return to Nevèrÿon, is of course his explicit foray into the genre that I am arguing *Phallos* evokes by effect.

2 J.R.R. Tolkien, "Foreword to the Second Edition," *The Lord of the Rings,* 1954, 1955; Houghton Mifflin One-Volume Edition (New York: Houghton Mifflin, 1991), xv.

3 Steven Moore, *The Novel: An Alternative History, Beginnings to 1600* (New York: Continuum, 2010), 100.

4 Oscar Wilde, *The Picture of Dorian Gray,* 1891; *Complete Works of Oscar Wilde,* Collins Classics (London, UK: HarperCollins UK, 2003), 17–167, 70.

5 Tim Dean, *Beyond Sexuality* (Chicago: University of Chicago Press, 2000), 89.

6 Ibid., 167.

7 James Warren, *Presocratics* (Berkeley: University of California Press, 2007), 64–65.

ABOUT THE AUTHOR & CONTRIBUTORS

SAMUEL R. DELANY is the winner of two Hugo and four Nebula Awards and is a novelist, critic, and professor of English at Temple University in Philadelphia. He lives in New York City. His fiction includes *Babel-17* (1966), *Nova* (1968), *Dhalgren* (1975), and *Trouble on Triton* (1976). Other works include his series of stories and novels, Return to Nevèrÿon, collected in four volumes (1979–87), *The Mad Man* (1995), his Stonewall Prize–winning novel *Dark Reflections* (2006), and most recently *Through the Valley of the Nest of Spiders* (2012). His critical essays have been collected in several volumes, *The Jewel-Hinged Jaw* (1978; rev. 2009), *Starboard Wine* (1984; rev. 2012), *Longer Views* (1996), and *Shorter Views* (1999), and he has published two books of interviews. Wesleyan University Press is planning shortly to return to print his major critical work, *The American Shore* (1974), a study of a text by the late poet and fiction writer Thomas M. Disch.

KENNETH R. JAMES is completing his PhD in English at SUNY Buffalo. He received an MFA in film and media arts at Temple University, and has worked as a scriptwriter for educational documentaries, a freelance producer for Maine PBS, a producer of political advertising for environmentalist organizations, and the manager of a public access station. He has taught screenwriting, fiction writing, film history, film aesthetics, and media studies at Colby College, the University of Southern Maine, and the Maine Media Workshops. He is the editor of volume one of Samuel R. Delany's *Journals,* forthcoming from Wesleyan University Press.

ROBERT F. REID-PHARR is Distinguished Professor of English and American Studies at the Graduate Center of the City University of New York. He is the author of *Conjugal Union: The Body, the House, and the Black Ameri-*

can (1999); *Black Gay Man: Essays* (2001); and *Once You Go Black: Choice, Desire, and the Black American Intellectual* (2007). He lives in Brooklyn.

DARIECK SCOTT is an associate professor of African American Studies at the University of California, Berkeley. His research interests include twentieth-century African American literature; creative writing; gender and sexuality studies; and race and sexuality in fantasy, science fiction, and comic books. He is the author of *Extravagant Abjection: Blackness, Power, and Sexuality in the African American Literary Imagination*. Scott also is the author of the novels *Hex* (2007) and *Traitor to the Race* (1995), and the editor of *Best Black Gay Erotica* (2004).

STEVEN SHAVIRO is DeRoy Professor of English at Wayne State University. His wide-ranging interests include philosophy and critical theory (Nietzsche, Heidegger, Saussure, Chomsky, Lacan, and Foucault), postmodernism, new media, cinema, and science fiction. He is the author of *Post Cinematic Effect* (2010); *Without Criteria: Kant, Whitehead, Deleuze, and Aesthetics* (2009); *Connected, Or, What It Means to Live in the Network Society* (2003); and *Doom Patrols: A Theoretical Fiction about Postmodernism* (1996).